About the Author

Tony Bury, born in 1972 in Northampton, England, has had a passion for writing songs, poems and short stories since an early age. He has taken it more seriously since having kids, writing several children's books and screen plays as well as the Alex Keaton series of crime novels. *Edmund Carson – The ONE. The Only.* is the second book in the Edmund Carson series.

Edmund Carson – The ONE. The Only.

Tony Bury

Edmund Carson – The ONE. The Only.

Vanguard Press

A CIP catalogue record for this title is
available from the British Library.

ISBN 978 1 784653 69 9

Vanguard Press is an imprint of
Pegasus Elliot MacKenzie Publishers Ltd.
www.pegasuspublishers.com

First Published in 2018

Vanguard Press
Sheraton House Castle Park
Cambridge England
Printed & Bound in Great Britain

Dedication

For Bethany and Alana who still love their dad…

Chapter 1

"Finally, I think I am going to have to sit down for a minute, if that is okay?"

I place Kate at the head of the table. I take a little lick of her neck to give me some energy. The smell is still strong, so strong it does the trick. I sit in the empty chair.

"That really took it out of me, you know, getting you lot to the table.

"I know, but I really wanted to. Besides, I think when everyone is dressed nicely, it is better for the cameras. Tiring, but better. I am getting better at getting girls to put clothes on now... I am not sure that's something I should be proud of though, or say out loud. Anyway, my fans, they have started to expect a level of dignity from me. It is not like the early days. And theatre, they like the theatre of my profession.

"Eddie, do you mind if I just help myself to a drink? This is thirsty work.

"Thank you."

He looks grumpy, but he is a good guy. I get up from the table, and head around to the other side of the bar.

"Don't worry, I will fix you all a drink for when we kick this off. Just a quick half of something for me, and then we will sort it all out."

I grab a glass and pull on the nearest pump to me. Just like they do on TV. It is harder than it seems. I now have half of something called Cornish Rattler. I am not sure about alcohol. I don't think it's ever going to be a great taste, but it is cold and available, which is what I needed.

"Sorry, before we start, has everyone introduced themselves?

"No? Oh, okay, shall I do it?"

I go around to the end of the bar, pick up the booking in register, and take it back to the table. I sit back in my seat.

"This should help. First, let's give a big thanks to our hosts. This is their place. It is lovely, isn't it? I can totally recommend the curry. Didn't know I was even a curry liker until I got here. So, this is Eddie and this is Jenny. Eddie will correct me if I am wrong, but you cook, and Jenny works the bar, is that right?

"Thought so, been coming in for a couple of nights now. I am sure you have noticed me? What am I saying, everyone notices me! But never expects me. I have been staying in a caravan down the road.

"Yes, that's right. You know the place? It is lovely and they are lovely hosts as well. Amazing people. Very supportive.

"OK, a little bit more about Eddie and Jenny as they are kindly hosting, and paying for the drinks this evening."

I knew that would get a round of applause.

"I think they have a couple of girls who are off skiing. Is that right? I was listening to your conversation last night. Such a shame. They are going to be so upset to have missed this. I will sign a few things for them, if you like? Should keep them happy.

"Good. I personally never really wanted to ski. I think it has something to do with the cold. Always thought of myself as a warmer holiday type of guy. Not that I have been away, but Thailand or somewhere like that would be nice, I have heard good things about it.

"Yes, thank you for noticing. With a body like this I was made to be topless on a beach.

"Spain. Spain would be nice too. A lot closer.

"Let's have a look then. Oh! before I get to the official residents. Gary and Kate… Joining us at the last minute. I must say, that threw me a bit. Must be good friends of Eddie and Jenny, right?

"Thought so, I did see you arrive around seven. I was sitting just over there. Very loud entrance, I must say. I had wrongly presumed you had left. Imagine my surprise when I was just finishing up with Lisa and I heard you stumbling into the next room. That is some effort in the bar, you two. What, six, seven hours? And you were hardly taking it slow. Very sensible not to drive. I am so glad you could join us for this. I am sure you would have been kicking yourself tomorrow when you read about it in the paper."

I look down at the booking in register. They have a lot of people stay here.

"So, we also have Jo Taylor and, I am presuming, your husband? In the book he is just a plus one? Jo, I am not one to judge, so if you just want to keep it as plus one that is fine?

"Nigel, okay Jo, and Nigel. Thank you." I am not sure he is a Nigel. There is a look in her eye that tells me she is available if I wanted too. A bit of strange if I ever saw it. Maybe if I get time, let's see how strange she likes it.

"Then we have Ian and Ceri, Lisa and Simon, and Amanda and Ian. Another Ian? I can't say I have met many Ian's and now I have met two in one night. Although Ian and Ceri, I am not sure you have the same tastes as Amanda and Ian. You two, I don't mind telling you; you shocked me a little. And that is not an easy thing to do, I can tell you.

"It is okay, don't be shy, we are all adults here, we can all learn new things."

Jo is looking directly at me now. I knew there was something about her.

"Shall I tell them, or do you want to?

"There is no reason to be embarrassed. I am sure we all experiment at times. Don't we?"

I return the look. I can tell most of the people in the room agree. Maybe it is that kind of hotel. Except for Gary, he doesn't look adventurous in that department.

"Okay, I will tell them. There I was lying under the bed, you know, waiting for them to finish dinner and retire, when they came in all frisky and pulling each other's clothes off. It was adorable. I mean, you must be well into your thirties now. I didn't even know that happened at that age. Anyway, I can just about hear them talking. Then, the next thing I hear is the snap of handcuffs. I nearly wet myself. You can imagine. Here

12

I am, under the bed, and the first thing I think is…they have worked it out, in my head, they are the police. I didn't know whether to lie still or jump out and run. A few seconds later I hear another set of handcuffs. I am thinking they are both police, and I am royally fucked. Sorry, royally screwed. I am trying to cut down on my swearing. Then, I hear Ian here, get up, and go to the end of the bed. He is tying Amanda's feet to the bed. It's at this point I twig what is going on. I can't tell you how relieved I was. I mean, I am hardly in my nineties, let alone the hundred mark. But by now I am thinking, good on them, let's let them have some fun. Well, five minutes later he is at her like a jackrabbit. I mean, a man of his age? She is screaming his name and everything. I must admit, I do like it when the woman screams your name. Makes you feel special, doesn't it, Ian?"

He knows what I mean.

"Don't be, it's perfectly natural. Anyway, amazingly, it turned me right on as well. I could have taken care of myself there and then.

"No, I don't do that. It did sound fun, but three's a crowd. A few times I have been curious I must admit. Do any of you all remember seventeen at the school? What am I saying? Of course, you do. She, she nearly got me there, her and seven. Not their real names. I always seem to forget their real names. I was tempted for a moment, even laid down with them."

I have a flashback to lying on the blanket. It gives me a shiver.

"Too many hands everywhere."

"Anyway, back to the story. Twenty minutes later it's all done. Ian is up and going to the bathroom and Amanda is

13

shouting at him as she is still blindfolded and tied to the bed. Naturally that was my moment. I came from under the bed and then worked quickly and silently with Ian in the bathroom. He was head down in the sink, washing his face. Didn't see me coming, did you?"

"I am sure you would have. You're a fit-looking bloke. Anyway then, back to Amanda. I have to say, by then I was tempted. The sight of you tied up on the bed, and blindfolded, that was very tempting. All I could think about was if you would notice it wasn't Ian. I mean, I know you would as not very many men are as well, well, you know, endowed as me. But I could have gone halfway in or something. Kept you guessing?

"I know, I really should have. That is nice of you to say, Ian, but I checked my watch, and time was getting on. I am glad I cracked on. I still had to visit…"

I check the book again. It is only for effect. It will make her smile.

"Lisa, another Lisa. Two Ians and two Lisas, how weird is that. Anyway, I still had to work with Lisa, and even then, I didn't know about our drunken friends staying the night… and Eddie and Jenny. I will say though, it must have got the old juices going as Lisa and I,well, we had our own little moment, didn't we?"

She is certainly smiling now.

"It's okay. You are single now. That's why you are down here, isn't it? Couldn't help hearing you on the phone over dinner. Think you are better off without him. There are plenty of other blokes who would love to spend time with you."

It is always important to make them feel important. It is not always all about me. Most of the time it is, but not always.

"Thanks. I had a feeling I was going to be a lot better. Let's hope that is a sign of things to come for you."

She will never have as good again. Hopefully things will improve though. I shoot a look over to Amanda. Just so that she knows she helped to start the old blood boiling. She loved that. I can see her trying not to grin too much in front of her husband. Makes it a little awkward. I am getting used to awkward though; all the women's eyes are fixated on me now.

"Am I single? Now there's a question."

The question that was always coming.

"Without a real answer, I am afraid. I hate to use the phrase 'it's complicated' but it is complicated."

I try not to make eye contact with Lisa as it's not fair. She has probably spent the last hour thinking about a long-term future with me.

"She, my complicated friend, is coming down tomorrow as it is Saturday and it is, well, you know. I have booked into a little B&B in Wadebridge. The Bridge on Wool. Funny name, but apparently they have a few nice rooms.

"Is it? How funny is that? You drink in there a lot, do you Kate?

"Oh, Gary does. Doesn't surprise me.

"Anyway, yes, so I don't normally spend time in hotels, but every now and again it doesn't matter. People aren't really expecting me to come and stay. I suppose people are so starstruck that they don't really believe it is me. The hipster beard is helping. That, with a hat, hides most of my face, something us celebrities are used to doing.

15

"You like the beard? I am not sure. It's always itchy. I prefer clean-shaven, which I will be tomorrow as we will be uploading photos tonight. It is always good to change after a big event. Tonight, is a special night.

"Thanks. I know, it does make me feel a little more macho, I guess. Anyway, that's the introductions done. We need to crack on, I think."

I get up from the table, and go out of the front door into the car park. I need to make two trips, but finally I bring all the boxes in.

"You know, I did all of this myself this afternoon. It took ages,but I think you are going to enjoy it all. The sandwiches are egg and cress, and cheese and onion. Sorry, they are both my favourite. I did think that maybe one or two of you may be vegetarian, so I played it on the safe side. I don't know why, but I always think of Cornish people being healthy. Other than those big fuc—, sorry, no swearing. Big pasties. Those Rose ones are amazing. Have you had them? They can't be good for you."

I lay out everything on the table in front of them.

"No, you don't have to wait till it's all set out. Dig in, guys. I have sausage rolls; I even made them with my own two hands, and… wait for it…"

I pull a plate out of the bag. I can tell they are all holding their breath as I can't hear them breathing.

"A cheese and pineapple hedgehog!"

I knew that would get a round of applause.

"You know, my mum and my nan both made these for me. It's the only time you ever want to eat cheese and pineapple at the same time. I know nowadays some people do it with little onions or gherkins, but it is never the same. Cheese and pineapple is always the best. And, I found this great cheese! Seriously strong. Not just strong, seriously strong. Really does the job.

"No, not on a pizza Gary, that is just wrong."

What is up with that guy? Pineapple on a pizza. I think he may have drunk a little too much this evening.

"We haven't quite finished yet, some jammy dodgers, pink wafers, snowballs, and then for the main event."

I pull out the cake.

"My birthday cake!"

Another round of applause.

"I have a confession. I didn't bake it. I am not sure I would even know where to start. There was a little bakery, next to the fudge shop, I think, in Wadebridge, they did it for me. It looks good though, don't you think?

"Yes, I know. I am only eighteen. It is right there on the cake. I look a lot older, don't I?

"I have accomplished so much already, I know. I just have a couple of other things to get from the car, and we are done."

I go back out to the car and fetch them.

"Balloons. What is a party without balloons eh? And party hats. Even got some of those whistle things that extend. Can never remember what they are called, bazookas or something like that?"

I tie balloons to the back of everyone's chair. I make sure that Lisa gets two, and then I give them all hats. They seem to be having fun. I then go back behind the bar, fetch some champagne, and place it on the table.

"Sorry, does anyone want anything different? I know this alcohol thing is an acquired taste.

"You do, Gary? And Kate? And you, Ian? Two pints and a large white wine."

I go back behind the bar and pour the drinks. I am a good host. I could have run a pub. Chatty, good-looking. It would have been full of girls every night. Just coming to spend time with me. I get that, and it is good for business; I am good for business.

"There you go. Now I just need to set up the iPad and phone so that it takes pictures and records the party. My fans will be expecting something tomorrow, I am sure of it. You know my Twitter accounts are in the millions now. I do love this social media thing. Instant recognition for your work.

"You all follow me? That is great. I will make sure I tag you all in."

I go to the end of the table and place them both on a small dividing wall that splits up the dining area. I check through the phone. It's the perfect height for both.

"Now, before I hit record, my plan was to come around, we all sing happy birthday and then I open the champagne, pour some glasses and then we tuck in. Does that sound like a good plan?"

They all nod in agreement.

"Cool. Ready, go."

I press record on both and get into position.

"Happy Birthday to me, Happy Birthday to me, Happy Birthday, dear Edmund. Happy Birthday to me."

Big round of applause and pop goes the champagne. Perfect. I run back around and turn them off.

"That was perfect, everyone. I just need some selfies for Facebook and Twitter, if that is okay too? I am sure there are millions of people dying to be where we are tonight."

For the next ten minutes I take selfies with all of them. A few more with Lisa as we did have a bit more fun together. A little taller than I like normally, but you can't really tell lying down.

"That's so perfect, everyone. Just give me five minutes to upload... That's YouTube done. Selfies on Facebook. Me and the gang. Happy birthday to me. Gary still not sober. Amanda and Ian loved up. Perfect, they are going to love those two. It is important that I don't make it all about me.

"I know, I know, just Twitter to do, then we will get on with the celebrations. My fans aren't as lucky as all of us to be together tonight. Hashtag Happy Birthday #Eighteen #NansPineapplehedgehog. That will be enough for now. You are all right; all work and no play makes Edmund a dull boy... See, I am putting the devices down."

Cheeky gits give me another round of applause at that.

"Great idea, Jenny, some music... Is it behind the bar?"

I go behind the bar, find the stereo, and put some music on.

"Isn't this James Blunt or someone? Hardly dancing music? Oh, I see, it's on random. They won't all be like this? My parents used to listen to this stuff all the time. They were into the soppy love songs, and eighties and nineties music. Sometimes it would be on more than the TV. Never understood that. Why listen to something when you can watch something?"

I go back to the table. They are all staring at me. I think it is going to have to be up to me to start the dancing. Yes, that is it. They are all smiling now. Waiting to see who I choose. I must do the right thing.

"So, would you care to dance, Lisa?"

It should be her first. She put the most effort in this evening.

"It doesn't matter, I will lead. I am a great dancer."

We get up and everyone claps again. We start to dance. I start to hum the tune into her ear as we dance. I can feel her rubbing herself closer to me.

"But it's time to face the truth; I will never be with you."

The song finishes. It is a bit of a sad ending to the song, but girls love it when you sing in their ear, especially the slow songs. It's always the personal touches that make a difference to them.

"What? No, it's just a song. I am not saying that I don't want to be with you. It is what he says. I think he actually wants to be with her, but she is too pretty for him."

That should do it. Women always fall for the "you are too pretty" line.

"Really, it's not like I knew which song was going to come on.

"Okay, if you want to."

I take her back to her seat. Women can be so funny sometimes. Here I am dancing with her at my birthday party, and she wants a fight. I don't think she is over the whole "it's complicated" point. That must have stung a little.

"The other Lisa, how about you? Do you fancy a dance?

"I am sure you were checking me out. I am sure your husband won't mind."

I give a little laugh so that he thinks I am joking. I am not joking, she was. I walk over to collect her and then change direction and walk back to the first Lisa. I whisper in her ear.

"I am sorry about the song. We can have another dance soon. While we are on that subject, can I ask just one little favour? If you happen to bump into Miss Walker while she is down here, can you not mention what happened in the hotel room? You see, she gets a little jealous about that sort of thing. Especially if she saw how hot you are."

Fuck me!

If looks could kill. Wish I hadn't given her the old, how hot you are line now. I go back to Lisa number two. At least she doesn't look like she would stab me in my sleep.

"Now you're talking, some old school Scritti Politti. This was my dad's favourite song."

I grab Lisa up to dance. I will try a little of the humming and singing with her too. She will not be so pissed at me.

"We tried together to discover…"

She is lapping it up, and this is about relationships and stuff as well. I escort her round the dance floor. She is quite light on her feet you wouldn't even know she was dancing.

"Spoils it all for love."

The song ends. We share a moment. One of those moments that tell you if her husband wasn't sitting two feet away, my singing would have got me so laid, so, laid.

"I love that song. I can see why it was my dad's favourite.

"No, my mum's name wasn't Patti. I did wonder about that when my dad used to play it all the time. Maybe it was

21

another girl in his past, although not sure he would have ever got anyone as nice as my mum. My nan used to say he was punching so far above his weight with my mum.

"You have never heard this song? What! Never? Quick story: I was what, twelve, maybe thirteen years old, and a girl called Vicky bought this for me. She used to come over a lot and obviously heard my dad playing it all the time. I thought it was so sweet. A girl spending her pocket money on me. I think she was a year younger too. Then we broke up. Out of the blue, just like that, she packed me in. About six months later I was dating a girl called, called, what was her name? Zoey, Zoey Shellswell. She only went and bought me the same song when we broke up. I figured, at first, it reminded them of me after listening to it all the time at my house. Then I found out they meant me. Don't feel sorry for Loverboy, was supposed to be me? Where that came from I don't know. Think they were saying I was some kind of prima donna. I don't know where they got that from? Should have just been thankful I let them spend time with me.

"Yes, still have the records at home at my nan's. Yes, records, not CDs or downloads; real records. They went through all that trouble to point it out, they bought an actual record. I am worth it, of course. I bet they miss me now, especially given the fame.

"Wait, is this One Direction? Jenny, really, how can you go from Scritti Politti to One Direction? Time for some food, I think."

I escort Lisa back to her husband and start on the food. I make a mean cheese and onion sandwich. I fill everyone's plates – they are hardly touching the food – and then take some more selfies. I want my fans to know how much they enjoyed the party. I can't imagine how many people will want to come to my nineteenth. May have to hire one of those celeb DJs.

"They are good, aren't they? My nan says I always add a bit too much onion, but that's how I like it. She used to say I could eat an onion like an apple. I probably could."

I clear the food plates and light the candles on the cake. I make a wish. I wish for my nan to have been here. I miss her. Since I have become one of the A-list celebrities, they have hidden her from me. She hasn't replied to any of my messages. I should just pop by. Problem is, there are probably shrines to me outside the house. I am sure they will be looking at a monument or something. I must be the most famous person from the town, ever. I guess it's for her own safety, or else she would be mobbed by fans daily. That's not good for a woman of her age.

I blow out the candles to a round of applause. I give them all a piece of cake and then start the selfies all over again. These are going to go down a storm on Twitter and Facebook. A million likes, I am sure.

"Jesus! Is that the time? It's nearly six a.m. That is your fault, Gary and Kate. If you hadn't have stayed at the bar so long, we would have had more time.

"I am afraid so. It's been an amazing party and I loved the fact that you could all share in this with me. Ohh, but before I go, and this news come as a surprise to me too, you have all put me into triple numbers! I didn't know this was going to happen, but it's all thanks to Gary and Kate for being sensible and not driving home. This is a great birthday present, I have now worked with one hundred people!"

At least, I think it is a hundred. I lose track. I know it is close. I also knew that would get a big round of applause. Rightly so. I am amazing.

"I am now officially bigger than the top ten put together.

"I know and only eighteen, although I do have a plan to retire at twenty. Well, twenty-something, I can't do this forever, no matter how much fun I am having.

"I know it seems young, but I need to have a life, maybe a couple of kids of my own and, you know, travel the world. I have money, I don't do this for that. This has been all about being the best at what I do."

Finally, a smile from Lisa. She knows what I do best and has had a taste of it. One of the lucky few, hundred.

"Movies? Maybe. I am a great actor. Always have been. I have already read about someone wanting to make a TV series on my life. I can see that running for what, five or six series at least.

"I know, all of this at eighteen. I think we already said that, Gary." He should really stop drinking at some point. He keeps repeating himself.

"My friends, we digress, and I really need to get a move on. Joan and Fred are going to be wondering where I am till this time of the morning. Their hospitality has been great, and I need to say my goodbyes before I head back up north.

"Definitely. I will be coming back to Cornwall, it's a lovely place. The people I have met have been wonderful too. Genuine is the word I think I would use.

"You know what? I am going to leave the food and the drink, and you lot party on into the early hours. You are on holiday, well, other than Jenny and Eddie, but the kids are away so enjoy yourselves.

"Okay then, one last selfie then all together."

I lean down by the table and take a selfie that has us all included.

"Okay, I am off. Thanks for everything. It has been truly great. Thanks for sharing my birthday with me."

I walk out of the bar. They were some nice people, although that Lisa got a bit clingy at the end. I think that's just the fame thing. She will be dining out on this night for months to come, I am sure.

I get back in the car and drive it back to Joan and Fred's caravan. The lights are on, so they must be up already.

"You two are so lazy, you haven't moved off that sofa for days now.

"Just to see some friends down the road. You know the Pickwick?

"I just need to pack up my stuff, shower, maybe get some breakfast, and head to Wadebridge.

"No, it's fine, you two stay there on the sofa; I will do it. I only want something small, I have stuffed myself on cake and sandwiches."

Fuck!

Didn't mean to say that. Should have really invited them to the party as they have been nice hosts.

"I know, but I couldn't help myself."

Don't think they picked up on the fact it was my party. Thank God, they are old. Probably wouldn't have wanted to be out this late. Old people go to bed early. I jump in the shower. To be fair, Fred and Joan could do with a shower also, they haven't moved off that sofa for five days now. They are beginning to smell a bit. After I shower, I head to the bedroom to lie down, and look at pictures of my party. That was fun. The perfect way to start the eighteenth celebrations, and I am at least one hundred; I think. The press has the numbers all over the place. It is why I need to keep going. Yes, I need to keep working so there is no doubt, from anyone, that I am the greatest! Everyone will know it… I nod off.

FUCK ME!

It's midday. I must have been more tired than I thought. I dress and pack in less than twenty minutes.

"You are still both there! Want me to turn the TV over? Channel 4 all day can't be that interesting?

"No? Okay, no problem. Listen, thanks for everything. Enjoy the rest of your holiday. I know you are going back in a week but enjoy what's left. Get some fresh air. Cornwall is lovely.

"Really? For my birthday? That's so generous of you. I will leave you my car to get around in. Yes, your four-by-four is so much nicer."

They did know it was my birthday. I must have told them at some point. I go over and kiss both on the cheek. They really need a bath.

I take the keys off the side, get in the car, head out of the campsite, and over towards Wadebridge. The last thing I need to do is be late, and piss her off on our first weekend together in ages.

Chapter 2

This place could do with a motorway or something. Everywhere you go there are just bushes and trees. The roads are so little; you can hardly get a car down them, especially these big cars. I drive into Wadebridge. It is very picturesque, if that is the right word. I park at the end of the road from the pub I have booked us into. It's a public car park that tourists use so nobody will look for the car there. I head into the pub. There is a few people in, but they all look local. I wonder if Gary and Kate will be in today? Maybe sleeping it off would be a better idea for them. Barmaid is quite fit. I knew I would make a good bar person. Attraction is everything.

"Hello, Sir, can I get you a drink?"

"Hi, no, thank you. I have a room booked for the night?"

"Oh, okay, love, what was the name?"

"Mr and Mrs Walker."

She will like that, the fact I booked it in her name, and that it is Mr and Mrs. We haven't really discussed it, but it does give her a view of what I am thinking about for the future. Our future. In the future. Way into the future. Wait, maybe I should have just said fiancée.

"Okay, there you are, just the one night. Is your wife with you?"

That's a good question. I thought she would be here by now. I looked at the train times yesterday, and it got in thirty minutes ago?

"I am sure she will be here soon. She is travelling down from London."

"Good. Shall I show you to your room?"

"Yes, thank you."

The barmaid walks around from the bar, and we head back out the front door. Then into a second front door on the right.

"This key is for the front door, and this is for the room. You are in room one."

"Thank you."

I follow her up the stairs. Nice figure for an older lady. I would. Well, I would if I wasn't so excited about seeing her. Need to ensure I have my A game. It is important the limited time we are together I show her what she is missing.

She gives me the key, and disappears. Nice room, it has an en-suite, a big bed; all good. I lie on the bed, and pull out my phone to look at Twitter.

What the fuck!

Twenty retweets of the pictures last night. Twenty? I get that for saying hi. And only nine added it to their favourites. Nine? That's shit. What is going on with this lot lately? I am working my arse off here. When I started on Twitter I was getting a thousand retweets an hour. I put a lot of effort into last night. Cheese and pineapple hedgehog and everything.

@thedandan Predictable you psycho!!

Predictable? I am not predictable. I am Fucking Edmund Carson.

@lisastanton #Boring.

Boring? Me? Who the fuck do they think they are! I am seriously pissed off now. I open Facebook.

What? It's the fucking same! Three likes. Three fucking likes for a night's work?? And look at these comments.

Same old Edmund, knew he would throw a party. It's my birthday, of course I am going to throw a party!!

Hey freak, give yourself up, you bore me! Who is this loser to call me a freak? He has a fucking picture of a cat as his profile picture! A cat sado!

At least Jack the Ripper was unpredictable... Bastard!

What! I am better than Jack. Who the fuck does, wait, Darren Gosling, think he is... I tell you, he should be on my list. Then we will see if he thinks that is predictable. An hour working with that knob, he will see how creative I can be.

It's like they don't want me to entertain them. Not everyone of them can be in a classroom, don't they know that? It takes skill and time to do what I do, and keep out of sight. I spent days planning that party, and this is the thanks I get? Next year no party for them. I will just spend it on my own. They can cancel the celeb DJ too.

I get up and start walking up and down the room. Why are they like this? You don't see any other superstar getting this much shit. Hell, James Cordon sings in his car and three million people watch. Three million just for a sing-song in a land rover.

"Knock, knock."

I know that voice. Immediately I head to the door. It is cute she didn't actually knock on the door. I open it. She is stunning.

"Hey you."

That instantly calms me down. She has that effect, as soon as I seem to be losing it, she is there. Ready to put me back on track. Maybe that's it, a thing of beauty. She is a thing of pure beauty in a dark world. Little black dress and everything. Every time I see her! That little black dress makes me remember why I work so hard. She deserves to be with someone like me.

"Hey, what took you so long?"

"The train was delayed. Something to do with leaves on the line, I think. Besides, it's a long way to Cornwall."

I kiss her. God, that feels good. It feels like the first time. Every time feels like the first time with her. We move over to the bed. I can't help myself, there is something about her which just gets me horny. I pull up the little black dress. Stockings, suspenders, and no pants. I know it is always the same, and that she does that for me but...

Fuck! That's so hot...

I am in her before she can pull the dress over her head. She is wet and hot already. She must have been thinking about me all the way here. I whisper in her ear.

"You were ready for me."

She whispers back, while taking a slight nibble on my earlobe, "I always am."

We are so in tune together. She just gets me. Deep down gets me. She knows what I need and when I need it. I lie back on the bed, and she pins me down. She is on top doing all the work. I just lie and watch as she slowly goes up and down on me. Slow and hard, slow and hard. It's everything I dream of; it's all I dream of. She keeps going and going and then leans over to whisper in my ear again.

"I missed you. Are you ready?"

I am so ready. I can't believe I have lasted this long. It's been months since I have seen her. Months since I have been inside of her.

"I am."

She speeds up harder and faster, harder and faster until we are both ready to explode. We do together. The sweat from her body is dripping onto mine as she leans down to me.

"That was worth the wait, wasn't it?"

"It so was. I have missed you this last couple of months. It's just not the same travelling on my own."

Wait, I am not sure I wanted to say that. What if she wanted to travel with me? She lies back on the bed with me. I hold my breath for her answer.

"I know, but I have school work to do, and you need time to write."

Thank fuck for that. She is happy with the situation. I can't believe that school is still a school. It closed for like three days after the launch party. Three days and she was back to work. You would have thought that it would have become more of a tourist attraction. They would make so much more money from that.

"How is the book coming on? Have you written today?"

Fuck!

I was going to google something to update her with. I still can't believe she bought the whole, I want to become a writer

31

thing…Travel to find my voice… Find myself. I don't need to find myself; I know who I am.

"It's good. Cornwall is an interesting place. No writing today though, today is all about you."

"Yes, it is lovely down here. Anything I can read yet?"

"Not yet, not until it's complete. I want you to be the first."

Not that I have even started writing anything. I so want to tell her the truth, but after the school, who knew these people meant so much to her? It's not like they were family or anything. I enjoyed their company too, especially Seventeen, but I don't stay attached to it. Just must move on. She was only there for a week or so before I visited.

She said she couldn't even watch the news footage. She didn't want to know. I think she secretly knows. She just doesn't talk about it. I think she knows her boyfriend, I mean, friend that is a boy, I mean, a man. Manfriend! Yes, manfriend is the legend that is Edmund Carson, the ONE. I am sure she doesn't think there are two Edmund Carson's out there. No, she knows. I am the best. I suppose, no matter what, once you have had the best, it's hard to give it up. I am glad she isn't pushing the book thing too hard.

"Oh, please, Edmund, I would love to read something you wrote. You are a very talented young man."

She does know me very well.

"Next time we are together, I promise."

She is silent. Maybe I should write something just to keep her happy. I am a great writer. I wouldn't take me long to knock out a novel or something. What, a week? I could spare the time. She is smiling again now. She bought it.

"Shall we do something this afternoon?"

"I kind of like what we are doing now." I shoot a smile back at her. "Like what? What were you thinking?"

"I don't know, something we can do together. It's been so long since we spent some quality time together, Edmund. When are you coming back to London? I have a new place now, you know. You haven't even seen it."

"I know. I will be back in a week or so. I am nearly done down here, and I can't wait to see your new place... I know, I have an idea. Get dressed."

Need to get her off this subject. I have plans to complete before the ONE makes a return to London. We get dressed and head out of the pub. It's good that you don't have to go through the pub to come in and out. I head over the road to the local shop.

"Wait here. I will be one minute."

She waits outside and I come back out five minutes later.

"What's in the back pack?"

"It's a secret. Come on, I saw a little place when I was driving through earlier today."

We walk back past the pub, past another pub, and I can see another couple of pubs up the road. Must all be alcoholics in this town?

Three minutes later we are standing in front of the shop.

"Bridge Bikes. I thought we could hire some bikes and ride out into the countryside for a picnic? I have wine, pasties and cheese. Think that's what the locals eat down here."

"Oh, Edmund, that's a great idea. Very romantic. Just what we need."

She kisses me on the cheek. That's got her to stop thinking about me coming back to London at least. I am sure half the police force is waiting for me there. My fans have been screaming out for the return of the ONE. I know they have. I am just building up excitement. Creating a comeback is all about timing. I get her to wait outside while I go inside and sort out the bikes.

"A tandem."

"Yes, a tandem. What is up with that?"

She laughs so hard. Her smile is even cuter when she laughs. She is, without a doubt, the most beautiful woman in the world, and she is mad for me. She is so lucky that I like her too. Imagine all the women in the world and I chose her. That must be like winning the lottery for a girl.

We get on the bike and head out through those back roads again. These are dangerous for people on bikes. They should have like a cycle path or something. They do have one further on, and we go onto the cycle path.

"Are you all right back there?"

"Fine, Edmund. It's lovely. This was such a romantic idea."

"Are you sure you are peddling? I am watching, you know."

I can hear her laughing as we continue down the road. We bike for about forty minutes before we reach a nice spot by the sea. At least, I think it is the sea. It may be a big river as there is something on the other side. I swear though, she never peddled once on those up hills. The afternoon is spent drinking wine and eating pasties. Not great pasties. Not Rose pasties, they do them so much better, but she doesn't know that. So, she thought they were great pasties. We head back and drop the bike off at Bridge Bikes.

"Do you fancy a drink in the bar?"

"Not really, Edmund, I would much rather spend the night lying in bed with you. Let's pick up another bottle of wine and stay in and watch a movie or something?"

When we are together, it is as if there is not another person in the world. It is always just about me and her.

"Sounds perfect."

I stop at the shop and we head up to bed. We are naked and cuddled up within five minutes of getting into the room. I needed this. She knows I needed a reminder of why I am doing this. She always knows when I need a reminder. It is like she senses when I need a visit from her. I cuddle right into her.

Fuck, she is hot!

"Fucking alarm, why has that gone off? I didn't set the alarm?"

Did I? Why would I set the alarm? I reach over, grab my phone, and turn it off. I lean back. Nobody is there.

"Hello?"

There is no answer. I listen. I can't hear her. I get up and look in the bathroom. No, she is not there either. There is a note on the bed.

"My dearest Edmund, I didn't want to wake you as you looked so peaceful. I am on the early train this morning as I must be back in class tomorrow. I will see you in a week? All my love and kisses. Miss Walker."

She could have at least stuck around for morning sex. Morning sex is so hot. Wait, why would she sign Miss Walker? Isn't that odd? She is so hung up on that damn school it is affecting her brain. I lie back on the bed. I can't go back and see her in a week. I can't just have the ONE return, with no build-up. I need to do something special for my fans. Like my birthday party. I forgot about that. She interrupted my feedback. I get my phone off the side and look on Facebook.

What the fuck is wrong with these people!

Nobody is liking the party. What is it? I check Twitter too. I swear, I may as well not do all this stuff for them. I try to plan nice things, and it's as if they aren't interested any more.

Am I really losing it? Is that what is happening? The people I work with don't seem to be upset with the stages I create? What is it that's changed? Is it all too normal? Have I made my work too normal, and now people don't want to see it? I need a *CSI* day or a *Criminal Minds* one to see if there is anything new out there. Give me some inspiration. All good artists need inspiration. Or a muse. Is Miss Walker going off the boil? Is that why this is happening? Do I need a new Miss Walker? Maybe this is all her fault. She is the one that just comes and goes as she pleases. Maybe if I had a steady girlfriend it would make me focus more on the work. Maybe I need a steady girlfriend.

No, I need breakfast. My head is delusional.

I get up, dressed, and head downstairs. The door to the bar is open. I go in. There is a table set for breakfast.

"Morning, Sir."

"Morning."

There is someone behind the bar, but I can hardly make them out.

"Take a seat, and I will be with you in a minute. Tea or coffee?"

"Coffee, please."

I am still not sure about coffee. It's always overrated. I sit down at the window. It's raining again. Something about Cornwall. The place always has rain. Well, other than yesterday, oh, and the day before, but mostly rain.

"There you go."

The girl places the coffee down in front of me in a gigantic mug.

"Thanks."

"Milk and sugar are already on the table."

I just nod at her. I take a second look at her. Didn't really notice a minute ago, but she is quite cute. Dark hair, small, petite. Not Miss Walker cute, but doable. I would let her do me if she really asked nicely, and I do like morning sex. So, she would only have to ask once.

"Is your wife joining you?"

"No, she has already gone. Oh, and she wasn't my wife. They just made a mistake when booking us in."

Nothing wrong with giving the girl a bit of hope. She is smiling. She likes the sound of that. It's as close as I could say to her, I am single and doable. Damn, should have said she was my sister. That would have been even better.

"Oh, I am sorry about that. Well, it's just me this morning so whatever you want, I am here to make it for you."

There is a smile on her face. Whatever I want? That is a line, if ever I heard one. "How about I make you a full English breakfast? Cornwall style."

"Why not? Sounds perfect."

"Scrambled or fried eggs?"

"Fried eggs, please."

Now, that was a definite brush of the shoulder as she walked away. Maybe I should have asked for something more. If your girlfriend, who is probably affecting your work, doesn't stick around for morning sex, is it so bad to have some with someone else? Surely, she is practically giving me permission? Wait, I don't need permission. Who the hell does she think she is? She doesn't own me. I just let her have some time with me now and again.

"The papers are on the bar if you want to read them."

I turn around. She must be in the kitchen and just shouted that through as I can't see her anywhere.

"Okay, thank you."

Papers, I had forgotten all about them. I will be all over them by now. I get up and bring them all back to the table. I can hear her in the kitchen starting on the breakfast. I think she is singing along with the radio. That is cute.

What the fuck is this!

"Unsteady Eddy? The once notorious murderer has struck again at a hotel in Cornwall. Edmund Carson, aka the ONE, threw himself a birthday party at a little resort down by the south coast as he turned eighteen on Saturday."

What do they mean *"once notorious"*? I am still notorious. You can't become un-notorious. Can you? Fame lasts forever. Jack lasted forever. They even make movies and series about him today?

Fucking paper!

I open the next one. *Holiday Blues? Edmund Carson celebrated his eighteenth birthday the only way he knew how... Alone.*

I was not alone! The pictures are right there? What the fuck are they going on about? There are almost a dozen people at my party. There, right next to the egg and cress sandwiches, and fucking pineapple hedgehog! I throw the paper down. Last one.

Holiday from Hell. Now that's a better headline. I breathe again.

Holiday from Hell as Cautious Carson hides away on the Cornish coast.

Hides away? I am hardly hiding away. I am about eight fucking miles away. They are trying to wind me up, aren't they? What, with Twitter, Facebook and now the papers turning against me. It's as if they don't want me to work. It's as if they don't want me to be around? That's not how you treat a star, an artist? They should be worshipping me. These pricks use words like predictable and boring and cautious. Me, cautious? I am working my way across the country ensuring everyone gets to see my talent and do they thank me for it?

Do they fuck!

"Would you like one sausage or two?"

What! Oh yeah, breakfast. Forgot where I was for a moment.

"One, please."

How many other artists travel the country like this? Jack? No, he stayed in London. The Doc? Manchester. I tell you, artists like me don't come along all the time. I am one in a million. I should be treated like a god.

"We have some heart and kidneys if you like? I know some people like that kind of stuff for breakfast up north?"

What? What is she going on about? Does she think I am from up north? I am a southerner too. Although I suppose everything is north of Cornwall. I get up and head towards the kitchen.

"I am sorry."

"Heart and kidneys, bit of black pudding, that sort of thing. Mum says northerners like a bit of offal."

I whisper in her ear.

"I heard you, I was just saying sorry."

As soon as the knife goes into her neck I can smell the blood. I hold her by the head and let her neck drain into the pan of sausages in front of her.

Why is she making four sausages? I only said one. And why ask me when she had clearly already started?

Boring. How can they think that I am boring? I just don't understand. Am I not theatrical enough? After the school, do they think I just haven't had enough showmanship? Is that it? Not keeping it fresh enough. No new ideas. Maybe that's what it is, maybe I need a new character. It's what they do with those soap operas and stuff. Spice it up a little, a new edge.

Fuck, that blood smells good!

I don't know if it's her or the sausages, but that smell is amazing. The thing about warm blood, it just makes you feel like home.

I am hard just thinking about it. I pick her up, take her back into the bar and lay her on the table. She is in that stage still. I don't like doing them when they are at that, not talking to you, stage. Just not fun for either of us. Takes a while for them to come around and be thankful for the fact I have included them in my work. I go back and put the sausages on low. Don't want them burnt.

What if I introduce a new character, and they don't like it? The ONE, they love. Edmund Carson, I think they used to love, but maybe that is what is stale? Maybe I should return to the ONE for a while? Or maybe there is a way of testing new characters. Don't always need to claim the work. Maybe I claim the work if it's good. I am sure that street artist fellow didn't claim all his crap drawings or ones that went wrong?

Oh, I don't know, why are they making things so complicated? They should just go back to loving me like before. I make sure I turn the sausages over. I go back to the hot girl on the table.

"Hi, sorry, I was just checking on breakfast.

"Yes, sorry about that. They got me all wound up, and I am a little all over the place now. It really wasn't on my mind when I sat down for breakfast.

"Yes, thank you, I am Edmund Carson. It is so nice to be recognised. I was starting to think people didn't care anymore. Are you a fan? Please tell me you are?

"Do you know what, that is lovely to hear. I really needed that. It has been a real hard few months. Knowing you are a super fan is great news.

"I was thinking the same thing just now."

I go over and pick up one of the papers.

"They never do seem to pick the best photo of me. I think it is to wind me up. I think, they think that if they get me going, I will slip up or head back to London and have a word with the editor of *The Times* or something. They do seem to know me a little as I would like to work with that guy so much at the moment.

"They are okay, trust me, I have put them on low. The blood slows down the cooking too. Makes them a little poached."

She is really smiling now. I know that look.

"You know, I did think about it. When you brought the coffee over. No offence and all that, but is that predictable? It's what the papers are saying, and Twitter and Facebook. They expect me to work with you, have sex with you, and then run away? Their words, not mine.

"Thanks. I know, I never run away. That's not what they are saying though."

She is smart. I do like her.

"You are cute, and your blood smells so sweet and dark. I tell you what, it was all I could do to stop myself from bending you over the stove. To be honest, that was exactly what my intention was, after turning the sausages down."

That will start the motor running. She is smiling even more now, if that is possible.

"Yes, exactly, something special. All I can think about now is something special. Stepping up my game. Do you think that's why they are taunting me? They want me to do something bigger and better? They want me to escalate even more?

"Evolve, yes, that is exactly the word.

"Wow, I can honestly say I didn't expect that.

"Yes, that would be different, and I can't say it would be my first time, but I can definitely see that going down well with my fans. They do like a good setting. Sort of changes direction a little?

"Maybe we can have breakfast together?

"Okay, but it would mean we wouldn't? You know... I don't really think there is time to do both? I am quite the stayer in the morning.

"Do you know what? You are the loveliest person I have met. To sacrifice not being with me as well for the sake of my profession. I am going to ensure that this is all over social media. Just because we can't. There will probably be a line of men around the corner for someone as pretty as you."

I go back into the kitchen and check on the sausages. They are fine. The blood is making them smell amazing. I pick up the carving knife off the side and go back to her.

"I think you are right. Maybe just pull the T-shirt up, and tie it, in like a knot? Covers you up, but you can see the belly then.

"You have a real nice figure. The boys must go mad down here for it?

"Really? Maybe you should try London when all this is over? There aren't many girls as pretty as you up there."

Women are so easy to talk to. So easy to impress. As long as you remember to flirt a little and be polite, you can get anything you want.

"Yes, I would be happy to show you around. Not going back for a month or so though. Look, this isn't going to hurt, but it might get a bit messy."

"Of course, of course. Sorry, didn't think."

I go back to the kitchen, get some towels, and a large saucepan. I lay the towels over her jeans, and the floor beneath her. I then cut into her stomach.

"I was thinking, cut like a square out from just under the rib cage to below the belly button. Should be able to get at all the good stuff then. It will only leave a little scar. You will still look good in a bikini.

"No, not your heart. You have such a nice one, I want you to keep it."

Now, there is a line to use on a woman. She is wet just thinking about that. Hell, most women would be wet if I said that to them.

"I will be okay with liver and kidneys."

I cut away until there is a clear hole. I drop the liver and kidneys into the pan, and leave the entrails on the towels. I then sit her on the chair.

"If I just pull the back of the T-shirt over the chair. See, you sit up straight. It's a tight top.

"No problem. It will look great for the pictures.

"It will take me like five minutes to cook this up with the rest of the food. I never like to overcook these things."

I go back into the kitchen, chop up the liver and kidneys, and chuck them in with the sausages. The smell is amazing. A few baked beans, some toast; can't be bothered with making eggs. Beans, bacon, toast, and this will be enough.

I wish I hadn't cut a great hole in her now as this is turning me on. If I bend her over, it's not like I am going to notice, is it? But, what if more stuff falls out as I am banging her from behind. That's not fair on her, is it?

44

No, I am going to have to get me some tonight from somewhere else.

I cook up the food, and take it into the bar. I lay it out on the table.

"Looks really good. Can't wait for us to tuck in."

"No? You are kidding me. I wouldn't have put it all down if I had known.

"That is so sweet of you. A vegetarian as well, and all this was your idea.

"Are you sure it won't bother you if I eat? Because I can box this up afterwards and take it with me?

"You are great. Can I get you something? Anything?

"Sure, no problem at all."

I go back into the kitchen and pour her a bowl of Coco Pops. Cover it in milk and bring it back.

"Perfect. I will serve up, and then we will kick off with some photos, okay?"

I put the food on my plate. I make sure there is a lot. Breakfast is the most important meal of the day.

"It's okay, I will come over to you."

I take the phone out and start clicking away pictures of both of us and the breakfast.

"They are going to love this. Breakfast at…

"Tiffany? No way, no fucking way, that is your real name? I was going to say Bridge on Wool, but that is amazing.

"Breakfast at Tiffany's. That must be the most amazing headline ever. They are going to love that all over social media.

"Ha, ha, ha! Sorry, now that is the most amazing thing ever. I would have never even thought of that."

45

I take a couple of spoons of Coco Pops, place them in her stomach, and then take some more selfies showing them.

"So funny. You are such a delight, Tiffany. You have really cheered me up. All of this. This is exactly what I needed."

I stand up and put the phone back in my pocket.

"Just one more thing before we eat."

I lean over and kiss her. Proper kiss her. I can feel her surrendering to me as I do. She is so weak at the knees right now.

"Just by way of a thank you for this morning. It was destined to be an awful day, and you have really changed that. Made me feel alive again."

I sit back down and eat breakfast. It is amazing. Warm, tasty, rich. There is no better taste than fresh meat with warm blood. And young. Must be young meat. I think liver tastes worse with age. Must be all the things that go through it over time.

"These sausages are amazing, Tiffany. Are they from the local butcher?

"Thought so. You do a lot of that local stuff down here, don't you? Not a lot of supermarkets or like Costas coffees. It is all about the personal touch. Where I used to live with my parents you can't walk half a mile without an Asda or a Starbucks."

Takes me ten minutes to shovel it all down. All mopped up with thick bread with lots of butter. The butter and the blood go so well together. Proper Cornish butter too. They probably make it in this village somewhere. From Cornish cows, no doubt.

"That was amazing. I will wash this lot up and get out of your hair.

"If you are sure?

"Damn, Tiffany, you are right. It's almost ten fifteen, they will be coming to open soon. What is it on a Sunday? Eleven a.m. opening? I will just run up, fetch my bag, and then be out of here, if you are totally sure about the washing up?

"Thanks, I will be back in a minute. Eat some more Coco Pops, you have hardly touched them."

I run out the door, into the door to the right, and up the stairs. Shit, nearly forgot about the time. Maybe the papers are good at distracting me. Maybe that is working already. Would have been bad to let the landlady walk in mid breakfast. She wouldn't have been happy about that.

Fuck!

Too late, unless that was Tiffany screaming. Shit! Need to get out of here. I run down the stairs, and out of the door. It's a good job I don't have to go back through the bar to get out. That would have been awkward.

As I run past the window I can see there are now three people in the bar. Looks like a landlord and landlady to me. I walk around the side so that I can get a look at Tiffany.

I stop and wave through the window. Blowing a little kiss as I do. She will love that.

Fuck, that was close!

I am back in the car within five minutes and heading out of Wadebridge. Need to upload breakfast, but not until there is a little distance between us.

I am not running away. Just a little distance.

Fucking newspapers! I hate them!

Chapter 3

I prefer motorway driving. It's so much easier than driving around those dodgy roads in Cornwall. I really need to get a fake licence though. If the police pull me over I am screwed. I will probably lose my licence, before I even get one. I can't imagine my fans would be very happy about that. Me having to take public transport.

That is a big Asda. That will have to do. It's Sunday; there won't be a lot else open. Let's see if they have anything in there to inspire a new character. Tiffany was right, I must keep it fresh.

I pull into the car park and go into the store. I go over to the DVD area. Nothing new. All the box sets of *CSI* and *Criminal Minds* that are here, I have already seen. The new movies are still vampires and werewolves. What is up with kids nowadays? Sloppy teenage girl nonsense. Forbidden love and all that stuff. I bet Carl Carnegie is watching all that stuff in France. Probably thinks it is the way to get girls.

Although, maybe I could be a vampire? I do like the taste? Well, depending on the age. I wonder if it's like red wine. People say that is all about the age. Maybe that is why it is the blood of Christ. I get it now. Wine and blood. The same thing. All of this is connected really.

But is that boring? Been done before? So many weirdos out there dressing like vampires. Edmund the Vampire? Carson's Crypts?

No, the press is going to come up with words like toothless and vampdire. I can't be vampdire. It needs to be something new, something fresh. I need to be something fresh. Oh, that reminds me…

I walk over to the health and beauty section. Electric trimmer, exactly what I need. Whatever I am going to be, it must be shaven. Short hair and no beard. That will shock them. Totally new. Boybandish, that's what the fans like. They like you to keep changing your appearance. New hairstyles, new clothes. I pick it up and go back to the DVDs. There is still nothing, no inspiration. Maybe I should become a director. Make my own films. I would be good at that. I would be an amazing director, slash actor, slash producer.

What does my nan always say? Clothes maketh the man, Edmund. Clothes maketh the man. I walk over to George. George is a funny name for a clothes shop. It's like calling an electric shop Nigel? Who would do that?

Suits and shirts? No, that would make me look like a banker, and I know what the papers would do with that.

I don't know why I let them get to me. I know they are doing this on purpose, to unnerve me or try to make me make a mistake. I need to get them back on side. Like in the beginning, they couldn't get enough of me when I started. I was headline news everywhere. I am headline news.

Maybe I don't need to get them back on side? Maybe they just need another top story? But, I can't let them know it's me? Not until I have been working for a while. Let them use the lines "Move over, Edmund, there is a real man in town". Then boom! When they least expect it, I upload the lot and say, Surprise! It was me all along. That's a good plan. That's a very good plan. My fans will love that. The big reveal.

Fancy dress? Maybe. Superhero turns super baddy? Although Superman and Supergirl look too similar for my liking. Batman? No, he smells and they will use that, won't they. Must be something that they aren't expecting. Something nobody is expecting; not the press, not the people I work with. Something unexpected. Unexpected Edmund.

That's only fucking it!

That's it, I got it! Nobody is expecting that from me. Nobody is going to be fearful of it either. That's what makes it a genius idea. They won't see it coming. I take it off the hanger, and head to the counter to pay for my new character.

I need somewhere to get into character. Somewhere out of sight. And lunch, lunch would be good about now. Cornwall is a long way down there. I walk past the counter and back down to the food aisles. I need to start eating something healthy. A few weeks on pasties and wine are taking their toll. I grab some bananas. Hardly lunch but I need to keep in shape for my fans.

I never really noticed before, but you can tell a lot about people from what they shop for. Big trolley full, a dozen pizzas, ready meals, four loaves of bread, and twelve bottles of pop. I am guessing a rake of kids and a big house. Although to be fair, I wouldn't like to be the man that's done her a dozen times. She should be buying him some beer too. That gave me a shiver. She must be like forty-five, at least.

Small trolley, wine, fresh veg, couple of steaks. Date night. But blonde? Yuk! Can't get my head around that. Maybe it's a work thing. Maybe people in my line of work don't like blondes that much. More into the dark hair. Maybe it goes better with the blood. Vampires always seem to have dark hair and they are always pictured with blood. I wonder if that is where the tall dark and handsome thing comes from. That is what they always say about me.

Small trolley, ready meals for one, and six trays of cat food. Three bags of cat litter and a kipper. Cat lady. I bet her house stinks, and she has like a hundred cats. Maybe she wants to be a cat. That's what the kipper is for? For her to pretend to be a cat. There are some right weirdos out here today.

Shit! It can't be a work thing. That German guy; he worked with a lot of people, didn't he? He didn't have a preference. Well, he did, but he had an army to help him, so his number doesn't really count. I can't be compared to a war. Anyway, he liked blonde-haired people, didn't he? A bit too much. Tried to make the world blonde, if I remember. Fans do like to be like you. But, he wasn't blonde, he was really the opposite.

There is nothing wrong with being gay and preferring blonde-haired people, but he really did lose the plot about it all.

Basket, four cans of beer, lump of cheese, three onions, a small white loaf, and some rolls. Single male shopping for dinner. We have a winner. Would I prefer a cheese and onion sandwich or a banana? Simple answer.

I follow the old man to the counter. I pay, and then follow him into the car park. He is heading towards a little white van. Definitely the car of a single man. He opens the back and places the bag in.

"No offence."

I plunge my knife into his back before he turns to see me. I repeat it four times in quick succession, and before he starts to fall forward into the van, I drive it directly into his neck. I push him into the back of the van.

"I just can't resist a cheese and onion sandwich. It is probably my favourite thing to eat. Well, maybe second now, but I didn't know about the blood till I was like sixteen." I close the door.

I really need to work on that one-liner. The Tiffany one was good. Sorry, no, sorry, I heard you, I was just saying sorry. That is classy. That is something you would remember from a movie. Where no offence just came from, I have no idea. Not really the words they would want to hear? Maybe something like, you are welcome? You have been chosen? Something to show how lucky they are that I chose to work with them?

Not as much blood as I would have expected. Maybe it was because he was old. The blood doesn't pump as fast as it used to. And, a man, girls seem to bleed like a volcano. Smell better too. I head back to my car, and collect my things. Throw them in the passenger seat of the van. I get in.

What the fuck!

He is still trying to move about. He is like a wet fish on the riverbank. I jump over the back of the seat and plunge my knife back into his neck. At least a dozen times. I climb back into the passenger seat. He was a fighter for an old guy. I can smell the blood now. It's strong. Not turning me on strong, as this van stinks even worse, but strong enough to get the old heart pumping.

I sit back and look out the window. Not a person noticed me in the whole car park. They are all busy unloading shopping or dragging kids into the shops. People are really involved in their own little worlds, aren't they? Maybe I could do more outside. I know it's not the same, but maybe with a little inspiration, it could be something of a change for the fan base.

Keys! I get out of the van and go back to the back door. They are still in it. I take them out. Looks like house keys also. I get back into the driver's seat. Three miles. I bet this old boy lives less than three miles from here. Sat nav on. Click home. Two point one miles.

My mum was right, men are lazy. Women will shop all day for a bargain, but your father in out, and back in front of the TV. I can hear her now.

I follow the sat nav to Little Stoke. I park outside his house. It's small. Has a driveway, which is good as I didn't fancy dragging him into the house. I grab my stuff and then go to the back of the van. I grab his shopping.

"Really?

"I thought you would be fine in the van?"

I close the door and get back in the driver's seat. I pull off the drive and reverse back on.

"Okay, let's get you in the house."

I take the keys and open the front door. I walk into the house just to ensure nobody else is there. There isn't. He lives alone. He could do with a maid. What is up with some people?

I kind of live on my own and I always clean up after myself. Well, at least I pay the maid to. I leave a tip sometimes. I go back to the van and check nobody is around. They aren't. I drag him into the house and into the living room and place him in a chair.

"You're welcome. It is the least I could do after you offered me your home.

"It really does need a clean though.

"Don't worry about it. Nobody is ever expecting me. Think it is one of my charms. People love that they are not expecting me. Then BANG! I am here."

I go back out and lock up the van and close the door. I pick the mail off the floor, and put it on the side. There is only one name on the envelopes, so he must be alone. Although some of this looks like it has been here a week. He must have been stepping over it every time he came in. That is just lazy.

"So, Harry, is it? Harry, I am Edmund.

"Yes, Carson. You have heard of me?

"The school, yes. That was me. They all remember the school. Sometimes I would like to be remembered for something other than the school. There have been some other good ones.

"To be honest, Harry, there was no plan. I stopped by for some inspiration. I needed some help as I am in a little bit of a slump right now.

"You know, thanks for that, Harry, it was a good birthday party. But it doesn't seem to have gone down that well. The last three months I feel as if, as if I am struggling to please anyone. Do you know how that feels, Harry?

"Yes, I guess so, a bit like marriage. Well, if I am married to the media and fans lately, Harry, we need counselling. That is all I am saying."

"I don't know, but I will make sure I get them back on track. Shall I make us some lunch, Harry? I am rather hungry today for some reason. And then, then I really need to crack on."

That guy could talk all day.

"Good, cheese and onion sandwich it is then."

It's why I chose you, Harry. He said that like I was going to make something else. I am not a chef. Although I would make a good one.

"Don't worry, Harry, sit down. I can find my way around it all."

Hardly going to get lost. The kitchen is in the living room. This must be the smallest house ever. I stand up and walk to the sink. Looks like he hasn't washed up in a month. I start to look through the cupboards. Don't think I am going to find a clean plate in this house.

My bag. It still has some paper plates in from the party and cups. I get them out. At least that's a start. I grab a knife from the sink and then clean it the best I can. Think it may have been there a month. I make the sandwiches and take them over to Harry in the living room. He doesn't really have anywhere else to sit.

"Two cheese and onion sandwiches, and a couple of cans of Stella, Harry. Sounds perfect."

There is nothing like a cheese and onion sandwich. The beer doesn't taste too bad with them either. In fact, I think it is the only time the beer tastes good.

"Harry, I know we have only just met, but can I ask a question?

"Well, given the state of the place, I am guessing you live alone, right? And you are like what, forty? Fifty? So why do you live alone?

"You were? I guess she was the cleaner. What happened?

"Really? And you didn't know? Or suspect anything?

"Your own brother. That is just wrong. What kind of woman does that? I must admit something though, Harry. I occasionally worry about relationships too. Just between you and me. Not the brother thing as I don't have one, but the keeping interest thing. And if I am totally being honest, the being honest thing. I have this girlfriend you see…"

I dig out my phone. I scan through the pictures. I don't have a picture of her on my phone? That's odd. We are always taking pictures. All the time? Come to think of it, it's only her taking the pictures. I need to do something about that as she will think I don't care. It's probably because I do it with my job all day, you don't want to be doing it when you are at home. She must know that.

"Don't know why, but I don't have a picture of her now. We don't see as much of each other as she would like, and, Harry, I am not being one hundred per cent honest with her.

"No, not cheating on her. I wouldn't do that."

Best not mention that to a man who has had his heart broken by a cheater. And, by his bastard of a brother.

"This job I do; I haven't really told her about it. I am lucky that she doesn't watch or read the news that much, as I am all over it. You see, I worked with some of her friends. Friends may be a little much; people she knew. Well, barely knew, but I don't think she is going to like it.

"I think it is, Harry. Well, let's put it this way, I don't see myself ending up with anyone else. Now I am still young, and there are great things ahead, I am sure. But, Harry, my girl; she is amazing.

"Yeah, you are right, Harry. I do need to make more of an effort to keep her and to be honest. Honesty is the best policy. I will, I will go back and see her soon. I only saw her yesterday, so I am good for a couple of weeks. It is good to talk, Harry, you have really helped put my mind at ease."

I get up and throw the leftovers in the bin. He hardly touched his. Mine would have been better with a bit of blood.

"Do you mind if I get ready in the kitchen, Harry?

"Thanks."

Not like I can make more of a mess, is it? I fetch the clippers and my washbag. I empty the sink, and put the plates back on the side.

Time to lose the beard, I think, and then the hair. I take the scissors out of my bag, and have at them both. This is going to shock the world. They have never seen me like this before. I carry on cutting at my hair and beard until it's as short as I can get it with a pair of scissors. I unplug the kettle and then plug in the shaver. Number two all over should do it. It's hard doing this without a mirror. Ten minutes later it's done.

"What do you think, Harry?

"That's the point, mate. Don't want anyone to know it is me. It is a good look though. Extreme, but good.

"Is it okay if I use your shower? I have hair everywhere. Don't worry, I will make sure I clean up after myself."

57

I head upstairs, and then walk back down again. I clear up the hair from the sink, and then wash Harry's plates for him. Must be hard to be alone, and he is being so nice about the house and the advice and stuff. I go back upstairs, and take a shower. If I had time I would clean this shower too. I think it's dirtier than I am. But I don't; it's Sunday and I need to test out the new character. I dry myself on what I think was a towel, and stick on my underwear. I go downstairs and pull a suit out of the bag.

"Black suit, Harry. Think it will go?"

I get dressed, and then pull out the costume. I put it on.

"What do you think, Harry?

"You know, I wasn't, but now I think about it, it's the last thing they will expect from me. I have hardly been religious in the past. In fact, I have really tried to keep away from it."

I go into the hallway and stand in front of the mirror.

"Hello, Father Edmund. Hello, Father Carson."

I can't use my own name. I need to be someone else. He needs to be someone else. All good characters need a good stage name? Something catchy. It won't be as good as the ONE. It will be better. I look back in the mirror again.

"Hello, it's Harry. Father Harry."

I like it. Harry is someone you would trust.

"Harry, what's your last name?

"Chapman. Hello, my name is Father Harry Chapman... Has a ring to it."

"Is that okay, Harry? You don't mind me using your name? People will sit up and notice, Harry. That cheating ex-wife of yours for one. It will make you famous, Harry."

I go back into the front room.

"Harry, do you know if there are any churches nearby?"

He doesn't strike me as the churchgoing type.

"Not a church going man then, Harry? It's okay, I will google it. Where were we before Google, eh? Changing the world, that is what my nan always says. And, Harry, the woman is never wrong."

I go into the hallway, pick up one of the letters from the side and input Harry's postcode. There is a small Baptist church about a five-minute walk away from the house.

"Looks like we are in luck, Harry. I should be able to give this character a run out on a Sunday of all days. It is good to get these things started as soon as possible. Good to get the feedback too."

I start to pack up my stuff.

"In fact, Harry, is it all right if I spend the night? I could walk round then, as I don't really want them to see a man of the cloth pulling up in a builder's van.

"Thanks, Harry. You have been a really good host."

I grab the keys from the side, and head out of the house. It's literally only around the corner. I check the time. It's almost five thirty. I head straight there. The church looks almost like an old house. I was expecting something grander, with those windows and everything. I walk in as a couple are walking out.

"Evening, Father."

"Good evening."

I swear they didn't even look at my face. One look at the collar and it was heads down. Sinners, I am sure of it. Guilt will do that to you.

As I walk in the door I can hear the end of a song, and people getting up. The poster on the wall says Sunday evening prayers four thirty till five thirty p.m. Father Andy Flynn taking confession from five thirty to six thirty p.m.

I grab a seat at the back as the few dozen people walk out. Each one gestures and says evening to me as they do. I swear these people are looking directly at me and don't know who I am. This character is amazing.

There are three people still sitting next to the confessional booth. A couple, by the looks of it, and a woman on her own. The woman walks into the booth, slowly followed by a man I presume must be Father Flynn.

I move behind the couple. They aren't talking. Just sitting in silence. The woman is in and out in five minutes and disappears out of the church. The man walks into the booth.

"Evening, Father."

"Evening."

Should I say something like, "Evening, my child"? I am always hearing that on the TV. Then Fathers are generally old on TV. I am younger than her.

"Are you waiting for Father Flynn, Father?"

"Yes, I am."

Don't know why, but I so want to say, "my child". Just seems weird as she must be like forty or something.

"Something to confess, Father?"

There is a cheeky smile on her face. She is hot. I mean, I would do her given the right circumstances.

"No, not this time."

I just smile at her. She smiles back. Probably never met a Father as hot as me. Must be giving her confusing emotions. Sin and saint at the same time.

"You are new to us, aren't you, Father? I have not seen you here before."

"Yes, Father Harry Chapman."

I like the sound of that. I reach out my hand and shake hers.

"Pleased to meet you, Father Chapman. Mrs Alisa Slager."

There is silence. More silence. This pause is too long. Do men in service talk more than this? Has this silence gone on too long for me to say anything now? These guys always seem to be chatty on TV. Should I be chattier?

"I am sure he won't be long, Father."

Thank fuck for that. I was struggling there for a moment.

"Are you not confessing, my child?" That does sound better. Makes me feel all grown-up and stuff. Like a proper Father. She doesn't seem to have disapproved of it either, which is good. I am just a natural actor.

"No, Father. I am not the one who needs to confess their sins. My husband is the only person in need of that."

He shagged someone else, didn't he? I can tell by the look on her face. She is seriously not impressed with her husband. Although I am not sure how bragging about it to Father Flynn is going to make it any better.

"Confession is good for the soul."

"Confession is good for his health, Father. As, if he doesn't sort himself out, then it won't be this priest he will be needing. If you know what I am saying."

The curtain to the confession opens and out comes her husband. He walks up to the altar, goes down on one knee for three minutes, and then throws what looked like a twenty in the collection plate.

"Father."

"Mr Slager."

There was just a look, and they both got up to leave. Nobody else is in the church. I go into the confessional. Very small in here.

"In the name of the Father, Son and Holy Ghost."

I need to remember his opening line. I need to remember everything that he does in confession. If I am to take on this role, it needs to be perfect. Maybe I should have brought a pen and paper to write it all down. Or one of those Dictaphone things.

"Bless me, Father, for I have sinned. It has been a little over eighteen years since my last confession."

That is what they say on the TV, isn't it? Sounded cool.

"Time is irrelevant, my child. You are here now, which is the main thing."

Calm, cool, he must hear some good shit in here. There is a silence again. Father Flynn breaks it very quickly. I knew I should have done that outside, with Mrs Slager. All about the momentum. Keep them talking all the time.

"In your own time. Remember, this is your time to speak to God. Clear all the things that are burdening you, my son."

Burdening me? I don't think I have anything burdening me. Not sure what to confess to get this going. Not sure if I have anything to confess? Maybe feelings and stuff? That's what people do, isn't it? Share their innermost feelings. I am sure I have some of them.

"I don't really know where to start, Father. You see, I feel, I feel as if I am different than everyone else."

"We are all special, in our own way, my child."

They do say the child thing, it's not just on the TV. My child, my son. They say it and mean it? As if we are all their children.

"Yeah, I know that, but I wouldn't say special. More, more just better than everyone else, Father. I don't mean to be. Well, I do mean to be. I just feel I was born, you know, better than everyone else. I have skills other people don't have. I am faster, smarter, handsomer, not sure handsomer is a word, Father. More handsome. I excel at everything I do, and I can't stop it."

Not that I want to. I am great. He just doesn't need to know that.

"I am listening to you, my child. You are concerned that you are superior to everyone else that you meet?"

Concerned. Did he say concerned? Why would I be concerned?

"Yes, Father, that's the word, superior, superior to everyone else. That's exactly what I am."

"And, why do you think that you believe that, my son?"

What? Didn't he just hear me? I thought I explained it quite clearly?

"Sorry, Father? Because I am? For all the things I just said. I am just better, faster, handsomer, and just all those things. I was born that way. I just keep getting better. It is like a curse or something. Well, not a curse as I like it but you get what I mean."

Silence again, but it is brief.

"I understand. So, what is it that you want to confess, my child? You are ashamed of your abilities? Your ego? Your beliefs? These things are weighing you down?"

"God no, Father. Sorry, I mean, no, Father, I am not ashamed. I love my life and my job, Father. Sorry about the God reference, Father. Probably something you are not supposed to say in here."

"No problem, my son, and what, may I ask, is your job?"

"Jesus, now there is a question. Sorry, Father, didn't mean to say Jesus. Now, there is a question, Father."

I think it is because I am in a church all these words are coming into my brain. All I need to say is Holy Crap a ghost and that's the three of them. That is a good question though. What is my job?

"I guess, Father, my job is, I am a celebrity. You know, like a superstar. Not reality TV celebrity. A real celebrity. I mean, I am all over social media. I am the first social media star in my profession."

Never really thought about that. I guess I am the first.

"The TV and news channels follow me like a god. I hear they are thinking about making a film about me. So, yes, Father, I am famous, on all platforms."

"I am very pleased for you, my son. Sounds like an amazing lifestyle. May I ask you a question in return?"

I nod my head. Why am I nodding my head? I am not sure he can see me.

"How old are you?"

Oh, maybe he can see me.

"I am eighteen, Father."

There was a brief silence. It was brief, but longer than normal. He is thinking about something.

"I thought as much. So, this is in fact your first time in confession?"

"It is, Father. Sorry, Father, that may have been a bit misleading. I just thought that is what you had to say. Should I have made an appointment or something? Is that how it works?"

"That is not a problem, my child. Let me tell you how this works, as you put it. Confession is for you to try and repent for something that you believe to be wrong. Either legally or morally or spiritually. Is there such a thing that you wish to confess, my child?"

I don't know. I think I am a balanced person? Morally I am a genuine person. I am not fake, like most people.

"Nothing I can really think of Father. Not now."

"Then, you have nothing to confess, my son?"

Shit. I need to confess something as I don't know how these things end. Quick, think of something, Edmund. Make some crap up.

"Is cheating on your girlfriend a sin, Father?"

There is silence again. It must be. Cheating is cheating.

"Yes, that would be something I would expect to hear in confession. Do you love her, my son?"

Love is a strong word. I really fancy her, and she is hot as fuck, but love? Sometimes I tell people she is my girlfriend. That must be close to love.

"I think so, Father. We do talk about the future, and our future. That must be love, right, Father?"

"Then seriously think about why would you be unfaithful to her?"

I am not sure I can answer that question. Generally, I don't think about it. It just happens.

"I don't really know why. Is that odd?"

"There must be a point to this, my son. There must be an underlying issue that makes you do this while you say you are in a committed, loving relationship. You do not have to be married to be in a committed, loving relationship. Marriage is the bond that ensures it is forever and blessed by God."

Fuck, he is good!

"I guess it's the work, Father. I have never cheated on my girlfriend with anyone other than people I work with. I end up in the most ridiculous positions with some hot girls, Father. I mean, hot. We are talking seriously hot, Father. We are generally alone, and then one thing leads to another."

"Do you think you put yourself in these positions because you know what will happen next? Is it conscious? How do you feel at that point?"

"Horny, Father, generally I feel horny. And most of the time, Father, they are begging for it. I mean, begging. They can't get enough of me."

"What do you think it is that makes you horny, as you would put it, at that exact point? Is it purely physical? Is it the fact that you are cheating? Is it the way they look?"

"I have a type, Father. In fact, if truth be known, all the women I fall for, fall for may be a little strong, the women that take my interest, shall we say, Father, look very similar to her, my girlfriend, Father. They all look like her."

Never really thought about that in too much detail. That's a bit odd, isn't it? It is almost as if I am trying to be close to her by sleeping with other women. The ones that I just can't say no to, look like her?

"So, it may just be a longing to be with her? Do you see her very often? Is that what the issue is? You don't spend enough time with her. In your own way, you are trying to get closer to her?"

It may be. I think he has nailed it in one conversation. That is amazing. I did say I needed to spend more time with her just the other day.

"Not as much as she would like, Father. I work away a lot, but we are trying to work on that. We did talk about that this very weekend."

"Is that what it is, my son? It is just a pure desire to be closer to the woman that you love. Then, I think you know what is needed."

"I think it is, Father. Thank you, that has really opened my eyes up... Well, it is that, Father, and the blood. Once that is leaking out of them, it doesn't help with the horny, if you know what I mean."

Silence again. Still silence. Isn't he supposed to be filling the silence?

"Father? Are you okay?"

"Yes, my son. Did you say blood?"

"Yes, Father. You know, when you have cut their throats and they are bleeding all over you. Gets me turned on, Father.

Always has done. I think it's to do with the smell, the rich, dark, sweet smell as it soaks through the long dark hair."

I get lost in the moment for a minute. He is probably thinking about it too. I am sure he is. He can't get a lot of action, can he?

"Sorry, Father, I lost myself there for a moment. I was just thinking about it when I was in Asda earlier. Ten minutes after the blood, I am horny and they are teasing me to sleep with them. The blood is a factor, Father. The factor."

Silence. Shit! Think I may have got carried away. He is good. I didn't mean to say all that. I get up and get out of the booth. I am in the Father's side of the booth in seconds. He hadn't moved. I slide my knife straight across his neck before he knows what is going on, and I whisper in his ear.

"Can you smell it, Father? That's the smell. Blood is a very strong aphrodisiac. I mean, I am not horny now as you are a bloke. But, imagine that smell with a really, hot girl. I mean, seriously hot, Father."

He doesn't move. Just sits there. I watch as the blood runs down onto the collar. Something very strange about it. Almost scary. Religion and blood are scary things. No convulsions or anything. It's almost mesmerising. As if he isn't even there. Maybe it's a God thing. Maybe his soul just goes fast to the next place. Like an expressway due to the job. The blood is odd for an older guy as well. It still smells sweet. Because he is like good and stuff, I am sure of it. I am standing in the booth with him when I hear it, the curtain being closed on the other side.

"Evening, Father."

Fuck!

Someone has come to confess. I pull the Father down onto the floor in front of me, and sit on the seat. I am going to have to stand on him. There is no room in these things. What if a big guy comes in to confess? Wait, big people don't cheat. Why would they be here? Must be only hot people. I wasn't ready to do this so soon. I should have taken notes.

"In the name of the Father, Son and Holy Ghost."

"Forgive me, Father, it has been three months since my last confession."

"Go on, my son."

"Father, I don't know where to start."

My God, he sounds like he is going to cry. Silence. How bad can it be? He only confessed three months ago? Still silence. Shit! Father Flynn filled the silence. Not now, but before when I was on the other side. Must fill the silence.

"The beginning is always the best place to start, my son."

God, that sounds good. I don't mean God, sorry. I just can't stop saying God. I am getting good at this already. Is there really nothing I can't do?

"Father, firstly you have to know I love my wife."

Cheating bastard. Money is, he is a cheating bastard. Probably Harry's brother. How weird would that be?

"I am glad to hear that. Marriage is a very important institution."

Institution? Is that even the right word? Isn't that where you go when you go mad? Maybe that is why it is the right word.

"It is, Father, and you have to know I fully intended to honour my vows, but things have, well, been going south for

69

a while now. What started as an innocent drink, well, it's turned into something more."

"When you say more, my son?"

"Teresa my wife, she is a nurse. Works late and long hours, Father, and I, well, I was just a little lonely, that is all. I finish at like five p.m. and most nights she is not in till ten, sometimes eleven o'clock."

He cheated. I knew it. He is a cheater.

"It's not like I went to a bar or anything looking for it. I was just at home on Facebook;one thing led to another, and I started to talk to, you know, someone else."

"Talking is not a sin, my son."

At least I don't think it is, is it? Suppose it is, depending on what you are talking about. That Judas fella, all he did was talk, and I am pretty sure he isn't in heaven.

"Then we started poking."

"Now that is a sin, my son. God looks down on adulterers."

"No, I mean poking on Facebook, Father. It was just a piece of fun."

Twat! Should have picked up on that. I get poked all the time. Think I am getting into this character though. Looking for the judgemental side of everything. Pretty easy really.

"It just started as a joke. That is all it was supposed to be, Father, a little bit of fun. Then after a couple of weeks, the conversation got more, involved, shall we say, Father."

"I am sensing, my son, that this conversation led somewhere else, didn't it? Somewhere that it shouldn't have."

Silence. I think he is really scared about confessing this now, isn't he? It must be like talking to a policeman or something? Although, all he gets is a few words, and to chuck a twenty into the plate, isn't it? I don't know. I didn't get to the end.

"It did, Father. It really did."

"Go on, my son. I cannot forgive you unless I know your sins."

Shit! I get my phone out. I google confession. Do I forgive him or send him to hell or what do I do? I am sure there is something to do with praying and giving cash to get rid of your sins. Like Mr Slager.

"It started with a harmless drink, Father. It would seem we have the same taste in a lot of things. We know a lot of the same people, and it felt like we had known each other for ever."

"Go on."

Still googling, no idea what the fuck I say if he finishes.

"We started to talk about family, and what we really wanted out of our lives. We met again and again until one night she came around the house. My wife was at work and, well, one thing led to another."

"Temptation is just that, my son. You do not need to follow through on anything. You are committed to your wife, and you should honour your vows."

"I couldn't help it, Father, she was all I was thinking about, and I just couldn't help it. She had bewitched me, Father, bewitched."

"You could, my son, just cut the woman out of your life. Turn the laptop off, and return to your family. You know it's the right thing to do. There is nothing more important than family."

71

Wait, am I supposed to give him advice? Or is he supposed to come up with this stuff on his own? Father Flynn made me do all the work. Maybe I need to do that.

"That's the problem, Father, she is the wife's mother."

What the fuck!

I stop looking at the phone. I look up at the grid and press my face against it. He has his hands in his head, but I can see the grey hair. He must be sixty? Which means his mother-in-law must be like what, ninety or something. *Fucking freak!*

"I didn't mean it to get out of hand, but I was helping her upstairs to the toilet, and she asked me to come in. I was going to wait outside, you know, to help her back down. The stairs are tricky with a Zimmer frame, Father."

Fuck! Why won't my phone tell me what to say to get rid of this freak? Wi-Fi in these places suck!

"You see, I started to undress her in the bathroom and well, I was just doing it to help in the beginning, you know, make sure she doesn't trap the bag and everything."

"I don't need the details, my son. I think I understand what is next."

Fuck's sake, keep the details to yourself.

"One thing led to another, Father, and we were at it on the floor of the bathroom within minutes."

I don't want to hear this. I really don't want to hear this.

"Her bag exploded, Father. I had to hide the rug and everything, but it didn't stop us. We just kept going at it, Father. Father, it was the best sex ever."

I am lost for words. No, I don't think there are words.

"Father, it has started something inside me. I see the world differently now."

So do I, you freak. How will I ever look at an old woman again?

"Sin has that habit, my son. It can be addictive, but you can be strong. You can resist. Put it out of your mind. You said you love your wife. Just don't talk or think about it ever again."

For fuck's sake, I need to change the subject!

"That's what I am trying to say, Father. I don't think I can. I can't keep my hands off her. When I am not with her, I am thinking about how she looks. How she tastes. How her skin feels next to mine."

Like sandpaper, I would fucking think! Sandpaper, you sicko.

"I retired last year, Father, and I had a plan. Golf, gardening, that type of thing. Two weeks ago, I started work in an old people's home. Father, I tell you, it's tearing me apart. So many hot women, Father. It is like I had never seen them before. I am working late just to be with them. Father, the K-Y Jelly alone is eating into my pension, and I don't know how to explain it to my wife?"

"K-Y Jelly?"

"Yes, you know, Father. The stuff you use to, you know, loosen things up a bit. Father, I am worried I may break one of their hips or something. I tell you, the other night Mrs Parker, I thought she had died halfway through. Luckily, it was just her oxygen mask falling off. I got it back on in time."

Fuck it!

The knife goes through the grate, and so do I. Flimsy partition for a confessional booth. I just keep stabbing and stabbing at him until he stops moving. And, at fucking last, he

73

stops talking. The blood is strong, but I don't want to smell it. I don't want to smell his blood, he is freaking me out.

Calm! Edmund. *CSI* Edmund. I stop stabbing. I wore my gloves, that is good, but the more I lunge, the more chance that there is DNA left. I don't want them finding out about Father Harry Chapman until they need to. They can't link us together.

The booth is in pieces and he is under there somewhere. I look around. So lucky nobody else walked in while we were in there. I didn't even think about that. I need to be aware that anyone can walk into these places at any time.

What a freak!

I go and close the church doors. No more confessions. This priest job must be so hard. Any weirdo could come in and confess.

I sit back down in the aisles. I need to find a new church. One that looks more like a church, and I need to research the confession thing better. Surely you aren't supposed to listen to all of it.

I look over at the mess I have made. Do I leave them like that or stage it? If I stage it, am I putting it in more of an Edmund Carson style? Will it be too similar?

Think I need to leave it, and then escalate. All people in my profession get better as they go on. Then I can stage some scenes. Hone my craft as it is.

Need to also go back to Harry's and pick up my stuff. I go to the church door. There is a people carrier sitting in the driveway. I go back in and check the freak's pockets. He has keys, and it will be more use than a van. I take the keys and head back out, closing the door behind me. Hopefully it will be tomorrow before they find them, and Mrs Slager has my name. That will come out in a couple of days.

I get into the car, and start the engine. As I look to reverse out the drive I notice the wheelchair in the back of the car.

Sick bastard.

Chapter 4

The next car I get needs to be an automatic. Priests would have automatics, wouldn't they? Leaves more time for praying and stuff. Plus, don't they like have to wave at people as they go by? Or is that just the pope? I wave at the person in the car next to me. They wave back. I knew it, they all do it. You would think religious people would have a better taste in music. It's either Madonna or the Worship top ten. I mean, who listens to praise music in the car?

I switch on the heating and turn the music off. The radio must be better than that nonsense. How is it that you can't drive with your phone, but you can listen to music and talk to people next to you? Isn't that the same thing? The weather is miserable today. So frigging cold. I turn the heating up a little more.

"Morning, and welcome to today's show. Serial killers on the rise or fall? With Edmund Carson now missing from the public eye for over a month, and the rise of the serial killer Father Harry Chapman. We ask, is the Internet and movie world responsible for influencing these young men in their career choices? Are the police doing enough to stop this and

what responsibility does the media have in the publicity of these events? Then later we will be discussing, are reality TV shows taking over our television? And as always, we will be catching up with Henry down on the allotment as summer is soon upon us, so we will be pulling up our lettuces and spring onions. But first, this, my record of the week. Adele with 'Hello'."

Hello, it's me. I would. Something about her. She is not Miss Walker type, but she is not actually blonde though, is she? Plus, she seems to be getting hotter as she gets older. Something about the way she sings. Makes me wonder what else she could do with her mouth.

Wait, what do they mean missing for a month? It's not been a month? Really a month? It can't be. Can it? She is going to be so mad. I said I would go and see her in a week or so, and that was a month ago?

At least I am heading in the right direction now. She will be thankful of that. Well, I am no longer in Scotland so that's a bonus all round. I mean deep-fried Mars bars and Haggis. What are we, savages?

A month! I haven't had sex with Miss Walker for a month? I haven't had sex at all for a fucking month! Is there something wrong with me?

Fuck! And well, fuck!

Maybe they are right though. I never thought of it before now, but Edmund has disappeared. That's a bit stupid really? I need him to come back while Harry is about as well... And maybe the ONE. Maybe a one-night special with all three making an appearance. That way people won't start to wonder.

"So, before we go to the lines, Elle on email says, Jeremy, I think the media is totally responsible for the glorification of these sick individuals. If they stop covering them then they will stop doing what they are doing. They are just attention-seekers… Interesting point. On the line we have Dr Darren Payne, a leading psychiatrist, and Mrs Sarah Fitzgerald, a world-renowned journalist. Well, what do you think of the view that if we stopped publishing the events, the now called modern-day social media killers will stop, Sarah?"

"Hi, Jeremy. Journalism provides a public service with regards to matters like this. It is our responsibility to report the truth, and to warn the public that there are people like this out there."

"I understand that, but for people like Edmund Carson, who thrives on the publicity, do you think that you also have a responsibility to ignore his endeavours? Maybe if he knew that the world wasn't watching, it would make him stop?"

"Maybe, Jeremy. But, if you didn't know about him, nobody would be looking for him. You wouldn't know what he looked like? How freely could he pass through society then? With the huge rise in social media this gives us even more of an opportunity to find him. As you say, the world is looking for him now."

"Despite that fact, it doesn't seem to have helped us so far, Sarah?"

"No, unfortunately, he still seems to be able to evade the public eye. While at the same time still trying to throw himself in it. I do think it is fair to say though over the past three to four months the press has taken a different tone with him. While we still are reporting him, we are not publishing it in a *glorifying light as your listener has stated. It has purposely been what we call negative press."*

I fucking knew it!

I knew the bastards were winding me up!! All this time they have been doing this on purpose to fucking wind me up.

"Are you saying that the world's press has taken this tactic, to give Edmund Carson negative press, Sarah?"

"Well, not the total press, but certainly it has been for the top three news outlets in the country. Yes, Jeremy, and, so far, we have seen a change in his behaviour, haven't we?"

"We certainly have, Sarah. I wasn't aware of that. Dr Payne. What is your view on this tactic by the press? To almost wind up or, I guess, call out the serial killer Edmund Carson?"

"Hi, Jeremy, firstly, great show. Big fan and always listen. To visualise on Sarah's point. I don't believe poking the bear is ever going to be a good thing."

"Yes, Dr Payne, but you have seen yourself the slowdown, and the performance issues, with regards to Edmund Carson. We started this campaign in secret, and look at what has happened. He has not been seen or heard of in a month. Even his social media outlets have not been used?"

Performance issues, fucking performance issues, you can't use that and Edmund Carson in the same sentence… Bitch! Bitch! How dare she? People will be playing that clip repeatedly. I need to deal with her.

I knew I should have been tweeting though. That was stupid, Edmund! At least throwing the odd one out there just to say I am here. Still working. Or at least worked with someone in the last month.

"That may be Sarah, but it does not mean that he is not active. What it means is that he isn't publishing it. There may be one hundred reasons why this is. He may be hurt or dead or clearly struggling with conscience. Given his flair for the dramatic and the theatrical, maybe he is planning the next event. Something major. Something like another school. You don't know if the work you have done has just driven him to get bigger and bolder. Only time will tell."

It has! How are you going to feel about that? I am going to get more creative. I will get bigger and bolder. Bigger and better than the school. I will do something. I like him. He talks a lot of sense.

"No, Doctor Payne, we don't, but we are helping the best way we know. Edmund Carson is the only serial killer to ever officially hit the one hundred victim mark in the UK. We all have a part to play in catching this monster."

One hundred. One fucking hundred! I knew I was there or thereabouts, but that was weeks ago? They don't know all of them, surely! They don't know about Father Harry Chapman. That's why they are only saying one hundred. Are they counting the ONE into that as well or is she just saying Edmund Carson? The bitch needs to be clearer. Doesn't she know people are listening? But she said it now and it will be in the papers tomorrow. Or not – forgot the bitch writes the papers! And who the fuck is she calling a monster? I am hardly a monster, am I? That's a horrible word.

"Sarah, I think the best thing we can do is appeal to these disturbed individuals to come forward. I agree with Jeremy that they want to be heard. So, let's listen to their side of the story. A villain is just a victim whose story has not been told."

"Dr Payne, I think that is a great idea. In fact, Edmund, Father Harry, or indeed any serial killer, if you would like to call in, please feel free to do so. Dr Payne and Sarah will be with us to take some calls after Cold Play and 'Fix You'."

I turn up the radio; I like this song. Always envisage a teenager in a car, driving, and crying at the same time. The rain is coming down hard, and he is struggling to see what is ahead of him. He regrets not being with her. He wants to be with her all the time, so he tells her the lights will guide her to him. And she will fix, I mean, he will fix her. That would make it into my movie.

"And I will fix you." I could have been a singer.

Did he say phone in? Maybe I should phone in? Or is that just too weird? Who do I phone in as? Edmund? Harry? The ONE?

No, they are just baiting me to talk to them. They just want to trace my phone. Probably set the whole thing up just to do that.

"And we are back with Dr Payne, and Sarah Fitzgerald from The Times. We are talking about serial killers and the effect that they are having on society. We are focusing in on the way, we journalists, are reporting these situations. Sarah, I am going to start with you again. While you discussed the negative press campaign with Edmund Carson, it's not fair to say that this is the case for Father Harry Chapman. Over the last month I believe he has been headline news every day. Sometimes taking three to five pages. Why the difference?"

"I think, Jeremy, that this is a totally different situation. Father Harry Chapman is proving to be rash and haphazard in his approach. We believe the more we publicise him, the

more chance he will be found and quickly. The last thing we need is another Edmund Carson on the loose."

"When you say 'rash'?"

"Well, other than last Friday's wedding massacre, all of Father Harry's main victims seem to have been killed with some haste. Very impulsive, and not planned at all. He is a very opportunistic killer. So, the more we publicise him, the better chance people have of recognising him."

I fucking planned them!

I meant them to look like that. The whole point was not to let people know that it was me. Thanks for noticing all the effort that I have gone to. Wait, I didn't want them to notice the effort I had gone to. It just proves how good I am.

"It leads us to believe, Jeremy, that he will make a mistake."

"And, Doctor Payne, what is your view on that?"

"Jeremy, up until last week I would have totally agreed with Sarah, but Father Harry is escalating."

I knew it, I knew I was! I am getting so good at escalating business. It was exactly what I was trying to do. He really gets me.

"With most serial killers, the need to kill is impulse at first. That is what has happened with Father Harry. Impulse drove him to kill that priest at the confessional. And, as he has travelled the country the victims were all attacked with a knife or strangled at opportune times. Last week, and to quote Sarah's paper, a Kill Bill style massacre, shows us that Harry is getting a purpose. The fact that he knew of the secret wedding on the Friday, and managed to drug all of the eight people present."

"Dr Payne, he Rohypnoled the champagne."

"Exactly, Sarah, and to do that he must have planned the wedding, conducted the wedding and then made the toast in the church afterwards for them all to drink the drink. That is a far different cry from a strangulation in a graveyard. It took planning, and rational thinking. Father Harry is escalating into a more professional serial killer."

I do like this guy. Think it's the way he shows the skills I have. He would be a good mentor for people like me. He is probably consulting on TV shows like *CSI* and *Criminal Minds*. To make the stars shine a little brighter. A little bit of facts behind them makes them sound more real.

"So, Doctor Payne, Sarah, I will ask you the same question shortly. What do you make of the scene afterwards? Very Edmund Carson, I would say. Theatrical and a sense of purpose about it?"

"I would agree. I would also like to believe there was some remorse for his actions though. To leave the married couple praying at the altar, and the six guests in the pews. Struck me as how he wanted to remember the scene before he lost control."

"And the fact that the men were strangled, and the women had their throats cut, what would be your take on that? Why the difference, given we know that they were already drugged?"

"I would say that he had the utmost respect for women and a hatred of men. He wanted the men to suffer longer than the women."

I think I should visit one of these psychiatrists. Clever guys. Seem to know what they are talking about. Surprising really, as most people they speak to must be a little cuckoo. That shit must rub off at some point.

"And, Sarah, your view?"

"Well, Jeremy, I believe somewhat the opposite. I believe that Father Harry is getting full of himself. So much so he is trying to become an Edmund Carson. Maybe we have some responsibility with that by creating the negative press, I don't know. Maybe he is looking to fill his shoes. I believe the opposite with regards to the killing also. The women's throats were cut as he wasn't bothered about them. He would have had to spend time holding his hands around the four men's throats, be close to them. I wouldn't be surprised if there was a gay undertone of Father Harry."

GAY! Gay! I am not fucking gay!

I am not gay. There is nothing wrong with being gay, but I am not gay. I strangled the men as it is different to what Edmund would have done… you stupid cow. And, I cut the girls as I wanted to at least get the smell? Do you know how hard it is not to be me in that situation? I can't make love to them, I can't taste them, and I can't lick them. Hell, not even a nibble. It will give away who I am. You really don't understand how hard I am working to make this happen.

God, I haven't had sex in a month. I need to have sex tonight!

Gay? What is up with this woman? Is she trying to mess with my head? Again? Does she not realise it's not just me? Imagine the thousands of gay men out there she has just given hope to. Probably dumping their boyfriends now with the hope of meeting me.

"We have our first caller on the line, Maria. Welcome, Maria, what is your view on this situation?"

"Hi, Jeremy. I agree with some of what Sarah is saying regarding negative press on these monsters, but I don't believe we are going far enough. Why don't we cut it out altogether? No papers, no TV and no Radio, Jeremy."

"Ouch... Although I would gladly report on something else though if it were to stop all of this. I do understand what you are saying, but back to Sarah's point, how would the public know?"

"I am not saying don't let the public know, Jeremy. I am saying stop reporting on it. I spent a while living in America and they have the top ten wanted posters everywhere from the FBI. With Facebook and Twitter and Instagram hitting half of the world's population, a daily tweet, or blog or something with their picture on, and a number to call is surely enough. We don't need to know the graphic detail of everything they are doing? Surely, all we are doing is panicking the population."

"Sarah?"

"Well, Maria. Personally, I think that is a great idea and concept. Professional suicide for me, but I don't disagree with your view."

"Doctor Payne?"

"I think knowing their behaviours is key to catching them."

"I agree, Doctor, but I think what Maria is saying is that the public don't need to know? Is that right, Maria?"

"Yes, Jeremy. The authorities need to know everything, but we don't."

"Great call, Maria. Thanks for phoning in. Looking through Facebook, a lot of today's feedback seems to be very similar. Andrew writes 'Stop reporting on these nutters, and they will stop.' Kerry Stephens writes 'Jeremy, aren't you playing into their hands also?' I guess that is what we are here to debate. To the phone again, we have Darren Gosling."

Darren Gosling? I know that name. Where do I know that name from?

"Hi, Darren."

"Hi, Jeremy, Sarah, Dr Payne. Great name for a psychiatrist by the way. You could be in a Marvel comic. Yes, Jeremy. I want to pose a question, as either I am as mad as these nutters or most of the world's population is."

"Okay, Darren, what's the question?"

"Isn't Father Harry Chapman just Edmund Carson in a dog collar?"

Fucking prick!

He was the guy who pissed me off in Cornwall. He was calling me names then! It was on Twitter or Facebook or one of them. What did I ever do to him? Why is he getting all up in my business?

"Interesting thought, Darren. Dr Payne, could Father Chapman be the missing Edmund Carson? It would explain where he is?"

The missing Edmund Carson. They keep saying that. I think I have messed that up a bit. That is my fault. I should have kept him busy. He needs to be busy. Even if they are not wanting to report on Edmund positively, he needs to be there.

"Hi, Darren. Firstly, I think I understand your point as one serial killer disappears another arrives on the scene. This

may look like the case, but these are without doubt two different people."

I knew I liked this guy. He speaks a lot of sense. You tell the twat. He doesn't have a clue what he is talking about. Well, he shouldn't have a clue what he is talking about. He is not as clever as me. Nobody is.

"How do you know they are two different people, Dr Payne? Darren may have a point, and would it not disprove Sarah's theory also that the press has managed to curb Edmund Carson?"

Fuck, this guy is agreeing with him also? They can't both be thinking that Edmund is Harry. I am sure there are hundreds of people listening to this show. This needs to be dropped and quickly.

"Serial killers have an MO, modus operandi, which is Latin for mode of operation. Like all of us, a killer learns from each kill, something that is evident in Edmund Carson. You can see, as he has developed, he has a need to be more and more creative with his scenes. The last being his birthday party followed by the breakfast scene at the bed and breakfast. The difference here is that Father Harry Chapman is a new killer. The rage that was seen at the first church that he entered. The wilful destruction of the confessional booth. All show signs of a killer out of control. He has, I will grant you, developed over the last month and improved his MO, as we would say. This is because he has escalated. Or, I slightly agree with Sarah, it may be a homage to Edmund Carson. Generally, though, Father Harry is still full of rage. Remember the second church, for instance. The priest was killed with what was recorded as thirty-seven stab wounds."

That was messy. I was trying to play noughts and crosses on his chest for fun, but it didn't work out. Had to cover it up somehow. Not Edmund's style at all. That was the point though. I am glad he has got it at least.

"You say that, Dr Payne, but the altar boys you can claim were very Edmund Carson.?"

"I believe they were experimental. I think our serial killer Father Harry Chapman was trying to decide what kind of killer he is. As a killer escalates, they very often try to have their own style. And given the press revolving around Edmund Carson over the past eighteen months, there is no doubt that he will be looked up to, in a way. I believe that Father Chapman was just trying to emulate something Edmund would do. Even serial killers have idols. It is very natural for him to look up to him in that way."

I shouldn't have done that. The smell of the blood was just too strong in those two boys. All I could think of was the fry-up with Tiffany. I had to.

"Sarah, what is your view?"

"I hate to say it, Jeremy, but for once I do agree with Doctor Payne. I don't believe that Edmund and Father Harry are the same killer. I believe, unfortunately for us in the United Kingdom, we have two major serial killers on the loose. The similarity in the killing of the altar boys for me as well was almost a homage to Edmund Carson. Although I believe Edmund to be somewhat of a cannibal, I don't see that in Father Chapman."

That did taste good. A kind of sweetness about it. Almost cherry flavoured. I am sure it is something to do with living a pure life. They have a different flavour. Nuns must taste amazing. I haven't had a nun, and I haven't had a nun. In fact, I am getting nun either. God, I need sex. Sex with a nun with the stockings and suspenders on. That is what I need.

"Okay, thank you, Darren. It was an interesting thought, but it would seem our experts don't agree with you. Let's play one more record, 'Chasing Cars' by Snow Patrol, and we will be right back."

See, you prick, nobody believed that they are the same person. You must be a moron or something! I am too clever for this game. I am a professional; there is nothing I cannot do, and nothing I will not do to keep my fans entertained. I think I may have to visit you.

I turn the radio up, love this song. He really does play some good music.

"And we are back with Doctor Payne and Sarah Fitzgerald from The Times newspaper, we have been... sorry, what? Bear with me one moment, listeners, my producer has just run into the room holding a piece of paper. The paper says go to line one. Let's go to line one. Hi, caller, you are through to the show?"

"Hi, Jeremy, love the show. The music has been really good today."

"Thank you, and who can I say is calling?"

"Sorry, Jeremy, it's Father Harry Chapman."

"Father Chapman. It is certainly a pleasure to have you here. Not that we would have any doubt who you are, but how do we know it's the real you?"

"It is, Jeremy. I am sure Sarah from The Times has done her homework. She will know that the first person I took confession from was sleeping with his mother-in-law... who,

by the way, Jeremy, must have been about ninety. There is a topic for your show for next week. The girl in the graveyard? She was a hooker. So was her sister. Who, by the way, I am surprised you haven't found yet. There was an open grave and I thought someone would notice that I only half-filled it in. Bit of a tip there for you too."

"I am getting a nod from Sarah's direction, Father Chapman."

"Then you know it's me, Jeremy."

"It would seem we do. Thanks for calling in but what has driven you to do so? How may we help you?"

"Well, first, Jeremy, I would like to say hi to Dr Payne."

"Hi, Father Chapman."

"Hi. I must say you have spoken a lot of sense over the last twenty minutes I have really enjoyed it. So much so I was thinking about therapy myself."

"I would be happy to do that for you. If you just name a time and a place."

"Very good, Doctor. I may be new, but I am not green."

"Secondly, Jeremy, and I will try not to swear but that Darren guy, what a prick. Sorry, can I say prick on air?"

"That's fine, Father Chapman. When you say prick, do you mean because he compared you to Edmund Carson?"

"Yes, Jeremy. That and the kind of joke about comics. He is obviously some kind of nerd?"

"And, so that I and the listeners are clear, Father Chapman, you don't want to be associated with the serial killer Edmund Carson?"

"No, of course I don't. I mean we are two different people."

"With similar, let's call them hobbies, it would seem, Father Chapman?"

"Yeah, I am not too keen on you, Sarah. You haven't been very nice about me. I don't think I want to talk to you. Just Jeremy and Dr Payne."

"That's fine, Father. Is it okay if I call you Father?"

"Fine, Jeremy."

"Father, it's Doctor Payne, Sarah will stay quiet. This comparison to Edmund Carson has upset you? Why would that be, Father?"

"Well, we are two different people, aren't we? We both need to be judged on our own merits. I mean, I must admire his work as he is a genius. Some of the characters and scenes he has created with the people he works with are legendary, but we are two different people."

"Interesting, you use the same words as he does. Working with people? Do you base yourself on him? Are you trying to escalate into him?"

"No, of course not!"

"Do you see yourselves as rivals then?"

"No, not rivals or comrades. I have never even met the person. Which is not to say I wouldn't work with him in the future. He has done some remarkable work, and I have seen his photo everywhere. He is a true celebrity."

"So, Edmund is somewhat an idol to you?"

"No, not an idol. An inspiration to me, maybe, as I am sure he is to thousands of people. Just know, I don't want to be him, and I am sure he doesn't want to be me."

"But, you are both killing for fun?"

Does he really think we are doing this for fun? I am doing this for fun. This is work. Surely, he knows that? Does anyone have fun at work? This is all about being the best I can be. Me and Harry.

"*Father?*"

"*Father Harry, are you still with us?*"

"*Yes, I am here, Jeremy.*"

"*How about we change the line of conversation, Father. This comparison seems to have you a little upset. So, Father Harry, would you like to share with us where you are right now?*"

"*I am in the car, Jeremy.*"

"*Good, and heading anywhere nice?*"

I guess I am. I am heading down south towards her. Wait, he doesn't want to know that.

"*I am not that silly, Jeremy. The reason for the call, Jeremy, was just to point out that we are different people. I have my own reasons for doing what I do, and I am sure this Edmund Carson legend does too. We are independent.*"

"*I think we have that very clear. Would you like to share what your reasons are, Father?*"

Shit, what are my reasons? Not to be Edmund Carson, and surprise the world isn't going to work on here. Although I am sure I read somewhere this station has six million listeners, maybe this is the place to come out. Although I have just spouted that we are not the same person repeatedly. That doctor was getting into my head. This was not my best idea; to phone in. I think I should have left it alone. I need to get out of it now.

"*Religion, Jeremy.*"

"Religion. Okay, and what statement about religion is it that you are trying to tell us? Do you have beliefs that need to be listened to? Are you atoning for something that you want us to know about? Or are you just so set against religion that you want to kill all the people involved in it?"

FUCK!

I don't know. That is the whole point. I could say I want religion stopped. It does more damage than good, but everyone says that. I could say that I was abused by a priest, but that has been done too. Shit. I hang up the phone. It is my only choice.

"Father? Father, you have gone quiet again? I was just trying to point out, should I be afraid if I am a priest or a follower? Which do you hate the most?"

"I think we have lost Father Harry Chapman, listeners, but this is certainly a first. We will be right back after we gather our thoughts, and play this record. Simon and Garfunkel 'Bridge Over Troubled Waters.'

FUCK!

I pull the car over into the lay-by.

That wasn't good. That didn't go as I had planned. All I wanted to do was point out that we are two different people. It's all that Darren's fault. He started me thinking. He was the one who put the idea out there, and now it probably sounds like they are the same person. Doesn't it? Doesn't my nan always say if someone protests to much then, it's them. Certainly, it is on *CSI*.

FUCK!

Not good, Edmund, not good. I am going to work with that Darren fellow. I swear it. It's his fault. I need to find out where that prick lives, and go and spend some quality time with him.

His fucking fault! His, not mine.

Chapter 5

It's going to be fine. They didn't really pick up on anything. I'm sure of it. I don't think that Jeremy is that bright in the end. That Sarah and doctor just came across as arguing so that would have probably made people turn off anyway.

That says Kendal, isn't that some type of cake? I could go for cake about now. I come off the road, and head towards Kendal.

Teatime. I sound like my nan. Teatime is four o'clock, Edmund. We never had teatime at home. It was always breakfast, lunch and dinner. As soon as I went to live with her, she always had breakfast, dinner, tea.

I do miss her. Every day I miss her. It's been so long. I don't even know where she is now. How can they put her in witness protection when she isn't even a witness to anything? That doesn't make any sense. She hasn't done anything? Hasn't seen anything. I doubt that Brad Pitt's nan is in witness protection just because he is famous. Why would they do that to my nan? I know that fame has a lot to answer for, but I am sure she didn't want to give up her charities and stuff. She loved doing all that. Probably some plot to get at me. Like that Sarah cow.

Wherever she is, she will still be proud of me. Of all the work I have done, and the volume of work. She always said I would achieve great things, and I have. She will know our name will go down in history. Maybe not proud of that interview just now. Although she wouldn't know it was me, would she? Nobody would. She is probably still doing charity work. Just in another name; in another town. Hopefully down by the sea; she loves the sea, maybe Brighton. I should go down and see her there. I am sure she will be keeping a scrapbook of all my work. She loves doing things like that. I think it is a nan thing. Photos and memories. I wonder if Panini will come out with an annual. Like they do with football tournaments or Star Wars movies. Collect all the stickers, fill up the book. An Edmund Carson Limited Edition book. That's an amazing idea. Something for all the fans to keep. Maybe once you have filled in the book you send off a picture and get an 'I love Edmund Carson' T-shirt or 'I am one with the ONE'. That would be so cool.

I loved them as a kid, always keeping an eye out for the golden ones. They were my favourite and it was always the special people that would be made of gold. Who would be gold in my limited edition? My nan obviously, my parents maybe? Seventeen, she should be a sticker. She is going to love that. Probably me in different outfits like the ONE and Father Harry? Maybe the whole school will be. Like a dedication to them. It could be like the centre spread. Collect all the girls and put them in the correct chairs. That would be so cool.

Although it seems they only like me when I do big events like that. Maybe I should do another? That doctor thought I was planning one. Maybe I should be.

Alina. Alina would be a sticker. I had almost forgotten about her. She was a little nutty though. I mean, to recognise me, and still want to stick around. Especially straight after the school. Should have known really. The pink hair and the tattoos do kind of scream I am a little different. But oh, the taste. The taste was amazing. That alone should have made her golden. The sweetness and let's face it, she wasn't sweet. I am almost convinced she wanted me to work with her. I would imagine there are a lot of people out there praying that I work with them.

I am getting hungry now, and not for mint cake. It was Kendal mint cake, wasn't it? I don't know why I remembered that. I am hungry for real food. I never liked kidneys the way my nan did them, but sautéed with a little garlic, heart, liver… that is amazing. Now it's all I can think of. That and Tiffany. I wonder if you could swap it up a bit. Wonder what Tiffany's liver and Alina's kidneys would taste like. Sort of a mix and match. Like they do with sausages now. There used to be just sausages, now there is like a hundred different flavours. They like mix pork and beef. Like a cow and a pig. Must be the same sort of thing.

They have a castle here. It's been ages since I went to a castle… The school trip. I remember Carl Carnegie pretending to be king. He was such a knob, but I am glad we got to spend some time together before he headed off to France. I will have to go to that. I like castles. I would have been born a king in those days. Or at least a prince, and then a king. I have always been destined for greatness. I think it's in my blood. That's what they say, isn't it? It was in my blood to be a star, a king, a God amongst men.

I wouldn't have been very good at being a servant though. Can you imagine being a servant or a waiter? I couldn't be a waiter. Not even today. All those people demanding food and stuff. Serving them like a, well, servant.

You know, I must have passed a dozen churches in this village, or town, whatever it is. I think it's time for Father Harry to make a house call... A god's house call.

Or Edmund? All I can think of now is that Darren bloke. I need to make sure all my characters are active at the same time. That way idiots like him won't make shit up about me.

Maybe a message. Oh, that would be good. Maybe a message to the world from Edmund saying that he doesn't do religion. That's it, that's what I need to do, and a message to that Jeremy guy. Fancy putting that as a topic on his show. Isn't there like world hunger and stuff he can talk about?

Now that looks like a proper church. Loving the round window in the front and it has a rectory. All in one. Never knew what a rectory was until a week ago. Isn't that funny? I would have thought it was something to do with building if you had asked me. A rectory. A rect. Erect.

Fuck! I haven't had sex for a month!

Must have a family or something as that is not a small house, sorry, rectory. That's the type of place I want to visit. Good job I am dressed for the occasion.

I park the car and walk up to the church. It's amazing. Some of the churches I have been in lately are amazing. I don't really understand this religion stuff, but clearly some people do. They are well into it. I mean, to spend the hours to build these things, and they probably do it for free or at least at cost, as you can't overcharge God, can you? It must be a sin or something. It will be in his book.

I should write a book. I would be a good writer. Maybe an autobiography? I think the world will want to read my life story. Can you imagine? The book tours, the book signings, TV shows. That would be so cool. I mean, God got his son to write his, and it is still selling shitloads now. Two thousand years later, and it's not even a good read. It's a bit like Shakespeare. Seems they jumble the words up on purpose.

"Afternoon, Father."

I turn. There is another Father standing in front of me.

"Afternoon, Father."

"Is there something that I can help you with, Father?"

"No, that's fine I am sure you are busy. I was just passing through and I spotted your church. It looked so good, I wanted to pop in and look around."

"Why, thank you. It is home to us. Father Steven Collis, by the way."

He puts out his hand, so I shake it.

"Father Darren Gosling."

I don't know why that bloke's name came into my head. I hate that guy, but I can hardly say Father Harry Chapman now. I hate picking new names, it's so hard.

"So, Father, where are you heading to make you come through our little town?"

Where am I heading? Now that's a deep question.

"London. I have been visiting friends in Scotland over the last couple of weeks, and am heading back home now."

"Ah, Scotland, it is a lovely place. Whereabouts in London do you live?"

Nosey, isn't he? What is this, twenty questions?

"Wimbledon."

"Lovely. Never been. Huge fan of the tennis though."

He is smiling. I think he thought that was funny. It's gone quiet, yep, still quiet... Need to think of something. We do that. We fill the silence. That's why the twenty questions. I need to remember to keep asking questions. Wait, how long has it been silent for? Need to say something.

"I may stay the night. I drove past your lovely castle and thought it may be worth a visit also?"

"That's an excellent idea, Darren, there is the Castle Green Hotel which is very reasonable, and has a spa and a pool if you fancy a dip in the morning. My wife uses it every day."

Knew that was a big rectory for one person. Now I am thinking about how hot his wife could be. I mean, models don't normally marry Fathers, do they? Or maybe they do, to atone for a misspent youth.

"Sounds perfect, thank you. I will give it a look."

"If you are going to stay this evening, it would be amiss of me not to invite you to dinner. My wife is generally an amazing cook, and Jess and Aaron would be glad of a fresh face at the table. You know what teenagers are like. Never want to speak to their parents."

It amazes me how friendly people are to people wearing a white piece of card under their shirt collar. Wait, did he say teenage daughter and wife? Now, that is an Edmund Carson style night out.

"That sounds a great idea. Thank you so much. That is so welcoming."

"Look, I will leave you in peace. Feel free to look around and shall we say seven this evening? Just come up to the house."

"Thank you again, that sounds lovely."

People just look at it and immediately they warm to you. Trust you with their deepest darkest nonsense. Always respectful, and keep offering you dinner. It's such an icebreaker.

Idiots!

Nice church though. I would have one like this if I took this job up full-time. Painting these windows must have taken forever though. I reckon a church like this would take like five years to build. Those new houses near my nan's house; three months, and they were big houses. They almost built a city in what, like a year.

Did they paint those windows after they were put up or before? Wouldn't the paint run if you painted them upright? Or is that why all of them have that lead lining? They always look like paint by numbers to me, the crappy presents you get for Christmas. Maybe that's where they got the idea, Christmas mass or something. Paint by numbers must have been nearly impossible. You could never cover over X plus V plus all those Is. I wonder who invited real numbers. Someone looking to save time, for sure.

Think I need to check into the hotel. It's gone five and if we are eating at seven I need to make myself presentable. Well, maybe wash my face. These guys never change clothes. It is acceptable to wear the same thing all the time. No logos either. So, there is no fashion or high-quality Fathers. I think they may be missing a trick there. If they want to make even more money for the church, the odd brand logo would do wonders.

I head over to the hotel. Check-in was very simple. I am always surprised people don't ask for ID. Although I really need to start keeping a list of names I have used as I end up reverting back to the same ones repeatedly. *Criminal Minds* would have worked that out. That Penelope is a genius, blonde though.Yuk! But so clever.

Nice to have a hotel room for a change. I shower and get re-dressed. I switch on the news before I leave to see if there is anything about me on there. There isn't. Probably part of that Sarah's campaign to block me out. I see they are not blocking George Clooney out. Almost every week he and his wife are on the TV saving something. There is very little difference between us. I don't understand why he gets all the press. He could practically be my grandfather. Great grandfather nowadays, I would guess. My nan and him would make a great couple.

Fuck!

Maybe that's the difference – him and his wife are always on TV. Brad and Angelina are always on TV although I think they are headed for a fall at some point. She is too hot for him. Harrison Ford and that Legal girl. It's all about couples. Maybe the press prefers that. If you are in a couple, you get more press. Maybe I should speak out more about Miss Walker. Maybe have a celebrity wedding or something.

I want to say Flockhart. Harrison Ford and someone Flockhart. I could get that boy band to play at it. They do that type of thing at celebrity weddings. The one with the boy with shaggy hair. The girls love that. I miss my long hair. Think I want it back.

A wedding that will get me into *HELLO!* and everything. When I get to London I am going to float it past her. It's about time I told her everything. It will be hard to hear, but she worships me, so it will be fine. It's not like she would leave me, is it? I mean, who would even consider leaving me?

I get back in the car and head over to the rectory. There are people coming out of the church. Must be an evening session. Always old people. It's like they get to about sixty and start hedging their bets. Probably didn't believe until then, but with one eye on the graveyard they are looking up and thinking maybe, just maybe. I see Father Steven locking the door after them.

"Evening, Father Collis."

"Oh, evening, Father, didn't fancy joining us for evening song?"

"Didn't notice it was on, or else I would have loved to. Seemed to be a nice crowd though?"

"Yes, a few. Not as many as I would like, but we do have an abundance of churches here. So, if we all get a few, that is a good sign."

He finishes locking up and we head over to the house. I wouldn't mind a house like this. Bit of a garden with a pond and everything. We go in.

"This is my wife Sandra."

"Hi, pleased to meet you, Sandra."

I shake her by the hand like she is a bloke. I don't think Fathers go in for the kiss, do they? Maybe I should try the double kiss thing. The thing the French do.

"Sandra, this is Father Darren that I told you about earlier."

"Darren is just fine."

This house is huge. I don't know how some of these guys get such a big house. It's twice the size of my parents' and they had to work for a living. Do these guys get a wage? Should I have been getting paid all this time? Does he have a mortgage? Or is that what that plate is for? To pay their wages? Kind of relying on tips. What if you are crap at your job? How would you know you were crap at this job? The result doesn't come till you get upstairs? Maybe you don't get in? Is that why they have gates? To turn people away?

"And where are Jess and Aaron this evening?"

Father Steven talking brings my head back into the room. A lot of questions in such a short time.

"Jess is at a friend for dinner, but will be home by nine. Aaron is in his room. I think he is plugged in and online. Some shooting game, I think."

"Like ships in the night this family, isn't that right, love?"

"Yes, dear. Why don't you sit in the study with Darren have a glass of wine, and I will check on the lamb."

"Great idea. Father, if you would like to follow me."

We head out of the kitchen. Something about her. She is not exactly hot, and looks like butter wouldn't melt in her mouth, but I don't know. I reckon she could go a few rounds. Maybe it's just me. Maybe it's because I haven't had sex in a month. I mean, a month! I can't even remember the last time I played with myself. Surely that's not good. All that build-up inside? It can't be good for my like swimmers and stuff. I owe it to Miss Walker to keep them fresh for the next time we meet. They must be so crowded in there. They don't keep growing, do they? I am not risking the chance of it exploding? Now that has me concerned. I am doing damage to myself by being Father Harry Chapman.

"Darren...Darren?"

Fuck! Is he talking to me?

Oh yeah, I am Darren. I was waiting for someone else to respond.

"Sorry, I am so sorry."

"Deep in thought, were you?"

"Yes, sorry, I was thinking of home?"

"It is hard to leave, isn't it? Especially once you have a congregation. They are family to you, and you want to be there to support them whenever you can. But you must remember to switch off every now and again. Holidays are good for the soul."

"So true, Father, I say that all the time."

I don't say it all the time. I am not even sure what he is on about.

"I was saying red or white wine? Or, I do have a drop of sherry, if you would prefer?"

Sherry? Isn't that what old ladies drink? In fact, I don't even think they drink that any more.

"Oh, thank you, red for me."

"Red it is."

I thought that was what we were supposed to drink. Blood of Christ and all that.

"There you go. Yes, I was saying time off. I try as much as possible to get the odd day here and there. Tomorrow actually. Saturdays are normally my day off. Although if we don't go anywhere I do like to take a trip down to the old people's home to sit with them. It's very calming for them. Especially for the ones that can't make it to church."

"Is the church closed on Saturday then?"

"No, of course not. We are a good number here. We manage to cover each other the best we can to ensure we all get time off. Especially given where we are. The lakes are amazing. With summer coming up it will be very busy soon."

I want to say, lakes? As I haven't seen any. I did see a sign saying welcome to the Lake District, so I am guessing there are quite a few. I might like to see them though. Don't get to see the water much. Well, not since Cornwall anyway and what has that been, like a month? A month. No sex for a month. Might even be six weeks? What is that all about? Six weeks? Now all I can think about is my swimmers. Swimmers, water, my head is all over the place.

"Darren?"

"Sorry, I guess my head is all over the place today. Thoughts of going home. I was just thinking about the Lakes. They are beautiful."

I was just thinking about sex. Ever since the radio told me Edmund has been missing a month I can't get it out of my head. I am so surprised how easy you can get lost in your own work. I need to be mindful of that when I work.

"Have you been before?"

No, shit, just told him I had arrived, didn't I? I swear, I am getting more and more careless with these lies. I used to be so good. Maybe it's the lack of sex that makes me think so unclearly. I need more sex. I need lots of sex.

"As a kid, yes, I would visit with my parents, but not for many years."

"I wouldn't say many, Father, you can't be older than twenty-five now?"

Twenty-five? I don't look twenty-five, do I? Fuck, this job must be weighing heavily on me. I will be getting grey hair at this rate. I touch my eyes. I swear, I can feel a wrinkle now. Maybe two? I am only eighteen, for fuck's sake. Maybe I need to start using one of those moisturisers or something.

"Twenty-five exactly."

"Twenty-five. Twenty-five, such a young age."

Something about how he said that. Wait, he isn't one of those kiddie fiddler priests they are all talking about, is he? Telling me I look older than I am. Giving me alcohol. That's the type of thing that these weirdos do, isn't it? Next, he will be talking to me about girls. To see if I like them or not.

"Anyone special in your life."

I knew it! He is a fucking weirdo. How do they let these people do this job?

"No, not yet. I am waiting for the right person."

Shit! Should have said yes. Then the weirdo might back off. When a weirdo asks if you are in a relationship, you say yes, Edmund. It is fucking obvious.

"Oh, don't worry. You are still young. There is still time."

Not time for you, you freak. God, you meet all sorts in this profession, don't you? The people taking confession should go to confession. It's their souls that need saving. Should be part of the job description or something.

107

"Steven."

Saved by his missus. Poor cow. I bet she knows he is one. Hard to deal with though, given the job. I mean, who argues with the right hand of God? Must worry about lightning bolts and stuff if you do?

"I guess it's time to make the gravy. She has her skills, but gravy isn't one of them. Coming, dear. Come on, bring your wine with you. I will grab the bottle and we can finish it over dinner."

You first. I am not letting you follow me. Looking at my arse as I leave. I know I am fit. I don't need you watching it for me.

"After you, Father."

We head into the kitchen. Father Steven starts on the gravy.

"Aaron, come and get your dinner."

Mums always shout up the stairs. My mum used to always do that to me. I look at the stairs. A young boy appears in a hoodie, Game Boy in hand. He looks like he could be a fan of the ONE. Probably not the best forum to have that conversation though. It is a nice black hoodie. I should really copyright that look or something. People will be cashing in on it, I am sure.

"Put your hood down, and that game, Aaron. We have company."

"Oh, don't worry about me. I don't mind."

"But we do. I swear, my son would spend all his time with one device or another in his hand."

"I was the same at his age."

I don't think that came out right. There is a wry smile from Sandra. I knew there was something dark, down inside that woman. Her clothes aren't very flattering. Look like they come from one of my nan's jumble sales, to be honest, but there is something under them. I can tell a body from the way it moves. I need help, don't I? I am so horny I am imagining things. No, I am not imagining it. There is something under there. Something worth exploring.

"So, Darren, how do you like your lamb? Steven likes his almost burnt, but I am always in favour of the rarer, the better. I like it juicy."

She is saying that shit on purpose, I know she is.

"I must agree with you, Mrs Collis. The rarer, the better for me too."

"Sometimes I think my wife would eat meat straight out of the butcher's shop. Her steaks are still practically mooing when they get on the plate."

See, there is something behind those eyes. It takes one to know one, my nan always says. She is one. I am the ONE. Something needs to happen.

They serve up dinner between them. It was delicious. It has been a long time since I have had a home-cooked meal. Well, one someone else has cooked. Seem to have only cooked for myself since I left home. Oh, and Miss Walker, but she eats like a sparrow anyway. Never finishes her food.

"That was lovely, Sandra."

"It really was, dear. Didn't I tell you, Darren, she is an amazing cook?"

"I must agree, she certainly is."

Everyone turns as the lock on the front door goes.

"That will be Jess coming in."

I turn to look at the door. Please don't be blonde. Pretty please don't be blonde. Please, please, please... FUCK! It may as well be Barbie walking through the door. I never get what I want. Why do I seem to never get what I want?

"Hi, Mum, Dad."

She throws a smile in my direction. I am not really looking now. I was so hoping she would be a brunette. Aaron gets up and leaves the table. His hoodie is back up, and he heads upstairs.

"Hi, dear, this is Father Darren. He is just visiting us for the evening."

"Hi, Father Darren."

"Hi, pleasure to meet you."

I try and make it sound like I mean it. I am sure she can tell I am not impressed. I mean, some normal boys would probably be impressed by her, but I am not a normal guy.

"Jess here is our little superstar, aren't you, Jess? Studies with her friends nearly every night."

There is a smile on her face as her dad says that. She's lying, I can tell. Besides who ever heard of a blonde studying? Jesus, how stupid are your parents? Sorry, didn't mean to say Jesus. Wait, nobody heard me, it's just me. Well, nobody but, you know, him upstairs. What am I talking about? I don't believe in God. This job has me all religious. I knew it would have an effect. Can he hear me if I am thinking in my head? Surely not?

"Every night you say? What is it that you are studying, Jess?"

Boys, without a doubt, she is studying boys, or hair and beauty. Of course, he can hear me in my head. That's the whole thing about prayer, isn't it? He must have powers like that guy in the wheelchair that can read minds.

"I am studying to be a psychiatrist."

No way, whoever heard of a blonde Barbie-looking psychiatrist?

"Really?"

"Yes, we have a real brainy one here, Darren. Apple of my eye."

"That's amazing, well done. I was actually just listening to one in the car earlier."

"On Jeremy's show?"

"Yes, Sandra, that is the one. Very clever guy."

Oh, shit, she is looking at me funny now. Did he say my last name when I came in? I can't remember now. Did he say Father Darren Gosling because if he did she may have put two and two together? Crap. Crap. Crap.

"I do like his show. He always seems to put a fair opinion across. Although, I only caught the last of the supposed interview."

"Supposed? You don't think it was actually this Father Harry guy phoning in?"

"No, did you?"

"No, I didn't either."

"No, I can't see someone like that calling into a radio show. The other guy, on the other hand, I could have seen him calling in."

"The other guy?"

"You know the ONE, or Edmund Carson. I can see him doing something like that. Always seems to want the publicity, to be in the limelight. The Father Harry guy seems to have another type of problem. Both still very worrying."

"We were discussing that in class today actually, Mum. We concluded that he had a very quiet upbringing. Probably not a lot of friends, and a family that didn't really acknowledge him. There is always a symptom for why they do what they do."

Shit, how do these people keep getting these things so wrong? What is up with them? I had lots of friends. Well, lots of people wanted to be my friend. I just chose not to be theirs, that is all. And my parents? Always took notice of me. All the time. Except for the bike thing. Oh, and the what I like to eat thing. And never caring where I was. But other than that, they generally loved me. They must have. Why else would I have all their money?

"What do you think, Darren?"

Shit, I missed that, I think? Were they still on about the friends? Or are we on about something else now?

"What do you think about this Edmund Carson person?"

Got it, back on track. I don't think I should lead with I think he is amazing, talented, handsome and I am surprised he is not worshipped more. I am not sure they would agree with me.

"I think he is a very troubled young man."

"I think you are being too kind, Father."

"No, I believe we are all God's creatures, but at times we can choose the wrong path. Edmund is such a creature. He clearly, as you say, needs the limelight and not giving it to him could cause this country massive repercussions. Ignoring him is not advisable."

Wait, I think I said that too strongly. They may put two and two together.

"Do you know we discussed that in class too? And I agree with you. I believe that if you played into his ego, he would make more mistakes. This so-called negative press that everyone is talking about, is clearly the wrong thing to do. I wouldn't be surprised if there was another school being prepared as we speak. He will do something, I am sure of it. Something big that is going to shock the world."

I am quite warming to her. I wonder if I could get her a hat or something to cover the blonde hair. Then hopefully she is one of those girls that just shaves everywhere. It would make her doable at least. Bit of a reward for her support. She obviously has a crush on me, I mean, Edmund. Probably both of us.

"I think between the three of you that is enough talk about serial killers at the dining table. Hardly fitting conversation. Especially in this house. We must think about the poor people that these people leave behind."

Wait, I don't leave people behind? I ensure that I work with everyone that is in the room. Always. I included everyone in my work.

"Sorry, Dad. He does get grumpy when we talk Edmund."

Nice to know that they do talk Edmund. I am probably a conversation piece in all dinner parties.

"Now why don't we all have a slice of apple pie? I can tell your mum's been baking today by all the pots and pans, so I know there is pie around here somewhere."

"Not for me, Dad. I just have to finish some homework. Plus, I am on a diet, remember?"

She bends down and kisses her father and then her mother.

"Goodnight, Father Darren."

"Goodnight, Jess."

"Well, I guess that's more for the rest of us then. Do you fancy some, Darren?"

"Yes, please. One of my absolute favourites."

Sandra goes off and pulls a pie out of the fridge and a pot of custard. I love custard. I can't remember the last time I had custard. You just don't, do you. Unless someone is making it for you. It is not something you keep in the fridge. Oh, unless you are Sandra, I guess.

"Custard, Father Darren?"

"Yes, please, love custard... Is there a gent's room I can use before we eat dessert?"

"Yes, Darren, top of the stairs on the right. First door, can't miss it."

"Thank you."

I go up the stairs. I can hear them talking downstairs about appropriate dinner conversation. I don't think he liked that. I thought it was fine. I like talking about myself. I am kind of fascinating.

The bathroom door is open. In fact, all doors are slightly open. They are obviously a very open family. I used to lock my door all the time. Can you imagine your parents walking in on you when you are like beating one out? I can see Aaron in a chair. Looks like he is playing a video game. At least, I hope that is what he is doing. I don't want to walk in on that either.

I push the door open a little more. I can see he has headphones on. I stand behind the chair as he continues to play his game. Some kind of soldier thing. Jesus, it's violent. When he is shooting them, they are almost torn in half on the screen. These things are getting worse and worse I swear. Kids should stick to the Wii, bit of bowling or tennis, they are just as much fun.

I can't watch this anymore. It is far too violent for my taste, and should be for him too. He is only young.

I lean over and cut his throat from ear to ear. I wait a second and lean him back in the chair. The game is still going. I watch until he dies. Wait, he had like four more lives. These games never end, do they? I am out of the room and standing outside Jess's room. I can hear her on the phone.

"He is quite cute for a Father. He can't be older than twenty-one… It's not freaky. My dad is a Father… Shut up. They can be hot too."

She is talking about me. Made quite an impression, I think. I just need her to stop looking in the mirror as she talks on the phone. Blondes are so vain. I am sure that is why I don't like them. Brunettes are classier, well, they always seem to be. At last, I am in the room as she looks out the window. Before she knows it, my hand is on her mouth and the blade is dragging across her neck. As soon as the knife goes in, I can smell it. The sweet smell of blood. I didn't notice it as much on Aaron, but I guess that is the horny side of me kicking in.

My God, it's good. It smells so good. I wonder if it's like virgin blood. Father being religious and all that. I wonder if it is. I wonder if that tastes different. I know the age makes a difference, and the sex. Well, not if they have had sex, but whether male or female. I take a lick, I can't resist any longer.

FUCK, that is good! I have fucking missed that.

This is so Edmund's return. Sex, oh, sex, now that's all I am going to be thinking about over my custard, isn't it? Custard and sex. Now there is a thought.

I lay Jess on the bed. I will be back. Just need to keep an eye out for a hat.

I quickly go wash my hands, flush the toilet, and head downstairs.

"Sorry about that, call of nature."

They don't answer. Not really table conversation either, I guess.

"So, Father, a small or a large piece?"

"As much as the dinner was lovely, Sandra, I am going to have to say… large. It looks amazing."

She smiles at me. It is a knowing smile. I can tell. I am sure the taste of blood has just made her even hotter than she was before. Well, hot under the jumble sale clothes.

"I just can't refuse home-made apple pie and custard."

"Me neither, Darren, and my wife makes one of the best."

She pours lots of custard over my pie. More than over her husband's. I think that is a sign. It smells amazing. Either that or I still have the smell of Jess's blood in my nose. Maybe that's it. Blood and apple pie… and custard, it must be very similar to the bread in a cheese and onion sandwich. The crust would soak up all the juices. Just leaving that slightly soft, crunchy, dry but wet taste in your mouth. I will have to try that. I will have to try that soon.

"So, Darren, are you heading straight home tomorrow?"

"No, Sandra. I am going to take your husband's advice and see the lakes and the castle and then head home mid-afternoon. It will still be a long drive, but there is nothing like sleeping in your own bed."

What am I talking about? Sleeping in my own bed? I haven't done that for years.

"I agree. I often say it's the best thing about coming home."

It is not a coincidence that she is talking to me about getting into bed. It is clearly on her mind. Probably since I walked through the door.

"This is delicious, Sandra. You will have to give me the recipe."

"Thank you. Could I tempt you with a little bit more?"

"No, I couldn't. I think that is quite enough. There is no room left for pie."

There is room left; it is just not for pie.

"Good. Darren, do you know what I have in the study? A lovely bottle of port. The best thing for an after-apple pie drink. Why don't we leave Sandra in here to clear up and have a glass? I am sure it will settle that stomach."

"Are you sure, Steven? Sandra, I don't mind doing the dishes?"

"No, that's fine. It won't take me long; I will come and join you afterwards. I do like a glass myself."

We get up and head back into the study. That weirdo is trying to get me alone again. I am wasting no time. The blood is in my nose, I can smell it. As he opens the cabinet to get the port, I already have my hand on his mouth, and cut his throat. He is kicking a little bit, so I pull him back from the cabinet.

There is too much glass in there. She will hear it and then call someone. He is a fucking spurter though. It's everywhere. There is no way I am going to clean this shit up. He stops kicking, and I lay him down on the floor. I catch my reflection in the glass. I look like I work in a slaughterhouse. Where did that all come from? I don't think I even have another black suit for tomorrow. I look down at Father Steven on the floor. He looks about the same size as me. I lie down next to him. Yeah, about the same size. He will have clothes upstairs that I can borrow later. I am sure that is all he has in his wardrobe. Must be a very black wardrobe. I can hardly see him in a Hawaii shirt. I pick up the throw off the back of the chair and wipe my face as best I can. I then go back to the kitchen and peer round the door.

She is sitting at the table with a glass of wine. She hasn't touched the dishes. That's a bit odd. She said she was going to tidy up. She is drinking the wine like it is going out of date. She is just sat there, looking at the wall. I walk in.

"Hi. I thought you were coming to join us?"

Nothing. She is not saying anything, just drinking the wine. I sit down opposite her. She is looking at me, but not looking at me. She is looking straight through me as if I am not here. She just sits and takes another big drink of her wine.

"Are you okay, Sandra?"

She grabs the bottle and pours herself another glass. Still looking at me. There is something about her. Something dark. It is like she is mad at me. In her eyes, there is something in the eyes.

Fuck!

What is going on here? This doesn't make any sense. I am not sure what I am supposed to do now. This is out of character for her. Did she just hear that? In the study? Is that what this is about?

"I went upstairs."

Fuck!

"I went upstairs. I thought there is only a little piece of pie left and I am sure Aaron will want it. Not Jess, Jess is on a diet. Although she doesn't need to diet. I tell her that all the time. I think she has a boyfriend which she hasn't told us about. I think that's the real reason. I took it in to Aaron. He likes pie. I thought he was ignoring me because he had his headphones on so I hit him around the head."

She is just pouring herself another glass. The bottle is empty. She gets up. I don't know whether to dive at her or not. She isn't moving very fast. It's like she is in a trance. She walks over to the fridge. I stand up in case she makes a run for it. She doesn't. She gets another bottle out of the fridge and sits back at the table. Pushes a glass towards me and fills up my drink.

What the fuck is going on here!

She necks her glass, and pours some more.

"I thought he was ignoring me because of his headphones. I hate those headphones. I am always telling him not to wear them... so I hit him round the head. Just a clip like, just a little tip around the ear. To let him know that I was there... It came off. His head came clean off... And I just stood there. I couldn't say anything. I just stood there."

Fuck! I nearly choked on my wine. I hope that didn't sound like a snort. She doesn't seem to be laughing. Can you imagine how that must have been? I know I am heavy-handed sometimes. It must have been at least a little funny?

"I just walked out of the room. Left him there. Left his head where it lay. I then went to see Jess."

Now, I know I wasn't heavy-handed there. I knew I might want to visit her again. It's been like twenty-five minutes, so she must have been chatty by then? She would have told her mum about the crush she had on me.

"I could see the blood before anything else. It was on the window. It's Saturday tomorrow though. Arnold will be round, and we can get him to do the windows inside and out this week… She looked like she was sleeping."

She drinks some more wine. Then some more. Come on, say something? The silence is painful. Is she doing this on purpose and then at some point going to launch an attack on me? Has she called the police and this is a stalling tactic? I don't like it. I am nervous now. What the fuck? Why am I nervous? I am not the one acting like a freak here. She is.

"Oh, where are my manners? Have some more wine."

She tops up my glass. I take a swig. I daren't do anything else. That sparkle she had in her eyes is gone and it's almost a glaze now.

"And my husband?"

She looks directly at me. Fuck, I think I fear her. She is unnerving me, big time. She just keeps staring… And staring. I just nod my head.

"Okay, I thought as much. And you are?"

She knows who I am. I am sure of it. Although she may think I am Father Harry? Who should I say I am? I am all confused now. She has me totally off balance. Would she prefer I was a Father or not? What do religious people like? Is it a club? Would they like it to be one of their own?

"Edmund, Miss."

She doesn't look surprised. Did I just call her Miss? Why would I do that? She does have that look about her now, that look that says I am about to be put on detention.

"While you are here, you are Father Harry too?"

I just nod back at her. She takes another swig of wine. What the fuck is she doing? Just sitting there, drinking wine. This must be a stalling tactic although I can't see a phone anywhere?

"You know, I have feared death my whole life. Well, when I say fear death, it may just be a case of fear of getting old. Steven, my now late husband, I suppose, he used to ask me to join him on his visits to the old people's home every Saturday. I hated it. To see these poor people lying in their beds, unable to go to the toilet on their own. People having to feed them their meals and wipe their noses for them. That's not a life. Especially the couples. In bed next to each other. To see your other half go through something like that and not be able to help them. That is no life for anyone."

She is silent. She is obviously thinking about it.

"But I guess I don't need to worry about that anymore?"

I never thought of that. Imagine someone having to wipe your bum for you. Is this her way of saying thank you? She grabs the bottle for more wine. She really does need a...

"FUCK!" She didn't grab it for more wine! She hit me over the fucking head with it! Fuck, that hurts. I think she has cut my fucking forehead.

She is making a run for the door. I get up and chase her. She is in the hallway and unlocking the door. I rugby-tackle her to the floor. I am clambering up her. She is stronger than she looks.

"Get off me! Get off me! Help! Help!"

I am not sure who she is shouting to? There are no other houses near here. Hardly going to attract someone. She is punching and kicking at me. I knew she had fight in her. For a moment then at the table I thought she was going to disappoint me. We are both on the floor and now face-to-face. Fuck, she headbutted me. Who knew she had that in her?

"You're the wife of a vicar, for fuck's sake."

I grab my knife and plunge it into her side. The fight stops as she screams in pain. I put my hand over her mouth. The bitch is still trying to bite it. She doesn't want to give in, does she?

I put the knife into her neck. Hit an artery, by all accounts. There is blood spurting out all over the place.

I have fucking missed this. The smell, the fight. Oh my God, this is amazing. She is convulsing as well. I can feel her wriggling underneath me. This is such a fucking turn-on. I am hard; I can feel it burning through my trousers. She can probably feel it too. She will be wanting it. I want it. She stops moving.

Not like this, not in the hallway and not before her quiet time. It's been a month, I need something a little bit special, but I need it fast.

Chapter 6

"You know, from the moment I walked into the room, I could tell. There is a sparkle in the corner of your eye, it just screams out to people.

"It is flattering but I don't think it is just me. I am surely not the only person to have ever told you that you are a beautiful woman?

"Really? Nearly a year? I am almost bursting, and it's been like a month. Although I must tell you something, prepare yourself, this may be hard to hear."

She deserves to know. You shouldn't keep secrets from your wife.

"I am almost convinced he was hitting on me in the study. So, I have to wonder if that is the reason."

She doesn't look shocked.

"I am not surprised you had your doubts. My nan always says there is a gaydar. You know like radar. People can always tell if they look close enough.

"Kind of, I can't say that I always know, as there are always a lot of people looking at me. You know, I am glad I am making the effort now you have shared that with me.

Believe me, it's hard to set all this up while you are lying there naked. When I helped you up the stairs and started to undress you, I just have to say, wow. Just wow. I knew there was something under those clothes. But you, you have the body of a model.

"A year? Your husband hasn't been near you for a year and you look like that? Then I am sorry, Sandra, he is gay. And probably into some other shit too… Cause even gay men, they would be turned on by you. Trust me. Not that I am. I so am not. There is nothing wrong with it. Love is love. But you, you are something.

"You have the cutest laugh as well. Lights up the whole room."

She is lapping all this banter up. I know how to make someone feel special. It is a gift.

"I know, there is something about candles that just set the scene. They say that romance is dead. I don't believe it. It is just all about effort. People are just getting lazy nowadays.

"No, the iPad is not to film us. That is private between you and me. I thought afterwards we might upload something to YouTube or Facebook? Just as like a memory of our time together? And I hate to say this, I have been neglecting my fans somewhat. I need to get that back on track, and they so enjoy selfies. Especially with my friends.

"Yes, I was going to include all of us. I was going to make sure we were all in there somewhere. Still working it through my head, but we will come up with something. Returning to an Edmund Carson style evening.

"Right, I think I am done. A little mood lighting always does the trick."

I jump on the bed next to her.

"Now time for—

"Oh, okay. Yes, I can see that. And do you know what? I prefer being totally naked anyway. I can see how this outfit might remind you of your husband. I guess I was just that keen to, well, you know."

I get undressed and throw all my clothes on the floor.

"Thanks. You know, I don't even work out. I don't eat properly, but I just seem to be built like this. It is all natural.

"Yes, and built like that down there. Sandra, that's for you. That's how excited you make me."

I climb back onto the bed and then onto Sandra. I enter her slowly, she is a little moist. I think she must have been thinking about this since the moment I walked in this evening. I bet she was. Every time I spoke to her she will have become a little wetter. I bet they all were, to be fair. They all wanted a piece of me.

FUCK!

That feels good. I have missed that feeling so much. The slow pump as you go in and out. The tightness. You can just never get your hand to do that grip. Not even when you change hands. I lean down to whisper into her ear.

"Your husband is a fool."

She will love that… I almost burst out laughing then.

"Thanks. I think I am blessed more than others, but if he wasn't ever getting this hard with how you look, well then there is something wrong with him."

She knows there is something up with him. She has just never been comfortable talking about it. I think I bring that out in people. Openness.

I can feel the rhythm returning slow and hard, slow and hard just like Miss Walker likes it. It's the feeling as if you can't get any more of yourself inside of her. That's what the ladies like. Slow and hard, slow and hard.

"I can? A little rougher? Are you sure?

"I would hardly say I am a bad boy, but if that's what you have always wanted, I don't mind role-playing. In fact, I think I quite enjoy it."

I go faster, she is liking that. I nibble at her neck. The blood is still warm and makes my head spin. I nibble a bit harder as I go faster. I can tell by the look in her eyes. I know what she wants.

"Okay."

I flip her over. I enter her. Been a while since I have done this. Always tighter though. Makes your blood pump even more. I grab the back of her hair. Girls like their hair pulled. Not too much though, I don't want her head to come off.

Oh, that's good. That's good. What have I been doing for a month?

I am out of her and flip her back. I look directly into her eyes. Girls like that. Means you are serious when you are talking to them. I presume it means the same when making love.

"I wanted to be looking at you when we come together. You deserve so much more than him. You are a remarkable woman, Sandra."

I enter her again. I can see the blood dripping from the side of her neck. I go in for another nibble. A bite. The taste, the taste is something I've missed so much. Father Harry is okay, but there is nothing like being yourself. Especially with a woman. I go harder and faster. I can feel that she wants that. She wants a real man inside of her. She wants to feel a real man between her legs. She is ready. I can feel the build-up inside her. Her body is screaming for an orgasm. I can feel it too. I am close, closer. I explode inside her.

Fuck! That feels good. It's making me light-headed, I don't think I am going to stop. There must have been a pint in me at least. It just keeps pumping.

It stops. I kiss her neck once more and then her. Tenderly. She deserves it. Every woman deserves me once in their lifetime. She isn't saying a word. Thankful, I would guess. I lie down next to her.

"Sorry if there was too much, I said it's been a month. Must have been storing it all up.

"Wow, three and still going. Must have been building them up yourself.

"That was good though. Not only are you hot, but good in bed too. You would be surprised how often that is not the case. Both don't always go together."

I would go into detail, but I am sure women don't want to hear about other women.

"If you don't mind me asking, how did you end up here? A life in the church and all that. Fascinates me a little that some people have, what do they call it, the calling?

"Really? From school? So, you have never, you know? With anyone other than Father Steven?

"Wow, that must have been love. Don't think I could have done that. And he has never?

"Yeah, I suppose. Who really knows what people get up too.

"I wouldn't say you have been missing something. I have been with a few women, and some aren't worth the effort. So, you can have good sex and bad sex. Was it good sex? Tell me at least it was good sex.

"Only once, eh? Then maybe it wasn't. You are missing a lot then. Sorry, I didn't mean to say it like that.

"Thanks. I do like to put the effort in, and at least now you have experienced the good. Who knows what will happen next?

"Next, thanks for reminding me. Yes."

I get up and grab the iPad. I lie with Sandra and we take some selfies. Tasteful ones. All cuddled up in the blankets. We look quite good together. I put the iPad down. I am so tempted to take more risky pictures. I am sure my fans would want to see more. It has been so long for them.

"No, that is totally up to you. You decide if you want them posted or not. I am happy I just have them."

Think ruder ones are out of the question if she is worried about the tasteful ones.

"I am sorry about the Aaron thing, by the way. I keep my knife so sharp that sometimes I forget, and it just seems to go too deep.

"I know, but I am sorry, all the same. I didn't want to scare you."

I am sitting on the end of the bed. Time to start to decide what comes now.

"I love that little laugh you do, it's so cute. Look at you all snuggly in that duvet. It's like one of those photo shoots that models do. The ones that make you feel all warm and cosy on a cold day.

"I would love to get back in. I just need to think out the plan.

"Thanks, that's so sweet. It's this whole Edmund versus Harry thing. I need to show the world that Harry isn't Edmund.

"Yes, we know that, but I am not ready to let the world know that yet. You won't tell anyone, will you?

"You are amazing, Sandra, just amazing. I think this is the start of great things for you.

"No, I was thinking the church. But I did the whole wedding thing as Father Harry and that is kind of Edmund Carson style. I shouldn't have done that.

"Yes, the family thing is kind of my thing. You really do follow my work, don't you?

"Yes, that's it. It's homely, and it will show that we are different.

"The sex thing is a difference. But one look at you and there was no way I was going to pass that up.

"Is it okay if I borrow some clothes? I think your husband and I are about the same size.

"Okay, not everywhere. That is very true."

She does make me smile.

"Thank you. Just some shorts or something while I set something up."

I go through the wardrobes. I was right, he must have like ten outfits of being a Father. Who has these many costumes in their wardrobe? It must be, so he always has some at the dry-cleaning. I must remember that when creating a character. I find some shorts and a T-shirt. I jump onto the bed and kiss Sandra.

"I will be back. I will set everything up and come and get you."

I head out of the bedroom and down the stairs. I can feel a spring in my step. Probably just deposited a stone in her. I go into the study.

"Yes, sorry, I was just, well, just upstairs talking with your wife.

"Yes, they are all fine. Just relaxing.

"Of course, I can, no problem."

I pick him up off the floor and put him in the chair. I go over to the cabinet and pour us both a glass of port.

"There you go. I knew this was what you were after."

I sit in the chair opposite and take a sip. That's just bad. It's nearly as bad as the stuff we drink in church with the little biscuits.

"Yes, it is a little smooth."

I don't want to piss him off. Although from the look in his eye he is picking up where he left off. He can't take his eyes off my legs.

"Yes, sorry, hope you don't mind. Spilled wine down my suit. Sandra is sorting it all out for me. Lovely wife you have there."

He doesn't mind. I think he prefers me in shorts. There is something off about him.

"Can I ask you something?

"It's a little personal. I was just talking with your wife and she seemed a little upset?"

I am awesome at the Fathering thing. What I wanted to say was, why haven't you banged your hot wife in a year? But it came out as she is a little upset.

"I know the work is long hours, but weren't you just talking about spending quality time with your family? That's the most important thing, right? I sense you don't practise what you preach, Father. Your wife doesn't feel that you practise what you preach. I sense from her mood. You are not as close as you should be?"

I love my nan, she always has these little sayings that just stick in your head. Practise what you preach. Always seem to come out at just the right time. With the right people, as well.

"Father Steven."

Oh, fuck, I think he is about to cry. He is starting to well up.

"Father Steven?

"It's fine, Father, probably better to get it off your chest. It is what we do."

I can't believe this guy wants to confess here and now. If he starts with the K-Y Jelly crap like that other guy, then this is going to get messy.

"Okay, just start wherever you want. This is what we do, right? Try to forgive."

How do you cry and talk at the same time? He must have been wanting to tell someone his story for such a long time.

"For six months you say?"

I take another sip of the port. What am I doing? If you have a glass in your hand you just keep drinking it. No matter how bad it tastes. I knew the guy was gay. I can spot a gay man a mile away. I think it's because they are always checking me out. You can tell when a man is looking at you. I mean, really looking at you. And he was. It's natural he would be, I am a beacon for all sexes. I could tell.

"And his name is Eugene? No, you don't meet many Eugenes.

"Oh, I see, so he will be covering tomorrow then? He is in the game like us? When I say game, I mean profession, not on the game. You know, like when you pay for it. Not that you would. Sorry, this is taking a wrong turn somewhere."

Lost myself in his conversation for a moment. I also keep forgetting that these people do this out of choice. Not just for fun. Not a game.

"Listen, I think you just need to be honest with your wife. Tell her the truth. Let her move on too. She is still a young sexy woman. You are both living a lie that can be resolved very easily. You can be happy with Eugene, and she can meet a nice man herself.

"That would be nice. Thanks for thinking of me, but I am fine. I am not looking for anything serious right now. I have to concentrate on my career."

I can hardly say I just banged her, and I have a girlfriend at home, can I? She would make my top ten though. Okay, fifty. Okay, one hundred, for sure. It might just be the sex talking and the light-headedness. Can you concentrate on a career in the church? Will he buy that? He doesn't really know me. He doesn't know if I am looking for promotion. Might be wanting to be a cardinal or, you know, the man himself. Pope Edmund Carson. Has a ring to it.

"Why, thanks, yes, I am, Father Harry. Well, Edmund Carson is my name. I know, I know you weren't expecting that, but please don't tell anyone yet. I am just sharing with you and your lovely family.

"Father Harry is one of my characters. I am not in character tonight though. Edmund's return.

"Not a clue at all? That's surprising, but good to know. It's good to know I can still surprise people. I think we need to get on now if that is okay?

"I was thinking all in the kitchen for starters?

"Sure, I will, it will be my pleasure."

I walk over and help Father Steven to his feet. I carry him through and sit him at the head of the kitchen table. It's good he is still dressed. Would have felt a bit funny undressing him. Especially as he has spent the night undressing me with his eyes.

"If it is okay with you, let me just go and look around."

I look under the sink for some tape or rope. There is nothing but cleaning products.

"Thanks, I will look there."

I walk back past the study and head towards the back of the house.

There was a garage to the side of the house. There must be a connecting door. I go into the garage. Nice car, but these religious people do like people carriers. Must be all the lifts they give people. I bet they don't leave gyppos at the side of the road either, or those blokes with number plates. Not sure what they are doing on the side of the road. Always imagined that their car must be crashed somewhere and all that is left is the number plate. That would be a lot of crashes as they are everywhere. Fathers must pick them all up, all God's creatures. Probably in the Book.

I find rope and tape. The tools in here are amazing. Maybe he manages all his own repairs and stuff. You would think builders would do it for free? I really need to get another go-bag sorted. Mine is just out of everything. It's costing a fortune to do this job and there is no payment. I mean, other celebrities get paid, millions. But me? Nothing.

Fuck! It's Sandra.

I haven't seen one of her movies in a long time and she is gorgeous. She is Miss Walker gorgeous. Every time I heard that name tonight, that was the person running in the back of my head. She knows how to get paid for her work. She was paid what, eighty million for one movie? All she did was float about in space. I could have done that. I really need to think about getting paid for my work. Maybe advertising. They do that on Facebook and Twitter now. Maybe I should speak to movie studios or something to advertise on my page. Or maybe some product placement money. Miss Walker taught us all about that in her class. Most of the time you don't even notice and they get paid billions for this stuff. All these tools. I could be sponsored by Black & Decker or something. Or get the ONE sponsored by Nike. They would be cool. I could just have a little white tick on my outfit. I wonder if McDonalds will sponsor me once they hear my life story. I was there when my parents had their accident. I have eaten there so much over the last twelve months. They could even name a burger after me. A Carson burger. Now that would be cool. I am back in the kitchen.

"Sorry, got carried away with my own thoughts for a minute then.

"No, I found them okay. I was just thinking about that space movie with Sandra Bullock. Every time you said your wife's name there was a thought in the back of my head and that was it. Just come to me.

"*Gravity*, yes, that's the one. That's it with George Clooney."

There is a fucking surprise. Hottest woman on the planet and he remembers the bloke who was in it for what, ten minutes.

I lift his jacket and tape him to the chair, so he is sitting upright.

"Comfortable?

"Good."

I put his elbows on the table and tape his hands together in the prayer position. They drop down. I put them up again. They drop down again. They won't stay up. I think he is doing it on purpose.

"Fuck, this is hard. It just won't work.

"That's a great Idea. I am sure you have something too. You have quite the collection in there."

I go back to the garage. There must be something here. I look through the tools. I pick up the biggest one, it looks like a gun. I pull the trigger.

FUCK!

It is a gun... well, a nail gun. That fucking thing was powerful. I walk over to the wall. The nail is almost buried in it from ten feet. I like this. I like this a lot. I take it back into the kitchen.

"Look what I found.

"I know, it is so cool. I like it. No, I love it."

I undo his hands from the tape. This is going to look way better. I lean him forward a little and place his elbows on the table. I tap a nail into each elbow.

"Fuck, that is cool. They are not going to move now."

Straight into the wooden table. I then put his hands together and put a nail through both. Literally through both.

"Sorry, I will try that again."

I try again. It goes straight through again. The nails are in the cupboards opposite now. This thing is amazing.

"Sorry, it's just too powerful. Is there a setting or something?"

I look, there is, and I turn it down.

"That's got it."

The arms are stable, but he isn't. He keeps falling to one side. I try resting his head on his hands but it's not working.

"I'm sorry, but it won't look good for the fans unless it really looks like you are saying grace. Can't be slumped over to one side.

"I know, I need to fasten your head, so it doesn't move.

"No, the hands are too thin. It won't work.

"That is a great idea. You guys have been so lovely this evening."

I go off to the study and come back with a copy of his book. Well, Jesus' autobiography. Or is it God's book? Who wrote this? I am sure it wasn't some bloke called Gideon. There are no Gideons in the Bible, are there? Or Nigels? Or Tonys? Funny how these names are all new.

"I tell you, you can turn to this thing for anything, can't you? I am going to write a book like this one day. Something that lasts for two thousand years and is still selling."

I rest his head on his hands, balance the book in front of them and put a nail straight through the book. Through the hands and into his forehead. I move my hand away.

"Solid as a rock.

"I was just thinking that, a couple for safe measure."

I wasn't thinking for safe measure, more for fun. I really need to get myself one of these. They are so much fun. Almost makes me wish I was a carpenter. Maybe that's why he has it. Feel closer to the boss and all that.

It's done. He really looks the part as well.

"See, that is good. I think a good family dinner while saying grace is a great idea. Your wife came up with it. She is a remarkable woman.

"Yes, of course they will all be joining us. I am just about to fetch them."

I leave the kitchen. As I enter the hall I see the hat and scarf rack. I pick up the scarves and take them upstairs with the nail gun. They are going to come in handy.

"Hi, Aaron."

Twat. As soon as I said it, I realised he isn't going to be responding, is he? His mum knocked his head off. I can see it in the corner. I wonder how many times his mum said she was going to do that if he didn't behave, and then she did. I need to apologise again about that. It must be still playing on her mind.

"Sorry, Aaron. I forgot. Don't worry, it doesn't change anything. Just makes it hard to talk, that is all."

I go over and pick his head up. I can tell by the look in his eyes he isn't mad at me.

"I am sorry. Something to do with cutting the vocal chords, I think. It has happened to me, by accident of course, a few times.

"But I am going to try and attach your head to your body. Else it really doesn't make a good picture. Thinking about it, best I do this downstairs though, if that is okay? I don't want to attach it, move you, then it comes off again. Who knows where this thing will roll."

I walk his head down the stairs with the gun and the scarves, and rest them on the table. It's probably a good job that his dad has his eyes straight at the Bible. I will put him directly in front, so he doesn't see this bit. Although technically, it was his wife that knocked his head off. So, I don't really have anything to apologise for.

I go back upstairs and help Aaron down the stairs.

"Yes, it's Aaron. I am going to put him opposite, if that is okay. Where we all sat for dinner.

"It's his seat. Even better. I would like you to all feel at home."

I pick up his head and the scarf, and try to wrap the head to the body. It's tricky. Makes me want to tie the scarf over the head, but that's not a good look at the table.

That's it! It is not a good look at the table. I can use that. I tie the scarves as good as I can and sink a couple of nails through them into his neck. I then do his hoodie up while holding the head and pull the hood over him.

I sink a couple of nails through the top of the hoodie.

"It's okay, I am just putting him into the prayer position."

His dad looks a little upset, I think. He doesn't like him in the hoodie at the table. Aaron is still all over the place. What am I missing here? I stand back and look at him.

Fuck! He is not secure to the chair. I lift the hoodie up and tape him to the chair; then put it back down. I stick a couple of nails into the back of the hoodie, and into the chair to make it tight. He is really sitting up now, and his head looks stable from the tightness of the hoodie.

I go back upstairs and into his room. I start looking around the room. He must have it somewhere. I find his Game Boy. I take it back downstairs. I nail his hands to the side of the table, and then place the Game Boy in them. Perfect. Looks like a proper teenager at the table.

Now for the blonde. I head upstairs, into Jess's room, and stand over the bed.

"Sorry, I thought you were sleeping there for a moment. You looked so peaceful.

"Yes, it has been a while. I didn't think it would take this long either.

"To be honest, your mother makes a great pie. And then there is this thing with your father. It is quite intense, but not really my place to discuss. I am here now though; that is the main thing."

I shoot her a smile. I know she wanted one. I know she wants more than that, to be fair, but a smile is enough for now.

"Really? Not even a little bit. I thought my pictures were very lifelike?

"So, do you think I should get a new camera or something, if they are not doing me justice? It might be why I am losing followers? People need to know how hot I am."

I sit on the edge of the bed to talk to her. That is a little concerning that I don't look that good in pictures. I mean, it is flattering to know how great I am in real life, but not everyone will get the opportunity to be up close and personal with me. No matter how much they would like to.

"On a scale of one to ten then, just so I know what I have to work with?

"Six to seven? And in real life?

"Eleven? Really, are you just saying that? Or is this just a ruse to get me to spend more time with you?"

I stand up and look in one of her dozen mirrors. I am a gorgeous man. I can't see why the camera isn't capturing me better?

"Really, the whole class? That does make more sense. Maybe I am appealing to the more intelligent person. I am concerned that I am not really getting the fan base that I am used to. Or even the one I deserve."

I am going to consider this. Maybe get one of those cameras with the big lenses. They are all the ones the press use. So, they must be better than a phone or an iPad. All the other stars get shot with those. Should I employ someone to do it for me, like a professional or something? Problem is, they will probably want to cash in on my fame. Say they were helping me work. No, maybe I just need a timer or something, so I can be in them, and a tripod. The world needs to know how good-looking I really am. Good-looking people are always more famous at everything they do.

"Sorry, was just thinking about what you said. I think you are right. A better camera may be the solution. One with all the pixels and stuff. HD.

"Yes, to upload to my Twitter, Facebook and YouTube accounts. That's the plan, like all the other people I have worked with."

I am glad she is so plain talking. This is good feedback from your fans, and you must listen to your fans.

"Sorry, sometimes you hit an artery, and it does make a bit of a mess. I feel that I was a little excited tonight. With you and your brother. It had been quite a while since I was Edmund. Well, you know what I mean. It had been quite a while since I could be myself.

"No, I totally understand. Of course, I will help you."

I know how vain girls can be. I suppose my pictures will be the talk of her school. Especially if they are all talking about me already. I do like that. The thought of being a topic in class. Must be thrilling for them. And Jess will be so popular for just being part of them. It must be a privilege to work with me. I wish I could open the opportunity up to more people. Maybe I should do a lecture tour or something for their classes. That would be a good idea.

"So, what kind of thing were you looking for?"

I start to go through the wardrobes. I find a little black dress. Every girl in the world has a little black dress. None of them look as hot as Miss Walker does in hers, but they all have one.

"How about this?

"That's true, hardly screams family dinner, and something more colourful would be good.

"Maybe something white? Wait, no, this is perfect. Summery. Has all the colours and flowers. I so love the summer. Damn, that was who your mother reminded me of,

141

the woman in the summer film. You know, the one that is not a love story. Something about a hundred days, or was it five hundred days. It was her laugh. Your mum has the same laugh."

That woman has me thinking of every superstar in the world. Is it her or just the sex? I mean, I do like sex. My head is full of hot women and sex.

"Okay, I think this looks good? Maybe put your hair in a ponytail or something?"

I go over to the bed. She doesn't have an impressed look on her face. Think it may have been talking about her mum like that. She must think I was interested in her. Probably jealous. I sit next to her.

The blood still smells strong. I think there is something about teenage girls. The smell is drawing me to her. I take a little lick from the side of her neck. There is a sweetness in younger blood that makes it so much more addictive. That should reassure her that she is attractive too.

"It does not tickle. It was just a little lick.

"Hey, you are flirting with me. I was just, you know, seeing what you taste like."

She does have a cute laugh like her mum. Unless she is just trying to copy her mum's laugh now? No, you can't fake that. And a beautiful smile. She has such a beautiful smile… And blonde hair! Blonde hair, blonde hair! It can't just be that my mum has blonde hair that puts me off.

Black hair, perfect. Even red, red is good. Not ginger red, but red like tasteful. I don't know, ginger might be okay? I can't think of a ginger girl. Is that odd? Even brown like her mum. In fact, where has the blonde hair come from? Her dad's not blonde?

"I am going to need to get you undressed.

"No, not for that, stop giggling at me. I have rules, you know. Besides, your parents are just in the next room."

I don't have rules. I just know I am not going to be able to perform with that hair. Ginger! That girl off *Doctor Who*, she was a ginger. She was doable. In a geeky sort of a way. I start to undress Jess.

"It does come out. I didn't think it would either, but it does. It will just go back to white. My nan is really good at getting blood out of clothes."

She has a great body. This isn't helping. Not many girls in my class looked like her. Right size waste, and up top. All sort of in proportion. She is nearly naked now and I can't help but stroke her body. Something about a naked body. All fresh and clean. Especially one so firm and young...

"Of course, I can. Where are they?"

Lost myself there for a moment. I walk over to the drawers and try them. Fresh underwear and bras. I hate bras. They are so fiddly. If it weren't for the sight of them off, I wouldn't bother changing them. Black as well. My mum used to say nothing good comes from a girl in black underwear. My dad must have been so bored. I unclip her bra. That's nice, really nice. I pull down her panties.

"What the fuck? You are not blonde?"

Her hair is blacker than her mum's. And really, girl, you need a trim. Girls nowadays do all that shaving and stuff.

"Out of a bottle? And all that psychiatrist stuff. That's because you are clever, not blonde, isn't it?"

I am fixated by that much hair down there. I suppose it is not something you talk about with a vicar's daughter. I need to stop looking at it.

"Kind of makes a difference, yes. I don't have any rules about non-blondes."

She starts to giggle. I am on top of her before she turns back to look at me.

It's amazing. As soon as I saw that the collar and cuffs don't match, I was as hard as a rock.

"You knew all along, didn't you? That's why you were teasing me to change your underwear."

I am inside her. Oh, that feels good. I did think for a minute I might have to trim the bush before going in, but it's all good. Being on top of her, the aroma of the blood is strong from her, and the bed. It feels amazing. It smells amazing. I am going at her fast. I don't need to savour this. I am back to my best now. I just need to... I open my eyes. The blonde hair hits me like sunshine. I get a shiver down my back. I don't like it. I keep going, but I can feel myself slowing down.

"No, no, nothing is wrong."

I keep going. I am trying to keep my eyes closed but they keep opening. I don't want to think about my mum, but she keeps popping into my head. This can't be right. I can't think about this and my mum at the same time. What do I do? I don't want to, you know, in my mum. I need to stop. She is going to be so disappointed. Imagine when she tells the story. He stopped halfway through? She is never going to live the thing down. Not with all her school talking about me. Maybe she won't tell them. That would be the best thing. But she will know. Shit, I am not a nice person if I do this. It is not going to make me look good, is it?

Wait, can blokes fake it? Surely, a woman would be able to tell if nothing comes out? Wouldn't they? I hear women fake it all the time. With normal blokes, not me, of course, but that's what they say?

Really? What is the alternative? I must do it. Don't I? I can't. I whisper in her ear.

"Are you close?"

I can tell she is. If I time this right, she won't notice, she will be all tingly anyway. If she is like her mum, she will be too busy orgasming to notice. I keep going. Something about not really being into it. I think I could be here for hours. Women are so lucky there are people like me out here.

She is close. I make the noises. A few grunts and collapse. She will never know, although I am still rock-hard, that is kind of a giveaway.

"Excuse me. Quick bathroom break."

I run out and close the door behind me. I am across the hall and standing at her parents' bedroom door.

"I was just thinking about you. So, I came back."

Her eyes light up. The sight of me naked in a doorway with a rock-hard dick will do that for a woman. I am on top and inside her so fast. Now that feels like a real woman. Eyes wide open as I look at her. The sparkle in her eyes tells me that she has been lying here thinking about this for the last hour. None of this slow and hard. She has had that. This is the hard and fast I can't get enough of you sex. Probably more sex than she has had in the last two years now.

"I know."

I can feel that she is ready. I am ready. This time it's for real. Wait, is that a song? Fuck, that's good. I get the giddiness also. I love that feeling. Stars and everything. I collapse on the bed next to her.

"I so needed that. See, that's the effect you have on real men, Sandra.

"Ha, I bet you did too."

I take a breather. That was close. I suppose that is almost a threesome if you are in and out of different women within minutes? Is it? No, it can't be, they weren't even in the same room.

"Nearly. Sorry it has taken so long. I was chatting with your husband. I think you were right about him, but I think that is something you should discuss yourselves. Your son is playing video games. And, yes, I corrected that little mishap. And your daughter is getting ready. I will come back and get you real soon. I don't want you trying to walk downstairs on your own. Your legs must be like jelly now. I tend to have that effect on beautiful women."

"Yes, a little nap. Not every day you get it twice.

"Ha ha, not every year."

I get up and go back to Jess's room. She is still exhausted on the bed.

"Are you okay?

"Still, eh? Tingly all over."

She didn't notice. I guess men can fake it too, but honestly, who normally would? Why would anyone fake it? Either you do, or you don't. I think it is really all about us.

"Wait, it wasn't your first time, was it?

"Oh, good. I thought you probably had as you knew the rhythm and everything. You were quite good."

Wait, should you use the word quite? Is that good or bad?

"Thanks. I have been told often that I am really quite good at it."

That should make her feel better. If I am quite too. I get her dressed. She is giggling every time I touch her. I am trying to not make eye contact with her while I do, as it's an amazing laugh. But that hair is going to freak me out. I take her downstairs and sit her at the table.

"She does look pretty doesn't she, Steven?"

I think I am going to leave her hair flowing. I quite like it that way. With a few streaks of red in her hair. Well, blood, but it really does work. I think praying like her father. I sense she has that good girl look about her. Even though I know I am not her first.

I take the nail gun and put her in the same position as her father. She is a lot lighter, so she doesn't need the book to keep her steady. That looks good. I go back upstairs and into the bedroom.

"So, they are all at the table.

"What's up? There is no need for all that."

I go over to her. She is very upset. She didn't hear me talking with her daughter, did she? Nah, I closed the door and everything. Besides she was hardly a screamer when it comes to sex.

"Is it because of your husband? Don't worry, he is downstairs and so engrossed in his book. Well, the Book. You know the one I mean.

"No, of course he will never find out. I am not going to tell him, but really, I don't think you need worry about it all, he has his own little secrets.

"Maybe this will just be a new chapter for the both of you."

Fuck, I even sound like a priest. Maybe I need to go back to being me full-time before it's too late. This stuff sticks with you. That's the last thing I need. I get her dressed and take her downstairs.

"See, everyone is at the table."

I put her in the chair. She is all right now. No more tears. The sparkle is back in her eye. I think she would go again if I wanted to. I could. I think I could go all night. She would like that. Wait, if they are saying grace, they need to be saying grace over something. That's the deal, isn't it?

"You sit down. I will see if I can rustle up some food. For the whole grace thing."

I go to the cupboards. They are all kind of full. She must do a lot of cooking. Well, a lot of shopping at least. Probably cooks for the parish.

"You guys must do a lot of entertaining. Looks like you almost have your own supermarket here."

Lots of bread. Tinned stuff in the cupboards. In the fridge there is left-over dinner and apple pie. Oh, I was going to try that, wasn't I? With a little help from Jess or Aaron I am sure it will taste great, but hardly a dinner in a rectory. That's it, dinner in a rectory. I go back to the cupboards, and go through the tinned stuff. I find five tins, and grab the bread.

"See, there you go. Two tins of tuna, three tins of salmon, and two loaves of bread.

"Yes, Aaron, two loaves and five fish.

"Or was it five loaves and two fish?

"I know, right? You wouldn't believe that there was enough fish to fill five loaves? It must be right.

"I did see that, Steven, next to the church? Hobby of yours, is it?

"No, that's just wrong. I can't go and get some innocent fish. Poor fish, what have they done to anyone? Besides, it's the early hours now. People will be coming home from nightclubs or walking their dogs soon. Last thing they need is to see me with a banding net scooping the church's fish up.

"It is good. Thank you, Jess. I think it works perfectly."

I tape Sandra to the chair and leave her hands in her lap. I whisper in her ear.

"You are amazing, beautiful and hot as fuck, remember that. I think you can pray afterwards. Your husband will have some things to say first. Then a new chapter for you both. I am so going to leave you my number."

I get up and go fetch my iPad. Fifteen minutes of selfies later, I think we are done.

"I am. I am going to put them all up on the website.

"Okay, okay. Just a couple now. Twitter or Facebook?

"Okay. Hashtag Edmund doesn't do religion, but if he did. And tweet. That should get the fans excited about what is to come.

"Edmund and the best apple pie ever, Hashtag hungry.

"Edmund and the Family at Dinner, Hashtag bible food. I am sorry I was going to put like the verse, and the numbers thing, but I don't know them. I would look them up, but your dad has the book. Don't think he wants to let go of it either. Keeps him stable.

"Ha, yes, in more ways than one. Although he needs to re-read some of the points in there."

Shouldn't have really said that. Not my position to tell them the problems he is having. They need to sort it out as a family.

"Think that's enough for now.

"It's been amazing. The food. Sandra, you are an amazing cook, and thank you all for the great conversations. There are some things that you all need to talk about, but that is more a family thing, I sense. You have all really helped me connect back with myself. It's been far too long being Father Harry. I can't thank you all enough.

"Sure, Aaron, I can leave the TV on for you."

I go over to the small TV in the corner, and grab the remote.

"You can tell it's a family house, there is a TV in every room."

I start to skip through the channels until I see a picture of myself.

"Look, it's me. I love seeing me on the TV. It's the best part of what I do."

I turn up the sound.

"Still at large serial killer Edmund Carson will wake this morning to the tragic news that his grandmother has sadly passed away. Edmund is now the number one fugitive in the UK and has killed more than one hundred people. It is said that his grandmother passed quietly in her sleep. It is believed

that she has had no contact with Edmund Carson since the horrors at Preston High School for Girls."

I drop the remote on the floor.

I can't breathe…

I can't breathe…

Chapter 7

I sink to my knees. I don't think my legs have the strength to keep me up; I can hardly feel them. I can't feel them. Surely it hasn't been that long? It hasn't been that long since I have seen her. I have only been to London... Wales. Scotland. Cornwall. Just all over really, but not that long. It's been over a year? Really a year? I can feel the tears rolling down my face, but I don't think I am breathing. I can't feel my heart beating. I can't feel anything.

I sit and bring my knees up to my face. I don't want to let them see me crying. I start to sob into my knees. I can't believe it? I can't believe she has gone. I was going to see her. I kept telling myself I was going to see her. I was going to Brighton. I am sure that is where she was. They would have put her by the sea. She loved the sea... Nan, I was coming... I was. I would have found you. I would have. Just to have dinner again together. Take you out, treat you. Buy you some flowers. I know your favourite. I would have even helped with the charity work. Just for one more day. Soup at the soup kitchen, you love doing that. I was going to take you that bottle of Advocaat that I bought. It's your favourite. It's in the car. You didn't think they made it anymore, but I found it, Nan. In a little shop in Scotland, I found it for you. I can't stop sobbing. My whole body is shaking.

What is up with me? I am cold. It wasn't cold before, but now I am cold. I can feel the chill all over my body. I am coming down with something, I know I am. And I don't have her to take care of me. I am going to get the flu, and I have lost my nan to take care of me. No more chicken soup or breakfast in bed. No more cuddles on the sofa under the knitted blanket she made me. No more nights in watching my programmes. If it wasn't for her watching them with me, I wouldn't be where I am today. The way she always wanted to watch CIS or that criminal thingy. She never got it right. I am sure she did that on purpose. Just to make me laugh. She could always make me laugh. I can't remember the last time I laughed; really laughed.

I am never going to hear her laugh again. I am still sobbing. I don't think I am ever going to stop. There is actual snot coming out of my nose now. I grab the T-shirt I am wearing, and pull it up to wipe my face.

I don't want to look up now as I know they will be all staring at me. They won't understand. They will have thought that I was always strong. Always. The job I do shows the world that I am strong, I am independent, but I am not. Not always. Everyone needs someone to love. Someone to be loved by. She loved me. She always loved me. Everything she did. Even before my parents' accident, she was there. I was the apple of her eye. That's what she used to say to me. She was the apple of mine.

She always had that little bit extra for you that you are not expecting. Extra pie. Extra 50p. Extra kisses, even if you don't think you want them, you secretly do. It was extra love. Some people have normal love, but nans have extra love. So much extra love.

I try to breathe, try to get it under control. I can't.

That's why she knitted scarves and gloves and hats for me. It's not because it's cheaper. I remember the time we spent at the wool shop. Wool was expensive, and I always told her it was quicker and easier to by a scarf, let alone the time it took to make one. The hours she would sit there with her knitting, I could buy a scarf for half the cost, and none of the time, but that's not what she wanted. She wanted to know that when you were cold, when the snow is falling, or the rain is chucking it down, she was the one who was keeping you warm. She was the one taking care of you.

I am cold now, Nan. I am so cold…

I still sob. I am a mess. I need to stop. I need to get focussed again. I pull the T-shirt back up, and wipe my face. I don't want people to think that I am soft. I get to my feet. My legs are still weak, I can feel it, but they are supporting me. I just hope that they don't give way.

They are very quiet. I know it's always hard to think of things to say at this point. People struggle with death. You must be strong. I am quite good at keeping things going. I will have to be the strong one.

"I am so sorry. I didn't mean for you to see that."

They are all very sheepish. They can hardly turn to look at me. I knew Sandra would break the ice. She has been a rock. She is an amazing woman.

"Thank you, all of you. It has just come as a huge shock.

"I know. I wish I had spent more time with her. That's all, more time.

"I think it was the only thing that she ever asked of me. I feel like I have failed her, and I have never wanted to do that."

I can feel myself welling up again. My throat feels like there is something stuck in it, and there are tears rolling down my face. I need to keep it together. I don't want them telling their story, and making it all about this. All about how they saw me fall to pieces. They need to be talking about the good times we had. Especially the girls.

"Anyway, where was I? I was just about to say goodbye. I was thanking you for a great night. Such fun."

The word fun sticks in my throat. I don't want to talk about fun. I need to get out of here; I need to deal with this on my own.

"No, really, I am fine. I will be fine."

It is nice that they don't want me to be on my own. Why is it that nobody says the word fine, and means it? You may as well just say no. No, I am falling to pieces and I feel like my world is caving in. No, I will never be fine again. That is what you really want to say.

"Okay, maybe you are right... just for a little bit."

I sit at the table. I think they are right; I am not ready to go out and face the world yet. I need a little more time to compose myself.

"No, thank you. I don't think I could eat anything. I don't want to be any trouble to anyone."

There is a silence again. Sandra is really trying though.

"That is a good idea. I know it's your day off tomorrow. Are you sure you don't mind? I could just lie down in the office?

"Okay, thank you. You are very kind. I promise I won't stay too late.

"That would be lovely. Thank you."

I cut the tape off Sandra and help her up the stairs. I whisper in her ear as we walk the stairs.

"Nice touch about helping me find clean sheets."

We lie on the bed together. She has her arms around me and I have my head on her chest. Just like my grandmother used to do when I was poorly, when I needed comforting. I start to sob again. I knew that my tears weren't gone. I feel like I am so full of them, they are overflowing.

"I am glad you are here."

I really am. I don't want to be alone. I guess without her I am always going to be alone now. There is no family left. Uncle George but I haven't seen him since my parents' funeral and even then, he isn't real family. I don't have a real family any more. I can't stop crying. I am glad there is only the two of us here. People shouldn't see me like this.

I don't think I will ever stop crying. My eyes are sore already. The tears are hurting my eyes. I can't keep them open…

I open my eyes. We are in the same position as we were when I fell asleep. She is still holding me.

"Thank you, Sandra. Yes, I feel much better. Thanks for staying with me while I slept. You didn't need to do that.

"Jesus, it's like eight thirty. I really didn't mean to sleep so long. It's not a good thing to do in my profession. I am not Goldilocks."

The thoughts of my nan and last night are still firmly in my head but it's time to get over them. At least put them to one side for now. I need to crack on with everything. The one thing my nan was proud of was my work ethic. So, I need to do this for her. She would want me to.

"Do you know, Sandra, I think I might. A little breakfast may be exactly what I need."

I think of all the times I would walk down stairs and my nan would have breakfast waiting for me. She always knew exactly what I wanted that day. Put on a brave face, that is what she always said. A brave face can hide a thousand worries.

I pick up Sandra and take her downstairs and tape her back to the chair.

"I am much better, thank you, Steven. I think a little sleep has done me the world of good. Your wife was kind enough to watch over me as I slept.

"We were just saying that very same thing. A spot of breakfast. Kids, are you hungry?"

I need them to see me back at my best. The real me. In full flow. It is important for them and for the press they will give me.

"It is okay. I will clear up the breakfast things before I go so the scene is the same. Certainly, one you will be discussing in class, Jess.

"Cereal it is. Steven? Sandra?

"Cereal for Steven and you, Sandra?"

I walk over. I can tell she wants to whisper into my ear.

"That's really kind. But, no, I don't think so. It's too much to ask, given everything you have done for me, and looking after me last night."

I lean down again.

"Are you sure? I mean, nobody will see?"

I whisper into her ear now.

"I love you. You are an amazing woman."

It's important that people know how you feel, as you never know when you might see them again. Love is a strong word. But I felt like I needed to use it today. I fetch a bowl and a knife and climb under the table. I don't want them to see me doing this. I must respect them as they have seen me at my lowest. Not that they will tell anyone. They are nice people. I get in front of Aaron and cut straight across his stomach. Because of the way he is sitting, only blood comes out. But it's sweet-smelling blood. I reach in and start to pull at everything inside. I cut at it with the knife. It is always easier to cut with the knife than just pull. I look down at the bowl. It's not a lot. I suppose the smaller the person, the smaller the insides. It's small but its smells so good. Looks good too.

I appear from under the table and throw a wink at Sandra. She just gets me, she really does. She is not Miss Walker hot, but as a person she is special. I set the bowl on the side and fix cereal for the three others and place it in front of them.

"Sandra, are you eating with me?

"Yes, no problem. I like it rare too. You will love this. I am not in the same league as your cooking, but I do make a mean breakfast."

I search through the bowl. Liver and kidney will be fine. I start cooking it up. It doesn't take long. It's barely pink when it is cooked. I serve it up and sit at the table.

"There is a little more in the pan, Sandra, if you need it. I find it very rich at times, and I am not overly hungry."

I cut a piece and feed her. I am glad Steven can't see me doing it as he is still behind his book. It would look a bit intimate.

"It does taste amazing. I think it's because it is warm. It really makes the sauce, doesn't it?"

Before I know it, mine has gone. I was hungrier than I thought. I stand up and go back to the pan. The blood is still warm. Warm, rich and sweet.

APPLE PIE! How did I forget about the apple pie?

"You know, it's all I could think about last night. Your apple pie, Sandra."

I fetch the leftovers from the fridge and spoon the warm blood across it. I go back and sit at the table.

"Anyone else?

"Thank you. Do you know what? I really needed this. I really needed to get back to myself. Father Harry was fun. But you must be true to yourself. My nan used to say that all the time. Edmund, be true to yourself. I get that now, and I will be. I will make her proud."

I eat the leftovers of the pie. It is amazing. Amazing. I think it would go great with lemon meringue as well. All that blood over the white peaks would look amazing. I clear the breakfast things and leave the table exactly how it was going to be before the news last night. Makes a good picture. That is a real Edmund Carson style family photo.

"I don't really know, Steven. I did think about heading back to London after the castle and the Lakes. But that doesn't feel right now. It's your day off today, isn't it?

"That's right. OAP home? Still going to be doing that?

"I agree. It would be good for you to stick around and help with Sandra. I think you both need some time together. You have a lot to discuss. Hopefully you can sort everything out so that you are all happy."

Not an easy conversation. Telling your wife, you are gay. But she knows. And she knows what she has been missing now. Which means I have done some really good work here. Think I have helped them all, a lot. And in their own way, they have helped me too. Helped me come back to being me.

"You know, I never thought of that? It might be exactly what I need now. I could do your rounds for you. Spend some time with the older generation. It will remind me of spending time with my nan. She was so into her charities and helping people. Seems like something she would like me to do in her memory.

"Is it okay if I borrow some clothes?

"Thank you."

I go upstairs and get dressed. Father Steven's clothes are a very good fit. Sandra must like guys of a certain stature. I come back downstairs.

"Okay, I really have to go this time. I would appreciate it if you didn't tell anyone about my little breakdown. She was very dear to me, and it's not really in my style.

"Thank you. You are so kind. I do hope everything works out for you all."

I leave. They were a nice family. I am glad I got to spend time with them. Oh, and I had sex. Good sex. They are the things I need to remember about last night. I am never leaving it that long again. I go back to the hotel and check out. I ask the receptionist for directions to the OAP home. There are like five in this place. Five OAP homes and a dozen churches. People come to the Lake District to die, don't they? I head to the closest one. I presume that's the one that Father Steven goes to.

I pull up outside. Saturday must be visitors' day as it seems to be very busy. Cars are pulling up everywhere. I guess it's a day off for most people, so they need to show up. Be nice to their parents or grandparents, I would guess. I head into the place like I know where I am going. The thing with this dog collar is, it is an access all areas pass to anything. People just nod at me all day. They never stop and say, hey, you, where do you think you are going? Generally the most I get is a how are you Father? Then they walk past fast. Sin is a powerful guilt trip.

I walk into what must be a communal room. There are at least five oldies all sitting in chairs. The TV is on in the corner. Not that I think any of them are watching it. It is a bit far away for old people. Maybe they should get one of those big flat screen ones for the wall. Some bloke is cooking on the TV. He is not one of the majors. I know them. He is just a Saturday morning cook. Cooking programmes. They seem to be taking over the TV. I look at the oldies again.

I guess I just sit and talk to them. I am sure they will want to talk to a Father. Talk about the war or something else that happened a hundred years ago? Or how old they are? Old people always want to talk about how old they are. It is like a badge or something.

They aren't moving very much? I think I may need a mirror or something to check that they are breathing. Imagine if they died there and then in the chair. I wonder how long it would take for people to notice. Weeks I bet.

"Morning, Father."

I turn to see a nun standing in front of me. I must look twice to check she is a nun. She has the most perfect blue eyes. They are stunning.

"Morning, Sister."

Why are Fathers Father and Sisters Sister? I know there is a Mother Superior. Is there a Father Superior? Is that the pope? But there is not a brother, is there? There is not a junior Father, is there? Wait, is a monk a brother? Maybe. I don't think I would want her to be my sister though. That's against the law or something, isn't it? Those eyes are stunning. She has me in a daze.

"We were expecting Father Steven this morning. He does like to pop in on his days off. Tries not to miss a Saturday."

Yes, I knew that this was the right place. This place was not the only thing Father Steven liked to pop into on a Saturday morning. That's what he was really doing with his days off, Eugene. A quick trip around the oldies and a quick fumble with Eugene. I can't get over the colour of her eyes. They are beautiful. She is beautiful. You could lose yourself in them. I could lose myself in them.

"Yes, I know. Father Steven has the flu. He didn't want to pass it around your lovely guests. It is okay, Sandra has him dosed up with tablets and chicken soup. I looked in on them on the way here."

That will put her at ease, the fact I at least know these people. Not that they ever think of not trusting me. I bet she is so hot under all that gear. Nuns are so hot. You just know they are good in bed. Appreciative. I just hope she isn't blonde. Blue eyes and blonde always seem to go together.

"Well, we are glad to have you here then, Father."

No, she is not blonde. Long, dark hair. A little longer than Miss Walker. A little shorter than Sandra Bullock. That's what she looks like under there. I can imagine slowly taking those clothes off without losing eye contact. Her eyes twinkling at the thought of me. With one hand, she would start to undress me. Then she would feel it. The size would frighten her at first, and excite her at the same time. Something she will have been dreaming about her whole life.

"Father?"

What did she say? Oh, yeah, Father.

"Sorry, Father Andrew." I shoot her a smile.

"Father Andrew, let me show you around."

Andrew, good name. Good job I saw it on the name badge of the guy checking me out of the hotel. She certainly has a body under there. I am getting good at seeing a great body under loose-fitting clothes. Even in that black dress. Even nuns have a little black dress. Must be a girl thing. Black dresses. Black dresses and stockings. Black dresses and stockings and suspenders. Nuns with blue eyes, black dresses, stockings and suspenders and black hair.

"Father Andrew?"

"Father Andrew?"

Shit, that's me. I can't keep it together. Once I have had sex, it is all I can think about. How did I last a whole month?

"Sorry, Sister, was deep in my thoughts. So, how can I help today?" That has her smiling again.

"Saturday is generally a busy day for us, Father. Lots of families visit. But Father Steven likes to normally visit people who aren't getting visitors. As I said, I can show you around, if you would like?"

"If that is what he would normally do, then so will I."

She walks me along the corridor. I stay a little back to check her out. Fuck, you can tell I have had sex. I can imagine every move with her. Starting with pulling that black dress over her head, just how I do with Miss Walker, every time we meet. I love the fact she always wears that black dress for me. With all the underwear. She knows what I like.

I bet it's been a while for her, that's why she was keen to show me around. Spend a little time with me to get the old juices flowing. Nuns have sex, right? I don't remember reading anything in the book to say they can't? They're married to the church, but married people have sex. Not a lot of sex, but they do have some. One little touch from me, multiples I can tell. Those eyes must look amazing all glazed over.

"In this room, we have Fred Scott. Across the hallway there is Susan Brady. They should keep you going for a while. After that maybe a quick cup of tea together. I am always interested in talking to new people."

I bet you are, Sister. Something about the way she said talking. She didn't mean talking. I can think of things we can do together that don't need a lot of talking. Hard to talk with something in your mouth sister.

"Sounds perfect. Thank you, Sister."

I go into Fred's room. He is sitting in a chair watching TV. I guess there is not a lot more to do in this room. Two chairs, a bed and a TV. I sit in the chair opposite him. Looks like a tiny bathroom off to the side. I am not sure my nan would have liked it here. I wouldn't have wanted her in a place like this. They probably had her in a big mansion, knowing how much I am doing for the country. Bringing fame back to the UK.

"Morning, Fred."

He looks at me and then back to the TV. I turn. He is watching something resembling horse racing. Or it may even be actual horse racing. There is a horse on the TV either way.

"How are you today, Fred?"

"Fine."

"How has your week been?"

"Fine."

There goes that word again. Maybe this wasn't a good idea. You know he doesn't mean fine. He is upset about something. I am not sure I was ready for this. I just came to do something nice. Something my nan would do with her day off. Not that she ever had a day off. She was always helping someone. I need this guy like a hole in the head today. I am not even sure why I am here.

"Do I know you?"

"No, Fred. I am Father Andrew. I am standing in for Father Steven."

He shakes his head. I am guessing not a fan of Father Steven.

"Oh, are you another one, you know, gay, like him?"

What the? I knew it. I just have a radar don't I?

"No, I am not gay, Fred."

"He is though, isn't he? Raving one, I would say. You can tell."

"Father Steven is a happily married man, I believe, Fred. He has a lovely wife called Sandra. With two lovely children."

I am not sure why I am defending the fact? He is. At least Bi. Although Bi, he would have slept with his wife more. She is well worth it.

"Happily married and doing an altar boy, by the looks of it."

Wait, he knows? I am not sure how to react to that. He probably is. Fathers wouldn't talk about that stuff, would they? Surely, they would all stick together. Like a gang. All for one and all that. It is like a secret club, isn't it?

"I am sensing you are not a religious person then, Fred?"

"I am as religious as the next bloke. Don't like all the nonces though."

"Nonces? What is a nonce?"

"You know, the men on men thing. Or the women on women. Either way. Just don't like it. Shouldn't be happening."

"Oh, you mean the gay community."

He gives me a look. Makes me want to smack him in the mouth.

"Are you sure you are not one? Talking like there is a gay community and all that?"

"No, Fred. I have a girlfriend. But there is nothing wrong with being gay, Fred. Love is love, no matter the form it comes in."

He is shaking his head at me. Is that what he wants to talk about? Maybe that is what it he is secretly hiding. Maybe he is a nonce too? My nan used to say that if you protest too much, then it is probably true.

"Oh, you are one of those, are you?"

"One of what, Fred?"

"One of those that will marry them. Let them be together and all that."

"I think I am, Fred, I believe marriage is something that is open to all people. As long as you love each other."

He is not impressed with that statement, I can tell.

"Don't you have to like pass an exam on the Bible or something before you get that job? Haven't you read it?"

"We are avid readers of it, yes, Fred."

I am trying to smile at him and lighten the mood here.

"Then where it says thou shall not... You do know it means you lot as well. You preach it to the congregation on a Sunday, and every other day now. So, you don't even respect Sundays any more. Isn't that like one of the rules? God's day? Don't shag the same sex, or your neighbour or a donkey. Adultery is against God. Most of the priests in the world are doing something dodgy with some young boy or girl. Mainly boys."

I think I am in shock. All the old people I have met up until now have been friends of my nan. Nice, warm, friendly people. This guy is a piece of work.

"Killing is bad, but you lot, you lot start more wars than anyone else. In fact, I think you start all the wars in one form or another. Don't steal and yet you are the wealthiest people on the planet. Collection plates. Charities. Fuck me, your houses, your lands are bigger than anyone's in the country alone. I can't imagine what you own worldwide. Even have your own fucking country. You guilt all these people into giving you money. Isn't that stealing? I am sure the only reason you all hang around old people's homes is to ensure that we leave you some money. Cause as we get a bit mad in the head and closer to death, we all try to secure our place in heaven. Why do you think your big fuckoff churches are full of old people? We believe, when we must. When we have nothing else in our lives... And another thing. Honour thy father and mother. Really, as soon as we are old, the kids put us in a home to deal with pricks like you on a weekly basis. Or those soppy nuns. Do you honour your father and mother? Do you make sure they are okay and taken care of on a weekly basis? Or are you just like the others? Fathers and mothers should be listened to and respected. Do you think they wanted you to do this job? Do you think you're honouring them by stealing off old people? Shagging young boys? And preaching whatever set of rules fits you today. No, you people, and religion. Makes me sick."

I think I am in actual shock. He was a frail old man when I walked in. That was a lot to take in for a short space of time. And Father Steven does this every week? No wonder he looks for love wherever he can find it.

"I think we shall..."

"Don't you read the commandments then, Father? Did it not give you a clue that He says He is a jealous God? He will punish the sins of the parents over the generations to come if you don't buck your ideas up. That's why we do our best and the younger generations fuck it all up. Treat us like vermin and house us away from everyone we love."

I get up. I can't listen to this prick anymore. If I had my knife I would just end his misery right here and now. Wait why don't I have my knife? I always have my knife? He is lucky, very lucky.

"Have a nice day, Fred."

Wow, this Fathering thing has calmed me. I almost meant that.

"That's it, run away. Faith is one thing but obeying the rules laid down is another. You are all the same. No real commitment."

I walk back and whisper in his ear.

"Shut the fuck up. You bitter, old, sexist, racist prick. You want to know how I respected my parents? I fucking blew their house up with them in it. Something that will happen to you if you don't keep your fucking mouth shut. People like you make me sick."

I turn and walk away. Then stop and turn.

"May God be with you, Fred."

I make the sign of the cross and then leave. I am outside the room. I close the door behind me and take a big breath. Not sure why I did that. Maybe religion is coming over me. Not what I expected really. I don't know what I was expecting. Maybe just some closure. Maybe the thought of seeing my nan in a place like this would make it easier knowing that she died in her sleep, in her big house by the sea. She probably spent her last hours watching the sea. That would have been nice. I am so glad she didn't end up like Fred. Bitter, old man. I walk across the hallway to Susan Brady's room. He can't be my memory of this place. Not today. I need to know I have done good today. I knock on the door and walk in.

It's the same size room with two chairs. A few more photos around the place than Fred's. In fact, a lot of photos. She must have a big family. She is lying in bed watching TV. I guess there is little else to do in an old people's home. I doubt they have a gym or anything. Probably a good thing, you wouldn't want to see all these wrinkles in gym wear.

"Hi, Susan."

She looks over to me. She smiles. It's the smile of a nan. Someone who is genuinely pleased that you are here. I think that's what I was looking for. She is the reason I came here today. I came because I missed that smile. Her smile.

"Hello."

"I am Father Andrew. I wondered if you would like some company?"

She smiles again at me. I can tell she does.

"Come closer, over here, Father Andrew, so I can get a good look at you."

I walk towards the bed. She holds out her hands and grabs mine and pulls me closer. Until we are almost face-to-face. Eyes are probably going, poor cow. At least, I hope that is the case. I am sure she doesn't want a kiss. Does she want a kiss?

"Ah, yes, it is you. I have been expecting you, Father."

Silly old girl doesn't remember we haven't met before. Head's probably started to go. Her smile is getting brighter though so at least I have done that for her.

"And how are you today, Susan?"

"I am as well as can be expected, Father. Ninety-seven, you know."

"I know, and how is everyone else? Are they treating you okay?"

"Oh, they are lovely, Father, you know that. Sit down, take a load off."

I sit in the closest chair to her bed.

"So how has your week been, Susan? Have you been up to anything interesting?"

"It's been a good week, Father. Much of the same. It is always much of the same."

"And have you had many visitors?"

"No, Father, no visitors. Not for a long time now… They all live so far away, you see. It is a bit of a trek to get here."

She starts pointing to pictures.

"There is my son Phillip. He lives in Australia. That's his wife Angela and children Jason, Alex and Freddie. And my great grandchildren Oliver, Tyson, Sarah and Annabel. They were all over last year but it's such a long way to travel and so expensive nowadays. Takes a day on a plane just to get here."

There is a little sadness in her voice as she said that I can tell. She must miss her family.

"And there is my other son. Carl. He is divorced, Father. Three girls though, Bethany, Alana and Grace. Has nine grandchildren too. Lives in London, Father. It's a long way to get here from London. He tries to see me once every other month. Tries to get the girls to come as well when he can."

"And who is the beautiful young lady, Susan?"

"That's my daughter Jennifer. We lost her two years ago, Father. But her husband still visits. They couldn't have children, Father. They weren't blessed. So, I think he is just lonely now. That's why he makes the trip up. But I love seeing him. He is family, Father. He is still family."

"Sounds like a lovely big family, Susan. You are a very lucky woman."

"It is, Father, it is. I have been really blessed, Father."

She goes quiet. Think all this talk about family may have her a little upset.

"It was better when Fred was alive to share it with, Father."

"Fred was your husband, Susan?"

"Yes, Father. Wonderful man. So big and full of life. Been gone now for ten years. I miss him every day, Father. Every single day."

"I am so sorry for your loss, Susan."

She is quiet again. I suppose they don't like being reminded about the past. Need to keep it lively. Keep the conversation going. That's what we do. There must be some good points about being here?

"You're still a young woman, Susan. I am sure you could have a pick of the bunch? I am sure it is party every night in here?"

At least she is smiling at that.

"Oh, I am old now. Old and tired. Too tired for all that nonsense."

"How can you say that? Look at you, in the prime of your life. In fact, I just saw another Fred over the road. I am sure he would be interested."

She laughs at that.

"I am sure he would, that grumpy old man, Father. I couldn't be like that, Father. Always has something to moan about. No, I have had a good life, Father, and I am just waiting for what is to come."

Now I don't know what to say. What do you say to a woman waiting for death to come? That is what she meant, right?

"And you, Father, anyone special in your life?"

As soon as she said that, there is a lump in my throat. I can feel it.

"There was, Susan. There was." That almost hurt to say. I can feel my throat swelling up.

"Do you want to talk about it?"

I am not sure if I do or don't. There must be a reason why I came here? I clearly need to talk to someone. Not Miss Walker, or else I would have gone straight home. I don't want her to see me feeling weak. She is besotted by me. That's not fair to her. Susan doesn't know me. I can say what I like to her. It is not as if she can tell anyone. Anyway, who would believe an old fuddy-duddy? I am smiling a little now. That is what my nan used to call them. She used to always tell me to watch out for her, to make sure she doesn't start turning into an old fuddy-duddy. She never did.

"I lost my nan recently."

That was even harder to say. I have never said that before.

"Oh, that's such a shame, Father. Were you close?"

"Yes, very. She raised me after my parents died in an accident. I always looked up to her. She always did the best for everyone. She was a remarkable woman."

"I am sorry, and you being so young too. So, you have nobody now?"

I ignore the, nobody comment. I have people. I am not alone. I have Miss Walker, she is always with me, when I need her to be.

"I don't think it has really hit me yet that she is gone. I didn't go to see her. I should have, I should have spent more time with her. I just lost track of time."

I can feel myself starting to well up again.

"It's very hard, Father. As you get older and turn into adults yourselves, your parents and grandparents aren't needed as much. My children have their children to look after, and their grandchildren. My husband Fred used to say that we have done our job, Susan. If they are happy and healthy, we have done our job. I am sure she knew that you were healthy and happy. Are you, Father? Happy and healthy that is."

There is a lump in my throat again. Makes me feel like I can't breathe any more. I didn't know I could hurt this much.

"I think I am?"

"It's something you need to know, Father. Not think. You are a young man and if you are not happy, you can change your life around. You have time. We only get one shot on this planet, Father. Depending on your beliefs, of course. You know, if you're not planning on coming back as a mouse or something?"

Think it was her turn to try and make me smile.

"Come here and give me a hug. It always helps me."

I do as she says. As I hug her, I can smell her scent. She smells like a nan. Never quite sure what the smell is. But it's a nan smell. Maybe a Werther's Original in her nightgown. I take a long hug. The smell brings a few tears to my eyes, but I fight them back. I wish I had the chance to hug her one more time, just once. Once so I would have known how proud of me she was.

"There you go, Isn't that all better now?"

"Yes, thank you. I think I needed that, Susan."

"All part of the service, Father. Wait a minute, weren't you supposed to be cheering me up?"

At last we are both smiling at the same time. She seems a lovely old lady.

"Before I go, Father, I would like a cup of tea. Is that okay?"

"Okay? I can do that for you."

I am not sure where she thinks she is going; she looks like she is a permanent resident in that bed. Maybe this has inspired her to go visit her family. I am sure they let them out, don't they? They aren't like prisoners in old people's homes? I go over and grab her small kettle and fill it in the sink in the en-suite.

"Are you going to be having a cup, Father?"

"You know, I think I will. Thank you, Susan."

Can't remember the last time I had a cup of tea. It was probably when my nan made it. I always drink water nowadays. Water or pop. I need to drink more tea. It will remind me of her. I make the tea and bring her cup to her.

"If you look in that top drawer, there is a little box of biscuits. Shortbread with real butter. The real ones, Father. I only keep them for special occasions. This is a special occasion, Father. I am so, so glad that you came."

I go and fetch them.

"You know, Father, Fred used to bring me a cup of tea in bed every day."

"Fred the grumpy guy across the hallway? I wouldn't have said he was the type?"

"No, silly, Fred my husband. Every morning he would get up to go to work, fix up his own pack and breakfast and before he would leave, he would bring me a cup of tea to the side of the bed. Kiss me right here and then disappear. Never saying a word. To tell you a secret, I was always awake. I just know he liked the thought of me sleeping another ten minutes. As soon as he left I would get up and drink my tea."

"That must have been lovely."

"It was, even when he retired. He would still be up at the crack of dawn and bring me my tea at eight a.m. I miss that so much, Father. Every morning when I see the clock tick to eight it reminds me, Father."

We both sip our tea. I try the biscuits. She is right, they are lovely. I don't think I have ever had shortbread before. I think I could eat a whole tin full.

"They were his favourite biscuits too. Those and Rich Tea. I used to say to him I would buy him a Hobnob or a chocolate biscuit, but he always liked the Rich Tea, and on special occasions a shortbread."

"A man after my own heart, Susan. Can't beat a Rich Tea."

"You make a good cup of tea, Father."

"Thank you, Susan."

We sit drinking our tea. She seems to be very reflective. Lost in her thoughts a bit. I hope it's not some kind of condition. Some old people do end up losing their minds a little. I hope that doesn't happen to her. She seems such a nice lady. Must be horrible to lose those special memories.

"Father, that was a lovely cup. I am glad we got to share it together."

"Me too, Susan."

"Well, I think that's enough for today, Father, don't you?"

"If you say so, Susan. I will let you rest. I am sure there are more people I can visit."

"Thank you. I am so in need of a rest. I have been waiting for you to help me with that. Edmund."

I freeze and then drop the cup on the floor. It doesn't break but the little bit of tea that was left over spilled onto the rubber floor tiles. She knows my name? She said my name, right? I wasn't imagining it?

"I am sorry, Susan?"

"I know who you are, Edmund. I knew from the moment you came through the door. I sit and watch the TV all day. Although you have been off the screen for a while, I know your face. When you spoke about your nan? I knew it was you. The news of her has been all over the TV today. Such a shame, dear, she looked a lovely woman."

I don't know what to say. She knows who I am. I can feel myself close my jaw.

"She did a lot for charity, your nan. They are saying nice things about her. But a lot of the chat is about you. People are saying that they believe you were Father Harry too? Is that right, Edmund? Were you that Father Harry? You certainly look the part now."

Everyone knows about Harry? What about the reveal? What about all the photos and everything I have stored up? What the fuck is going on here?

"They all know I am Father Harry?"

"No, dear, a few people are asking the question. But most don't believe it. Is it true though, Edmund?"

I just stand looking at her. She doesn't seem mad at me. I expected her to be mad? I am not sure what to do now.

"Yes, Susan. There was a plan. It was all about my fans, my followers. I wanted to entertain them a little more. Something to keep them looking up to me, I guess. Wait, did you say you were expecting me?"

She is quiet now.

"Not expecting, Edmund, but hoping. Praying."

Hoping? What would she be hoping for from me? It's not like she has… FUCK!

She is hoping for the end. That's what she means. She thinks that I am here to help her with that. That is what she thinks? Why would she think that?

"Whatever you have done, Edmund, you have done for your own reasons. I am not here to judge you. There is only one person who will judge you."

She means God, right? She means God will judge you. Me. She means God will judge me. She is silent again now. She doesn't seem to be afraid of me. There is even a little smile on her face as she looks at me?

"I've been here in this home a long time, Edmund. Over ten years now. I am a burden to my family and I just want to see my husband again. I really miss him, every day. I hoped you would come, come to help me."

She does, she is waiting for me to work with her?

"But you have your family, don't you? Phillip and Carl and all the grandkids? Great grandkids? They all need you?"

"As we are being truthful, Edmund, it's been a lot longer since I have seen them. I haven't even seen five of my grandchildren. Oh, they send me the photos but that's not the same. They have their own lives to live now."

"Still they might come and visit you soon?"

"They say they will, but they don't, Edmund. They are busy, and they don't want to be coming all the way up here."

"Then why did you choose to stay here? Why not stay in a OAP home closer to them? There must be homes down south?"

"Fred and I used to holiday here with the kids, and even when the kids had grown up we still came here. I thought it would bring me closer to him. I thought they would continue to holiday up here. You know, as I was here." There is the sadness in her voice again.

"And they don't, do they?"

"No, they seem to be all over the world now. The world seems to be so much smaller than it was in my day. They don't think twice about living in another country. They don't even holiday in the Lakes anymore. No, I came here to be closer to Fred and all that has happened is that I miss him even more. Being here makes me miss him even more."

There is silence. She is obviously thinking about him. Must be hard to lose someone after spending so much time together. It is hard to lose someone after spending so much time together.

"Susan?"

"I am tired, Edmund. I am so tired. My days just melt into one. I am lying in this bed day after day. I only get up for a weekly bath. My toilet bags are hanging at the side of my bed. I can see life out of the window, the comings and goings of other people's families, Edmund, and it makes me feel sad. I don't judge people, Edmund. Everyone has their own life to live. And I have lived mine. That is all. I have had my time."

She does look sad now. What a difference a few minutes can make. If you had asked me before the tea, she looked so happy. And now, so sad. It's a sad little existence stuck in this little room day after day. I am glad my nan's days didn't end up like this.

"I think it's time, Edmund"

I don't want to answer her. Was she only happy before the tea as it was her last cup of tea?

"They will just think I fell asleep. It will be fine. They don't even need to know you were here, Edmund."

Those words stick in my head. Just fell asleep. My nan just fell asleep.

She looks so sad now. My nan wouldn't have been sad when she fell asleep. She knew that I loved her. She would have been okay with the fact that we haven't been together for a while. She would have known that I loved her. That I thought about her every day. Wouldn't she?

She pulls the pillow from behind her head and holds it out to me. She really wants me to do this. She wants to leave us. There is a little smile on her face again now. I think it is there as a plea to help her. A plea to take away her pain and loneliness. A plea to send her off to see her husband. I walk over and take the pillow.

"Thank you, Edmund. You are a good man deep down inside."

I don't really know what to say. I look down at her. She needs my help. I lean over and kiss her on the forehead. Like her husband used to do.

"I forgive you, Edmund."

There is a lump in my throat. Feels like I have something lodged in there. I can feel my hands start to shake and my eyes are welling up again. But she smiles again. I know this is for the best. I take the pillow and cover her face. I press down as gently as I can. Those were her last words.

She hardly fights as I hold the pillow down. As I do, I can feel the tears rolling down my face. I have that feeling in my chest again like I can't breathe. It hurts. My chest hurts.

She stops moving. I take the pillow away from her face. I place it behind her head again. I brush the hair from her face. I lean in and kiss her on her head again and sit back down. I sit and wait. And wait. She doesn't talk to me. I don't know where she is, but she is not here. I hope wherever she is, she is with Fred, having a cup of tea.

I get up and leave. By the time I am in the corridor I am nearly running. I don't want anyone to see me crying. I get into the car and drive. I don't know where I am going, I just need to drive. I need to get away from here.

Chapter 8

It has been three weeks. Feels like the longest three weeks of my life. Three weeks until they can have my nan's funeral. How bad is that? Where do they keep the body for three weeks? People die every day. There must be warehouses full of dead people. Just lying there waiting to go into the ground. That's not fair to anyone.

The pain is still there but over time, it is starting to ease. I can feel it. Maybe after today, maybe once I know she has been laid to rest, I can breathe again. I can feel again. This numbness will disappear for good.

I should have gone. I know, I should have gone. I should have taken Miss Walker with me. That's what you do, you take the people you love to show them you care. To show that we are all family. They aren't even televising it. Famous people's families get televised funerals, don't they? I mean, the princes' mum got one. The ex-prime minister got one and she had been unemployed for about thirty years. Even those two gangsters in London got it on TV for their mum. Well, that's what it said on the movie. They must know people would want to see it. I get up and fetch a glass of water from the sink.

I look out at the fields in front of the kitchen. I can see why Susan and her husband used to holiday here. It is nice. I never thought I would stay here this long though. I couldn't drive any further. I didn't think I would ever stop crying. That was a hard day, but I am glad I was there for her in the end. The tears are drying up. Either that or I think I have run out of tears.

It's a great place, lots of little villages everywhere. I am just not ready to go back to London. I will be soon. I will go back. I will have a comeback. People like a comeback. Bigger and better than before. I need a comeback. I can't imagine what people are thinking.

I watch as the sheep graze in the field up the road. It is a few miles away. I can see as the shepherd and his dog turn up. The dog just circles them and they move. First one side and then the other. He is rounding them up. You think it would be in the dog's nature to jump on them. But he doesn't. He doesn't eat them, he just circles them. Dogs and wolves are the same, aren't they? Why wouldn't he attack? It can't be fun with him playing with his food? I mean, it's nature, isn't it? They disappear out of sight into the next field. I stand looking at the field for a while. It's empty. The field is just empty. The dog has rounded them all up and now they are gone. He has done his job. What does he do now? What does he do now he has done his job? There must be something more?

I go up the stairs and get dressed. I need to look smart today. For her. I check in on the girls before heading back downstairs. They are quiet today. Maybe showing me some respect. They know how much today means to me. They both smile at me as I walk into the room.

"You two have been in bed for days.

"I guess so. Love is a powerful thing. I do remember having a weekend in bed with Miss Walker. Seems a long time ago now. But they are the moments that you should treasure. Quality time she always called it.

"No, still no response. She will be busy with school, but I will text her again. She knows today is the day. She won't forget that. She is never good at texting me back. But she always turns up at the critical moments."

If truth be known, neither of us are good at that.

"Okay, I will leave you to it. You know you both came here to spend time outside, don't you? And you have hardly been out since we met. It is quite lovely out there.

"Okay, just bang on the ceiling if you need anything. Thinking I may make us a nice dinner later. Will seem a fitting way to end the day."

They are a nice couple. Summer in the Lake District is a great way to start a relationship. Although I know they are both into me, secretly. I can tell in their eyes they are always wanting me to stay a little longer. Especially Joanna. She knows what it's like to be with me now. Probably been bragging about it. She is only human. She really did help me get through that low point. People can really surprise you. Even if their girlfriend is in the other room at the time.

I go downstairs and sit in the chair. The bottle of whisky I bought from the local shop and the glass are next to me. Never had it before. But it's what they do on *Criminal Minds*. What Rossi and Co. do if they lose someone! Drink a whisky, neat. Sometimes ice. I go and fetch ice from the freezer and put it in a different glass next to me. I am not sure how much ice you are supposed to put in the glass. Always looks like a couple of cubes. I sit back down.

The paper says the funeral is at eleven. It's ten to eleven now. The press is going to be there by now. On the off chance of an appearance from me, no doubt. I will make one. Just not today. I will go down and see her. Take some flowers. I used to know a girl from a flower shop once. Maybe she could help me pick some out. Be nice to take her some of her favourite orchids. White and pink. I love that about her. So classic.

I don't know why but my stomach is churning. I suppose it's the thought of her being there without me. Without Mum or Dad, just Uncle George, I guess, although she does have so many friends. I bet the church is full. I bet they are packed up and down the rafters. With hordes of press on the outside photographing everyone as they come in. Wondering if they are me. Wondering if I am going to come in disguise. I could have gone. They wouldn't have been able to tell it was me. I could have launched a new character today. I don't want today to be about me though. It is about her. It is her day. It was her life they are celebrating. She was a special lady.

They still don't all believe I was Father Harry. Not everyone. I am sure of it. I don't think I can be Father Harry again. Not after this, not after Susan and the old people's home. No, when I return I will return as me. Or the ONE. May even leave Father Harry as a guessing game for some time. Maybe it is his turn to rest in peace.

They will be there too. Some dressed in uniform and some probably undercover to see if they can get close to me. They don't want me to be as famous as I am today. I know it. They are happy with the Jacks of this world. Long gone in history.

They don't care. I don't understand why, as without me they would probably be unemployed. I have done so much for them. You think they would be worshipping me.

I watch the clock in the kitchen as it turns eleven. I reach over and pour myself a drink and swill it around the glass with the ice cubes. Just because that is what they do on TV.

I then take a big gulp.

Fuck!

It's burning my throat! It's burning my throat! I give a shiver and grit my teeth. How do people drink this stuff? I put the glass back on the table next to me. Takes me a minute to calm down from the taste.

I am never going to be able to drink a bottle of this? I thought that is what people do. Drink a bottle, end up in a drunken state and then remember the good times. I get up and go to the fridge to see what else we have. A lot of cheeses, salad stuff, water, juice, Coke. No beer. I grab the Coke and sit back down. I guess the girls were trying to be healthy while they were up here. I pour some Coke into my drink and take another sip. It's better. It's still not great but it's better. I should have eaten. I have hardly eaten in three weeks. The food just didn't taste good. I guess it is the thought of never eating her cooking again. It was so bad at times it was good. Especially the sausages. She could never cook sausages.

Okay, let's do this. I add some more whisky and more Coke. I drink it down. It takes me three goes but it's done. I fill my glass back up again, then drop in a few more ice cubes. I watch as the ice melts into the whisky and Coke.

I don't think I know another way I could have spent today other than going to the funeral. I did think about going to a church. So at least I would have been in a church when it was going on. Father Steven's church is only ten miles away. I don't want people to know I am still around though. That much press would spoil the countryside. I hope there are orchids? White ones and white lilies too. She would have liked that. There will be. And I will take lots when I go. She will be able to see them. For sure. When she looks down on me. She will always be looking down on me. Always.

I take another drink. I just know I am never going to be a big drinker. I really don't like the stuff. I take another drink. She knew she was loved, that is the main thing. She knew that I loved her. I take another drink.

I remember carrying all those clothes to jumble sales every week for her. That was a good sign. Although wearing someone's clothes is a little weird. And the soup kitchen. I helped her out there too. Well, once. Lots of people wanting food for free. Wearing other people's clothes. That wasn't a good sign. I am sure there are enough jobs for everyone. Enough food for everyone. Why do some people have to live like that? Isn't that why we have governments? To make sure that people don't live like that? Not relying on my nan, to take care of all of them. I take another drink. It tastes a little better. Well, I suppose there is one thing, nan. If there is a heaven, you will be going straight to it. Straight through the gates. There were not many people as nice as you. She was always there for everyone. Everyone. I finish the drink and pour another. My head is starting to feel a bit fuzzy. This is the drunken state I was working towards, I guess. It doesn't take long with this stuff. Must be quite powerful.

Are nans still nans when they go to heaven? I mean, wouldn't they want to be like twenty again or something? Heaven is supposed to be perfect, isn't it? Your own little piece of heaven? If you are going to enjoy life, wouldn't you be in your prime? It says somewhere in the Bible about being reborn into heaven, doesn't it? Or taking away sin when you get in? Or am I getting confused? Because how would you recognise them when you get there if they are twenty? Like, if I am twenty, what if I went to heaven and ended up getting off with my nan? I am sure she was hot when she was twenty?

I take another drink.

What about the waiting stuff as well? Like Susan was saying in the home. If her husband is up there he has been waiting ten years. Surely, he has another woman by now? Or if he is in heaven and he is waiting for her, she is like ninety-seven when she gets there. He might think, fuck, you've aged, love.

I finish that drink and make another. This is getting easier to drink. Although that is the last of the Coke.

Oh yeah, you've aged, love. Maybe that's it. Maybe people in love don't see it. They don't see the flaws in each other. Flaws is a funny word. Why would you see a flaw in people? You don't see a wall in people, do you? Maybe you don't see how you age when you get older. If you are in love, I mean. I fancy Miss Walker because she is hot. Am I going to fancy her when she is like fifty and on a Zimmer frame? Grey hair and all that? Because I don't fancy fifty-year-olds now. Does taste change as you get older? Oh fuck, am I going to turn into the sicko? The one who likes old people. No, I can't do that. I can't turn into a freak. I need to stop that. I would take the pillow to myself. Holy fuck, what if you are married more than once? Who is waiting for you? Fuck, who is waiting for me? They all love me. And if in heaven you get everything you want, fuck, it will be like a pop star turning up. I can't be everyone's piece of heaven. Imagine.

I wonder if Melanie will be better in bed, in heaven. It is where dreams come true. I am going to be so busy up there. Where would I go to rest? Where do you holiday when you live in heaven? Can't be Brighton, can it? Holy fuck, is that why they are all old down there? They are holidaying from heaven? Heaven's holiday home is in Brighton where my nan was. Wait, that's why she wasn't ready to go. He just got confused and took another old person from Brighton.

Love is a funny thing.

I take another drink. I like this drink. All warm. Makes me feel warm.

It can make you a little bit crazy, this love stuff. I think it's designed to make you a little crazy. I know, I will go and ask the girls. I grab the bottle and my drink and head upstairs into their room. I knock before I go in just in case. Although might be nice to watch. Not join in but watch.

"Hey, I knew I would find you two still up here.

"Jack Daniels. I am not sure I like it. The Coke makes it better though... although I don't have any Coke any more. I don't know where it all went.

"Yes, thanks. Eleven o'clock... I was just thinking about love and I wanted to ask you two a question. What do you see when you look at each other? I mean, I know what I see: two extremely hot girls. But what do you see? You know, when you are alone and looking at each other?"

That will make them feel good about themselves, a little flattery. Well, Joanna. I am not sure Brooke likes me that much. Unless she is just trying to play hard to get. Some women do that. God knows why. It's not like she wouldn't enjoy me. Her girlfriend did. Wait, did I say that out loud? I need to watch that. I don't want to upset anyone today. Not today.

I take a drink. I am quite getting to like the heat of it. Makes me shiver but it almost feels like a good shiver. Like I can feel something. Like I am sensing her close to me. Probably here with me. She would prefer that. Why would she want to be where everyone is sad? That is just silly.

"Really? Both of you? Okay, I need to ask another question. How can you see a feeling? You say you can see love. But love is a feeling, isn't it? You can't see it? Can you? Surely you only feel love."

Wait, have I seen it? If I haven't seen it, have I even had it? I look around the room. Then I laugh to myself, I think I am looking for it. It is not like it is hiding under the bed, is it?

"My friend Susan just said that. She used to get a cup of tea in bed every morning without a word. She was a nice woman… So, it's the little things? The things you do that make the difference and show you love? Is it that you can see the little things? Expressions. Looks. Are they little things?"

I am not sure people do the little things for me. I can't remember the little things. Pineapple hedgehogs. They are the little things. I could go some pineapple hedgehogs today. Who is going to make them for me now? Nobody makes them anymore. Is the love disappearing from the world?

"Like what, Brooke? What are the little things that make the difference for you?"

I sit on the chair next to the bed. I look directly at her. I need her to know, I would do her. It will give her confidence. My glass is empty, so I take a swig out of the bottle. Fuck that is strong. But I bet it makes me look manlier though. She can tell how hot I am. She would turn for me in a heartbeat.

"You know, sometimes I get the feeling I don't do enough of that. I don't do enough of the handholding or looks as she walks into the room. I know I don't text enough, phone enough. It's not that I don't want to, I just forget. I get carried away with what I am doing so much I forget about other people? Do you think there is something wrong with me?"

I know there is nothing wrong with me. I am playing the vulnerable card. She is getting hotter the more I drink. Right there in front of my eyes.

"Thanks. It is a demanding job. And it's not like I plan to do this forever. Just until there is no doubt that I am number one. That was my plan.

"I am not sure. There is this doctor, you see. People say anywhere from fifteen to two hundred. If I am past two hundred I will be considered number one. No, considered is the wrong word. I will be undoubtedly number one. Then my thoughts were to settle down. Maybe London, with Miss Walker and have a couple of kids.

"Sorry, force of habit. She was my teacher. I guess I fantasised about her so much I always called her Miss Walker. It's a habit I can't seem to shake. Her real name is Emily. Beautiful name, isn't it?

"Walking home from another date actually. Yes, she pulled up next to me and offered me a lift. I think she could feel the tension, chemistry in the air when we were in the car together. One thing led to another, although it really didn't nearly. She went in to her house. I thought that was it."

I remember standing on that driveway. Thinking my life was about to end, on what was the best night of my life. It couldn't end like that. My birthday couldn't end like that. I didn't deserve that. She didn't deserve to not be with me. Imagine if that had ever happened, if she had not had the opportunity to be with me. They are looking at me? I have been quiet too long. Women don't like that.

"Then bang we had sex on the floor of her house that very night. We have been together ever since. Well, we are together as much as we can for two young people with demanding jobs. She is super good at hers. She was always my favourite teacher.

"I do need to make more time for her. I thought she would come today. Maybe she has gone to the funeral. That would be nice for my nan. To know that someone is there for her, from the family."

I take another swig. Miss Walker, Emily, she is family. She is my family. I am not alone. I will never be alone.

"Sure, sorry, that has been so rude of me. I will go down and fetch a couple of glasses? Unless you are okay to swig?

"Glasses it is then. Quite posh really, aren't you? The both of you. I was just thinking that with all the healthy food in the fridge."

I stand up. My legs don't feel right. I straighten them.

"Yes, thanks, I am fine. Strong stuff. Hit me a bit then."

I walk out of the room and close the door behind me. I go down the first few stairs and then my legs give way. I can hear the bottle smash on the way down.

FUCK! Fuck, fuck!

"Edmund."

"Edmund."

Oh, my head. I can feel it pounding. Feels like someone is having a party in there. Wait, someone is touching my hair? Who is touching my hair? Nan? Am I... am I already up here?

"Edmund."

I open my eyes slowly. It's a soft voice. One I recognise. As my eyes adjust I can see the long dark hair and the face, the face I love. I can feel the smile as it happens across my face.

"There you are, Edmund, let's get you up and on the sofa."

I do as I am told. I don't feel great but now I am lying on the sofa with Miss Walker kneeling beside me.

"What happened to you, Edmund?"

"I don't know. I think I lost my footing coming down the stairs."

"Looks like a nasty bump on your head, but at least it's not bleeding."

I raise my hand to feel it. Fuck, it feels like there is a golf ball in my brain.

"You're here? You are really here. I knew you would come."

"I am. Sorry, I meant to be with you for ten, but there was an accident on the M6. Traffic is a bugger."

"The main thing is you are here. I knew you would be here. I didn't want to be alone today. Not today."

I still feel fuzzy. She will know the smile is for her. It's not me gritting my teeth as my head really hurts. A mixture of bump and booze, I guess.

"I wouldn't be anywhere else, Edmund. You know that."

She gets up and climbs next to me on the sofa. Half on me. I don't care. She is little and doesn't weigh a lot. I can feel her cuddling into me.

"I have missed you. You do know that, don't you?"

"I have missed you too. You said two weeks, Edmund, you said two weeks."

"I know, I am sorry. Will never be that long again, I can promise you that."

I look her straight in the eye as I say that. Like Brooke said. It's all about the look. I know I am falling back to sleep. I can hardly keep my eyes open. I hold on tight to her as I do.

"I love you, Miss Walker. I love you."

I wake up. There is nobody on top of me. I feel out with my arms. My dizziness is disappearing.

"Hey, sleepyhead."

I turn, and she is standing by the sink in the kitchen.

"Hey, what time is it?"

"It's about seven thirty. I thought it best you sleep off the concussion. How are you feeling now?"

"Much better. Even better to know you are here. I felt for a minute then, like I had dreamed it."

"No, not a dream, Edmund. How about you light us a fire and I will make us some cheese and biscuits. I found a nice bottle of wine in the pantry."

"Okay, wait, I didn't even know we had a pantry."

She helps me off the sofa and leads me to the pantry door and then I push it open. It was already a little bit open. It is at the bottom of the stairs. I wonder if I hit my head on it. There is wine and beer in there. All different kinds of food. I have been shopping in the village daily as I thought the girls only liked cheese and salad. I knew those girls weren't as innocent as they made out. And now wish I had drank the beer instead of the whisky. My mouth is so dry. I go and grab a glass of water, I am suddenly aware of where I am. I walk over and kiss Miss Walker.

"A fire and a bottle of wine sounds like a plan to me."

I get up and start the fire. She starts making the food, but I go over and help her too. She is useless at that stuff. I practically do it all myself. I grab the wine and some more ice. Who doesn't keep wine in the fridge? Can't drink warm wine? I lay it all out on the rug in front of the fire.

"The ice, Edmund? For your head?"

"No, it's for the wine."

"It's red wine, Edmund. It's supposed to be room temperature."

"Oh, I didn't know that?" Did I? I thought all wine had to be chilled?

"You know, this kind of reminds me of our first time. Teaching me new things in front of a fire."

She smiles at that. She knows what that meant to both of us. It was life-changing. She is that type of woman. Life changing.

"Yes, Edmund, it does. Although it was G&T and you weren't hungry. Well not for food anyway. Or for drink."

I love the way she smiles at me. There is an innocence in her smile. Something that says she is mysterious yet fragile at the same time. Makes me want to protect her. That's my job. My job is to keep her safe from the world. There are some dangerous people out there.

"Dig in then."

"So how have you been coping? I know she was very dear and close to you. I do hope you just haven't been drinking all the time."

"No, I haven't. To be fair, I don't think I really like drink. I have been coping as well as I can. It came as quite a shock. I was with some friends for dinner and it just came out on the news."

I need to be careful not to say too much.

"I have been taking some time out, to get my head straight again. Felt for a moment there like my heart had been ripped from my chest."

"Think that time out was for the best. Is it working? Do you feel any better?"

"I think so. No, to be fair, I know so."

I do know so. I feel so much better knowing that she is here. Seeing her was what I needed. Always helps. Always as if it brings the focus back.

"Oh, look, a chessboard. Shall we play while we lie here, Edmund? Come on, show me how clever you are."

"If you like. I can take time out of my busy schedule to beat you."

I go and get it off the side. I never noticed that before either. I must have been walking around this place with my eyes closed.

"Okay, you be white and I will be black."

I adjust the board, so she has the white. I presume it's because she is pure and I am, well, not so much. People always think white wins every time. Not every time. Sometimes black wins.

"It's been ages since I played a game of chess."

"Me too."

That's not a lie. I was twelve and going to chess club for six months. Until Carl Carnegie joined and showed us all up. That kid had to be good at everything, didn't he? I would have been champion if it wasn't for him. I make the first move. She puts it back and then she makes the first move as she laughs. I knew white always went first.

"How's work? How is the school?"

"It's good. The kids are amazing and, yes, I am really enjoying it. How's the writing? Must be nearly done now? You are nearly done now, aren't you, Edmund?"

Something about the way she said that. How's the writing? As if she knows that's not what I am doing.

"It's good."

Her head goes down as she makes another move. She doesn't look back at me. I think she knows. She does, she knows I haven't been writing. She probably knows everything. Here I am lying to the woman I love and she probably knows everything already.

"That's a lie. It's not good. I don't think I can pretend to you anymore. I haven't been writing."

She is looking directly at me. It is not shock on her face. She is just looking directly at me.

"I haven't been writing. It's not what I do for a living. I am not a journalist. Well, not in the terms you would call one. I am more a blogger, you see. More a celebrity of sorts. I work with different people up and down the country. I do write about it. On Twitter, Facebook, YouTube, all of them. Not that Insta thingy. I can't get used to that. But I do write, just not books."

She is just looking back at me. I can't tell what she is thinking. There is something in her eyes. I can't tell if its disappointment or not.

"When I say celebrity, I mean, I can play, do play, other characters in my job. Up and down the country."

This isn't like I had thought. I sound like a babbling idiot. I wanted it to sound better, but I am telling this to the woman I love. The only one I have left in my life. Other than her I would be all alone.

"Like they do on the TV. Like that David someone. You know, the guy always on TV. Plays the wheeler dealer with a market stall. With the dopey brother and he plays a detective. And a wizard. I play characters for my fans just like he does."

Still nothing. I am going to lose her. I need this to sound better than this.

"I play different characters and work across the country, that's what I am trying to say. I won't be doing it forever though. I just wanted to be number one. Wanted to be the best. Wanted to be someone that you would be proud to walk out with of an evening. I thought as soon as I got to number one, we would settle down, maybe have a family of our own."

She is still quiet. We both are now. Surely the family thing must have turned this conversation around. Women love that idea, don't they? She works with children, she must be wanting some of her own?

"Characters?"

Is that a test? Is she asking if I am the Edmund Carson off of the news? The ONE? The ONE that was at her school? Is that going to make her mad? I don't want her to be mad.

"Yes, characters. I have a few. To keep my fans and readers interested in my story and help me get to number one. I just thought it would help."

In for a penny, in for a pound is what my nan used to say. I am just going to tell her. I need her to know me for who I am. It's a risk.

"Like Father Harry and the ONE. They are a couple of my characters."

She leans towards me. I almost feel like leaning backwards. She looks like she might head butt me. She kisses me. I wasn't expecting that. She kisses me properly. Like for real.

"I know, Edmund. I know."

She knows? How does she know?

"You know?"

"Edmund, I have always known. I was just waiting for you to tell me. I didn't want to push you into it. This is your decision. You need to know who you are. It will help in the long run. I am just so glad to be part of it, and now I can be for real."

She really does know. She kisses me again.

"I was going to tell you so many times. I swear I was. I don't know why it was so hard."

"I know. I could see it in you. The last time at the picnic you were almost bursting. But I don't think you were ready, ready to share with me who you really are. But, Edmund, I think you now know who you really are. Don't you? Everything that has gone on and then losing your nan. You know who you are and who you were meant to be? And as you said, it is not forever. It will be over soon and then we can start on the rest of our lives."

I do. I do know who I am and what I am going to do. She just gets me. She is part of me. It's like we were meant to be together. She is really is full of surprises.

"So, it is your move, Edmund."

"What?"

"Your move, silly. The game?"

I look down at the chessboard. All my pawns are gone.

"Hey, that's not right. They were there a second ago."

"You snooze, you lose, buster."

I pick up my queen and knock her king over. She has pounced on me before I could let go of my piece.

"Hey, that's not fair."

"You snooze, you lose."

She is now on top of me and I am pinned to the ground. I could get up if I wanted. She is only little. I let her pretend she is stronger than me.

"Now, Edmund Carson, when are you going back to work?"

"What? I would have thought that you would want to spend more time with me?"

"I do, of course I do, but as you said, the sooner you are number one, the sooner we get to start our lives together. And let's face it, you are hardly going to become number one hanging around here, are you?"

"I guess not."

"It is time to go back to being you. Or the ONE. He was special. Something about him scared London silly. Father Harry, I think Father Harry has had his day. Don't you?"

"I do."

"Not the last time you will be saying that to me Edmund Carson. Just remember those words."

Wait! What? What is she on about?

"I did think about leaving Father Harry as a mystery?"

"Yes, but if you do that, aren't you going to be longer getting to number one?"

"True. I hadn't thought of it like that."

"So tomorrow, up bright and early and back to yourself. Back to work. You must be well over halfway by now. Maybe even three quarters."

"I probably am…"

"Then back to it. We have our futures to plan together."

She leans in and kisses me. Even I know what that kiss means. As she sits back she takes off her black dress. Straight over her head. She always wears that black dress. She has the stockings and suspenders on. I know that it is her effort to keep a guy like me. But still she really does know how to do it. Dress up and keep me keen.

"Stay where you are, Edmund. Tomorrow you take charge. But tonight, I am the boss."

I lie on my back and she places me inside her. The heat is amazing. The heat from Miss Walker and the heat from the fire next to us. She slowly moves up and down and up and down.

201

I have missed this so much. She looks amazing on top of me, her black hair swishing side to side. She keeps pulling it back, so she can see me, and I can see her. There is a cheeky smile. Every tenth or twentieth stroke she grabs my chest a little harder. Just so I know that she is in control. She is, and it feels like heaven.

I can feel the rhythm getting faster, harder and faster. I can tell her style now. I know her and she knows me. She is fucking me like a bronco. One hand is holding her hair back the other hand firmly on my chest. She is looking directly at me. Without asking, without saying the words, we know it's time. It's time.

Oh my God, I think I nearly passed out again at that. I feel giddy. I feel like one of those cartoon characters that have all the birds flying around their heads. That was unbelievable. She leans down and kisses me.

"That's worth the trip right there. I do miss you, Mr Carson."

"It so is."

She unplugs and lies next to me on the other side from the fire. I turn and lean over her. Just to see that smile. That smile she has when I know that she is spent.

"Let's get to the time that there is just you and me, Edmund."

"I agree, and travel. Not UK travel but travel the world. I think you would look amazing in a bikini. And out of one."

"Sounds perfect. Let's do that."

She snuggles into me. I don't think we are going much further than here tonight. A quiet night in.

"Shall we watch a movie or something?"

"No, I think let's just lie here. They have some music in the stereo. It is quite nice?"

"Okay, stick it on and I will pour us some more wine."

I get up and stick the stereo on. She makes no effort to move. She really is spent. I pour the wine as well. I don't mind looking after her. She just smiles at me. She knows I will do anything for her. We snuggle back into together. The music starts to play and we sit and listen.

"Who is this?"

"I think it is Simon and Garfunkel. My nan used to listen to them. From the fifties or sixties, I think. The people that rent this cottage must have liked them too."

That was a good save. I nearly said the girls upstairs. But that might be a bit too much for tonight. I know they are in bed together, but they are naked nonetheless. I am not sure she will understand that.

"Sounds good. I like it."

"Yeah, it does."

We sit and listen and drink some wine.

"So, you are going to promise me to get cracking tomorrow, aren't you, Edmund? I don't like us being apart so much. I follow you. On all your media stuff. I follow you and there are chat rooms and everything. They are all crying out to see where you are, and what you are up to. It makes me feel quite good to be with you. Proud to know you are my man. The world needs you, Edmund."

"They do? That is so cool. I have neglected them recently, I know. And you. I have neglected you too much. I won't do that again. I am going to get cracking first thing, I promise. I will make it to number one, and fast."

I knew people still wanted me. I knew I had been letting people down. Now I am letting her down. I will never do that again.

She leans up and kisses me and then buries her head into my chest. I take a sip of the wine. It's better than the whisky, that's for sure. I look around the room. The fire, the wine, the music. This is what love is. This is love. It is the little things. I am going to have to thank Brooke somehow. Well, yes, somehow.

"How do you know all the words?"

"Sorry?"

"The words, how do you know them, Edmund? I can hear you singing them under your breath as the music plays. Nearly every song?"

"I guess I got used to my nan playing them. The words just stick in your head. My nan used to say it was an ear worm. When a song sticks in your head you have an ear worm. I didn't even realise that I was doing it."

She smiles at me. It's that smile that can melt you.

"Then sing one to me then. The next song, sing it to me."

"No, I can't sing."

"Please, Edmund, you know you are amazing at everything you do."

I think there isn't a thing I wouldn't do for her. The next song comes on.

"Hello darkness my good my friend…"

I carry on singing the song to her. She looks directly at me. I want this to be the way I end every night. I need to go back to work. I need to get to number one and then be with her. We were meant to be together. Loving the lyrics now, I come to think of it. I never really listened to them in depth before. Very me. Although I don't like the old friend bit. I am not old. This could be used as part of my comeback tour. I create the silence. I create a lot of silence. I could see this on one of my YouTube videos. Yes, part of the return of Edmund Carson.

Chapter 9

Nineteen. Seventeen, eighteen, nineteen. It's too many. I need to wait. Why is the northern line always so popular? Saying that, why am I on it? I mean, the central line goes nowhere, but that's why it's normally quiet. Some will get off at Camden. Euston and Camden. Those four are Camdenite's. Is that even a word? It should be. It is a cool one. All in black, piercings everywhere. I love Camden. Full of colour. By having none. Full of colour by having none. I am sure I read that somewhere. If not, that is mine too. Will go down as one of my sayings. I am on fire today.

Needs to be more than four. Comebacks must be bigger and better than the original. With a bang. And all in one day. The ONE has been away for far too long. I check my phone. Edmund has returned and the world knows I am Father Harry. All the photos I uploaded from Father Harry's work and the rectory and the holiday home are going viral. Love the going viral thing. Spreads around the world in one day. Twitter just hits everyone. Tomorrow's papers will be amazing. I am going to be all over them. He is Harry, Father Edmund. The Return of Edmund Carson. The return of Edmund Carson. I know it was a few weeks ago, but that still counts, right? They didn't know that was me? Seventeen. Seventeen, still too much. Seventeen was too much. She was so cheeky. I should go and see her again. I wonder if she is still at school. Surely, she will have gone home by now. She must have been in her last year there when we met. Oh yeah, it's the weekend. She won't be there anyway. Still don't understand why Miss Walker did her disappearing trick again this morning. We could have spent the weekend together. We could have travelled down together, we were going to the same place. It's not like it is a short journey. Why wouldn't we do it together? Seems to be more interested in me getting back to work. Is this what married life is going to be like? Her making me go out to work? Is that it?

She is probably planning our future. All the talk about settling down and stuff, probably looking at wedding dresses or baby clothes. A little Edmund running around. She would enjoy that. Fifteen, are you kidding me? Only two people off at Euston. It is a major stop. I suppose it's a good sign that nobody has come on.

Morning Crescent, then Camden and then it must be time. Lake Carson. Lake Carson sounds good. That's what they do, isn't it? Celebrities, they name the baby after where they were conceived. She has never asked to use protection. In fact, nobody does? I thought girls always asked for that? I mean, it's not like they don't teach it in schools. I was being taught it at twelve. District Carson. Sounds better than a lake. Sounds like I own a district. Big, strong. Any son of mine would be just that. Yes, District Carson. Three with headphones, two sitting down and one standing. They make it easy for me, and the two opposite would take no time at all. It's surprising how people don't look at each other on the Tube. Don't want to catch people's eyes. Other than Asian- looking people. Especially if they are carrying a bag. People look at them twice. What is the world coming to? They are no different than anyone else. I mean, wait, what the fuck! One, two, three, four, five, six, seven… Seven? Who the fuck gets off at Morning Crescent. It's now.

I dive forward and I have them both cut within seconds. I pull my hood up. I am on my feet and heading down the train. One of the stereo kids has seen me and started to move backwards. I slit the throat of the closest one to me. He still had his back turned. The other one turns and I have the knife in the neck of the fourth and he is on the floor. There is screaming. Lots of it. So glad it's not one of the new Tubes. Those things just go on forever. At least nobody is coming to help this one. Wait, we have stopped. We must be between stations. I keep walking forward. The stereo kid is in the corner, trying to get out of the window. By all accounts, he is never going to fit in there. The two girls are screaming and trying to get somebody's attention. I am not sure who to? The first girl I stab straight in the stomach as she tries to stand up to me. At least she tried to stand up to me. That's more than any of the others have done. I make sure I pull the knife up straight through her stomach and up to her ribcage and then back down. I am not making that mistake again. I turn and they are both standing in the corner now. The girl is in front of the guy but not by her choice. The train starts to move again. I head towards them.

"Some kind of gentleman, aren't you?"

He pushes her towards me. If it wasn't my comeback, I would probably have not worked with her. I stab her in the throat as she comes forward and she drops to the floor. The stereo kid has his back to me still trying to claw at the door. I stand behind him and stab and stab and stab into his back. I then pull his head back and cut his throat. Hard. I slice again and again. It comes off. He deserves that. The blood is everywhere. I stick my hand into the place where his head used to be and cover my hand in blood. I walk over to the window. I write *I AM BACK* in blood on the window. The train pulls into the station. I am off the train before the screaming starts. I take one quick look back as I start to run down the platform. *KCAB MAI.* Oh yeah, I forgot it only reads from the inside. Sounds like a dodgy Chinese takeaway. I am running up the conveyors before I know it. It's quiet for Camden but still there are a few people looking on.

Fuck! How high are these?

Ticket. Ticket. I put the ticket in the machine and wait for the doors to open. Then run out into Camden. I run straight up the nearest road. There is a pub there with toilets directly at the entrance. I've been to it before. I need to wash myself. I am into the front doors of the pub and down the stairs. I go straight into one of the cubicles. I wait a second. Nobody is following. I wasn't the only person running away from the scene. People scare easily. I take off the hoodie and put it behind the toilet. It's covered in blood. I can't wear it walking around here. I wait to hear that there's nobody else in the toilets and go out and wash my face and hands. There is blood on my trousers, but you can't tell. I look straight into the mirror.

"It's done. Seven. Seven is better. Seven is good. It is a good comeback."

Seven on one train in one go. No more on the train tonight. Comebacks are that. Leave them wanting more. That will be the next day's headlines. It's too late for tomorrow. Besides, tomorrows will be full of my return online. All the photos. That is tomorrow's news.

"Excuse me."

I turn around. There is a bloke standing in front of me. He is just looking at me. He smiles. I bring my knife up and put it straight into his throat.

"Edmund?"

Wait, what? He knows me? Holy fuck, Dan. Dan... Dan Grainger. From School. Fuck! Fuck, he is on the floor. Shit, I didn't mean to do that. I just thought... Oh fuck... I don't know what I thought. I didn't think.

"Dan?"

He is nodding at me. Fuck, I didn't recognise him.

"Sorry, Dan, it was just a reaction."

He is bleeding out everywhere.

I drag him and put him in a cubicle. Anyone can walk through here.

"Sorry, mate, you just came up on me and I have been working tonight. This job just takes over you. You know? People say never take work into your personal life. I guess this is why."

I close the door behind me and leave Dan in there. Give him ten minutes, he will understand. I just don't have ten minutes. I go back and have another wash.

"Think, Edmund, think before you act. Work is work."

Sometimes I forget all about the social part of life. I am back out, up the stairs and head down to the market. There are no police yet. Just a crowd of people. Nobody is ever looking for you to stick around. They always believe you are long gone afterwards. I walk through to the stalls and buy myself a new hoodie. A red one. Just in case. In fact, I think it is some sports one. LFC. Probably a football team, or basketball, that is fashionable nowadays.

Wait. Is that? Holy fuck, it is. It's a "I know where Edmund Carson Is" T-shirt. I must have one of those. I am famous in Camden. I have my own T-shirts. I knew they would have one. I knew it.

"Excuse me, how much are the T-shirts?"

"Oh, a tenner, please, love."

"Cool, I love it. I think they are so cool."

I hand her over a tenner.

"We have multiple colours."

I turn around. There are racks of them everywhere. How did I not see that? This is amazing. There is a T-shirt saying, "I am the ONE" in a love heart. In a love heart? Oh, shit, I just got that. That's very clever. I take out five twenties from my wallet.

"I will have one of each... All of them."

She wanders off and collects them.

"That's only eighty, love."

"No, I want the black and white "I am the ONE" T-shirts too. Very clever."

"Okay, whatever you say, love. Big fan, are you?"

I just nod at her. She packs them all up in a bag.

"Do you sell many of these then?"

211

"Been slowing down recently. But I hear that he has made a return online today, so I expect sales to go up again now. We all like a bad guy, don't we?"

I hand her the money.

"I guess so. Thank you."

"You are welcome."

"So are you, so are you…"

I wander out back into the street. I love this place. This is my real home. I think I will get Miss Walker to settle down with me here. I walk down towards the Stables Market. I can hear the police turning up in the distance behind me. But I don't look back. Nan used to say that a lot. Don't look back. Some bloke sang that song as well, didn't he? Especially if you are mad. Then you are really supposed to not look back.

All twists and turns in that market. Lots of shops. Shops and food. It was good food, I remember. Lots of bronze horses and stuff as well. I am going to stick to the high street area though. The shops are full of people. Mainly buying long black coats, and full of piercings on their faces. Seems every other shop is a tattoo parlour? Or selling Victorian black clothes. I think this is where vampires go to shop, or those gothic kids. They always wear this stuff too. But mainly vampires. Bloodsucking vampires. Wait, I am not a…? Am I? Sometimes I think it would be a good idea for me. A good character at least. My fans would like that.

Tattoos, I have never been sure about tattoos. Does anyone ever want to mark their body forever? What is worth marking your body for, forever? I go into the nearest tattoo shop. There is someone in the chair. It doesn't seem to look like it hurts. I stand and look at the walls. I look back in the chair. He is having his head tattooed. Right on the top of his head. I wander over. It's amazing. I thought he would be screaming. That's right on the bone. Or the skull, whatever you call it.

"Have a look through the books, he is nearly done."

I turn and see a woman behind the counter. She wasn't there when I walked in. Pink hair, must be thirty stone and covered in tattoos everywhere. The tattoos are enough, I am not sure she needs the pink hair to stand out.

I look back at the man in the chair.

"It's amazing, isn't it? It's his final sitting. Just some shading but it makes all the difference."

"Go on, have a look…"

The guy stops tattooing and I look at the guy's head.

"It's a skull?"

"Yes, and down the back of his neck is the rest of the skeleton. And if you look around the throat."

He turns the chair. The guy has a pair of hands tattooed around his throat. I am fixated by it. He will be being strangled forever. Forever. Who does that? The guy in the chair looks up at me.

"You don't have any tattoos, do you?"

"No, sir."

Felt like a sir moment. Anyone that hard deserves to be called a sir. He smiles at me and turns in the chair and the other guy goes back to work. The woman behind the counter beckons me over to her. She hands me three large books.

"Sit over there and have a look. We don't bite in here. Well, not unless you ask us to."

I believe she would bite me either way. Probably eat me. That's probably why she got so big. People come in here but never leave. Like that barber guy. *The Sweeney* or something like that. I take the books and sit down. There is a mixture of drawings and photos in the books. Who tattoos their boobs? This woman has paw prints on them. What's that about? You want people to know you have a dog? Or are you saying you are a dog? And Chinese letters. If you don't read Chinese, then why would you have them? How would you know they are true? It might say dickhead or something and you would never know? Unless you went to China to get them checked out. I keep flicking through the books. Knives. Knives and skulls seem to be very popular. Doesn't really say anything though, other than I want to stab you in the head? Bands. People seem to like bands. Around the arm. Looks very Indian. Indian and boy band. I guess they look all right.

Cartoon characters. Who would have a cartoon character tattooed on them forever? I have to ask the pink-haired lady that one. It is just too weird.

"Excuse me, miss, do people really have cartoon characters?"

"Miss? Been a while since I was called that. Yes, lots of people. *Tweetie Pie* seems to be the favourite now. Especially for the younger people."

I think she is saying that I am young. That is good after Father Steven thought I was twenty-five. I mean, twenty-five is old. Really old.

"Really? A little yellow bird? What does that say to people? You like birds? Canaries?" She shrugs her shoulders. I am sure she doesn't know either.

"I don't think it has to say anything. It is personal. I had a guy in here last week who had Bugs Bunny on his bum."

"You are kidding me?"

"No, I am not. Takes all sort. I am sure it must have meant something to him,"

I shake my head in disbelief and go back to the books. Bugs Bunny on his bum? What kind of weirdos are out there? I flick past all the famous people's faces. That's just wrong. I get to the names. Lots of them. Mum and Nan seem to be the most popular. Maybe I should have Nan. It would be nice. A nice way of remembering her. I flick through the book. There are quite a few designs. Different fonts and some with flowers and stuff. Orchids would be a nice touch. They have them anywhere from their arm to their leg to their chest. This one looks like an actual photo of his nan on his arm, in tattoo format. Maybe over your heart. That would be a good place for one. Always close to you then. Not sure how it looks in the mirror though, a bit like the train, I would guess. Wait, no, Nan backwards is, well, Nan? Surely, that's okay then?

I look over at the pink-haired lady again. I am going to end up looking like that if I start having tattoos, aren't I? People never have one. They always seem to have lots. Whole arms full. Or heads full in that guy's case. I close the book. I can't do this. Not now. I haven't even had a photo shoot yet. Not even released a calendar. After my first one maybe. That's what I will do. After the first calendar, I will have a tattoo of my nan. It will hit all the news and then that will be a nice way to remember her by. There are always image changes, aren't there? Keep it fresh, keep it real. I must keep thinking about that. Keeping it fresh. A tattoo will be a good way of doing that. It will make me look like a bad boy. She watches me close the books.

"You don't fancy it, do you?"

"No, thank you. Maybe next time."

I leave the shop. A quick glance to the right tells me there is an army of police down there. I should carry on walking a bit. That is a little close. The pink-haired woman thinks I am a wuss, I am sure of it. I am just image-conscious. It's all about the fans. She wouldn't understand that. I think her image-conscious days are behind her.

FUCK!

The northern line is probably going to be closed all night now. I am going to have to get a taxi or something later, or walk to Caledonian Road. That's going to be miles. Why does it take so long to clear up an incident in London? It's over. You know what happened and you know who did it. Take a few photos and move on. I am sure they are after more overtime. But do they thank me for it, do they…?

FUCK!

Photos! I didn't take any photos. What with the hype of the ONE's return, I forgot all about it. I am sure all the people on the Tube did though. There will be enough all over social media. I can tag some of them.

Blonde… No, I think that is yellow? She has dyed her hair yellow. Like the cartoon character. Like the bird. Only in Camden. That's why I love it here. I carry on walking. I can just about still smell the food court from Stables Market. I am going to have to eat later. All this work really builds up an appetite. That place has the best Mexican food. That wrap thing with rice and meat and chillies in it,that was good.

Pink hair. Both. Him and her. I know they say that people that stick together start to look like each other but that is ridiculous. Is it a statement? They can dress all in black but have shocking pink hair? You never look them in the eyes either. Like the guys on the Tube. People who look a bit different tend to divert your gaze. I can see people looking at them as they walk on the opposite side of the road. They are just people. Maybe that is a new character. One of the extreme versions. Pink hair, pierced face and a Bugs Bunny tattoo.

Perfect, and they have food. My knife is out from behind me and I follow them through the front door on the right. She is in front of him. I grab his head from behind and cut his throat. He drops to the floor without making a sound. I close the door behind me. I walk into the house.

"Just stick them on the table and take your shower. I will sort them all out."

I can see her through the kitchen already putting the shopping away. I walk up behind her, grab her head as I did her husband's and slit her throat. I hold her there as the blood starts to squirt from her neck. I can feel it hit the back of my throat and my nose. I have missed this. I have missed having the time to enjoy my work. I catch a reflection in the window of the two of us just standing there. She is quite cute. It was a good choice. We look good together. I lean in and lick her neck. It's warm. It's sweet. It's going to be supper. Well, afterwards. This is a night of comebacks after all. I take another lick. There is no greater taste than this. I catch our reflection in the window again. Miss Walker was right: this is me. This is what I was born to do. I carry her over to the sofa and sit her down. I then go and fetch her husband and put him on the sofa too, then take a quick look around the house to make sure they are the only people there. It's only small. Two bedrooms, and one isn't finished. I bet it still costs a fortune, for a house in London in the middle of Camden. They must be bankers or something. I am so glad that I have money to pay for ours already before the movie deals come in. I go into the kitchen and fix a glass of water. There are bills on the side. They are a Mr and Mrs. That's nice. People don't always get married nowadays. I think if we ever get a house together, I would like to get married first. I go back into the front room and wait for them. I sit opposite them on the chair as they sit there. Been a good ten minutes. I am still waiting. This adjustment time seems to be getting longer and longer. If I wasn't so polite, I would have started already, finally.

"Welcome back. Yes, sir, I am.

"The ONE, the Only."

I am kind of liking that line. The ONE meaning the ONE and the only. There is only one of me. Wait, is there only one of me? Father Harry? It is still a good line. I think I will keep it. Well, till we have kids then there will be a little me? Or maybe two? Boy and a girl. That would be nice. Wait, why am I thinking about kids?

"Been a while, yes. It's comeback night. So, the ONE has just returned down the road.

"Yes, exactly what all the sirens were about, and now it is time for Edmund to return. Again, return again. It is a whole thing, I don't mean to get into it.

"I did, yes. Did you see them? I put them all up this morning. Sort of cataloguing what's been going on over the last couple of months. I wanted to tell the world about Harry.

Let people know I have still been working. What did you think? That's what I meant. That was kind of a return too.

"Really, you didn't know? I am glad about that. Overall, you would say it worked then? Shocked the media and the fans? It was what I was going for.

"You are too kind.

"Oh, there you are. I was beginning to think that the cat had got your tongue. Little bit of a delay, I guess. It does happen.

"Yes, as you ask, you are my return. Comeback. Whatever you want to call it. It's a return to me. I must say it is long overdue.

"I don't know really. I think I liked the look of you. I mean, you look like a lovely couple and, to be honest, in this neighbourhood, I quite think that is a rarity. Normal people, I mean. I mean they are all normal. Just look normal is what I meant.

"Really?"

I am not sure how to respond to that. I mean, I was planning on sleeping with her but it's the first time someone's husband has asked me that straight out. It is a little weird. But he seems to be well read up on me. I can hardly say no, now, can I?

"I was thinking about it, yes…"

He is looking directly at me now. Not sure what's next?

"I am sure that's not a problem. Do you like to watch her normally?

"From the wardrobe you say? I hope at least it is a big wardrobe?

219

"And she likes to bring guys home, and you hide there. Why?... She does the business and then what?"

This guy really is kind of a freak. Maybe that's why he lives here. He likes the alternative lifestyle.

"What, straight afterwards? Like straight afterwards?

"You don't make her wash or anything?"

I think I may have spoken too soon about them being normal. They seem far from it. Well, he does. Maybe she just likes sex. Can't say I blame her. The more I get, the hornier I am too. If she isn't getting it at home with the wardrobe monster, then I don't blame her.

"Okay, I think that's quite fair. Shall we move this upstairs?"

I take him up first and place him in the wardrobe. I don't know how he fits in there every Saturday night. He is not a small person. I then carry her upstairs. I lie her on the bed and undress her. She is sexy. In an older thirty-something kind of way. Little bigger than I would normally like though. Especially around the belly. A few sit-ups and a diet wouldn't go amiss.

"Don't worry about it, we all put a little bit of weight on as we get older."

I try to make her as comfortable as possible. Although this is clearly not her first time. Not if she is bringing guys home every week so her husband can watch her have sex. Maybe if she was skinnier he would have a go himself.

"I do like black underwear. Tells me a lot about the woman."

There is the smile I have been waiting for. The one that says I know what is about to happen and I am ready for it. I didn't think it was coming. Maybe it's because she is lying down now, and her husband can't see the expression on her face. Time to strip off. I do, and I am on and in her in seconds. Fuck! That is warm inside her. Must have been waiting for me. Probably why she told him to go and take a shower. It feels good though. Oh, it feels good. Sex is great, but a bit like Pringles: once you start you just can't stop. I can't believe I went so long without it. I can tell by the look in her eyes she knows this is no normal Saturday night. Tonight, she is really getting seen to. There, almost glazed over now. I can hear a knocking. It's either the headboard or... or is he in the wardrobe knocking one out to the sight of us? Is that his thing? He is getting off on seeing me going up and down on his Mrs. Think it's the headboard. Nope, it's him. I can see from the look in her eyes she is ready. Fit to burst, I would say. I time it perfectly so we both come together. I bet her husband has never done that for her. Well, not from inside the wardrobe, that is for sure. I lie on her. I can hear her whisper.

"Thank you. I know, it's been said before."

I like it when they are grateful. She is having multiple. I can tell. That look when you know the orgasms aren't stopping anytime soon. That's the look she has. I am glad for her. She deserves it.

"Why don't I leave you two to do whatever it is you do now? I am going to go downstairs and look through the groceries that you bought and see what we can do about some dinner. For the three of us? Are you both hungry?

"Cool. Then leave it with me."

I get dressed and head downstairs. I can't believe that is what he wants to do with her after I have just been there. Yuk.

Just, yuk! I collect the groceries off the floor in the hallway and take them into the kitchen. Nice kitchen, seems to have everything. I start to unpack. Lots of vegetables, that's good. Coffee. Not really a fan. Fruit, steak. I do like a nice piece of steak. Sausages, eggs. Oh, how about a fry-up? Maybe a little something extra. I did see one of those cooking programmes. The naked bloke. One-pan breakfast. That sounds good. Milk, maybe a cup of tea. SMA powdered milk. Who has powdered milk? I mean, I have seen it in some of the hotels I have stayed at but never in a big tub like this.

"Fuck..."

I am on my back on the floor. Ouch, that fucking hurt. I slipped on something. The floor is soaking wet. I stand up. Where the fuck has that come from? I put my finger in it and smell. It's pee. She must have peed herself when I came in. I guess the excitement of seeing me. But I didn't think women in their thirties had bladder trouble. That's why she was so warm just now. It wasn't excitement, it was pee. Yuk. Wait, and he is about to go down on... that's just wrong in so many ways. I thought they looked normal. I place the powdered milk back on the side and run back upstairs to stop him before he throws up.

I knock on the door first before I walk in. Don't really want to see that.

"Before you...

"Wait, have you finished already? Why are you back in the wardrobe? I wasn't intending to go again.

"No, you were great, I was just thinking some dinner and then back to the hotel. It was a long drive this morning and with the comeback and everything. I mean, I would. You were

222

good and all that. I just need to be fresh for what is coming tomorrow. You know all the press."

She was more standard than good. Not a lot of activity. I like it more when they are totally into it. And the belly... Could feel it every time I went in. I can't imagine how it would impact on smaller men like the wardrobe monster. I am just standing, staring at her on the bed. He is still in the wardrobe, hoping I will go again. She is probably dry now. He has hoovered everything up. Did I just say that? That is just sick.

Camden colourful because of the lack of it. That is still in my head. She could do with shedding a couple of pounds. I mean, how does she hope to get men back here when she isn't looking after herself? I leave and go back into the spare room. It is not finished. It is as if they are preparing for... I go back into the bedroom.

"I am so stupid. You are pregnant, aren't you?"

How didn't I see that before? Her belly isn't fat, it's solid.

"Eight months? Why didn't you say?

"No, I am sure I would still have. I mean, you are still hot."

Am I sure? She is probably right, as that is now all that is going through my head. She is pregnant. That's what the milk is for. That is what the bunny wallpaper in the room is all about. I thought it was an odd way to decorate a spare room. She peed herself as she probably does have a weak bladder and the excitement of seeing me is too much. I should remember that when I am meeting pregnant people, old people and girls. I could have that effect on all of them. I need to be more considerate.

"No, I can't say I have. You are my first pregnant woman.

"He doesn't want to? And I guess you can't pick up random people either in that condition. They would probably think it a little weird. Even for Camden.

"No, it didn't feel weird. Just people may think it's weird. You know, pregnant women on the pull. I couldn't tell, honest. I just thought that you could have done with losing a few pounds.

"I can assure you it felt fine. Doesn't it?"

I look to the wardrobe. There is no answer.

"Do you know, you haven't even told me your names? Let us just start with that.

"Tim and Verna. Sorry, Tim, tell your wife it is fine. You know.

"How long?

"Since you found out. Come on, Tim, it's a natural thing. Women don't stop wanting sex just because they are pregnant. Step up, man. At least step out."

It's a bit weird he is staying in the wardrobe. Do you think it's symbolic? Maybe another one. Maybe that's why he isn't doing his wife and letting strangers do her. I tell you, we give the world a choice and they are voting with their feet. Well, just not their feet, everything else they have. Everything goes nowadays.

"I do have one question though. How does it feel for you? I mean, here I am poking you with a large stick.

"Yes, thanks. Very large stick. Does it not like knock the baby about a bit? I imagine it being in there like it's on a trampoline?

"Good, I am glad. I don't want to think I upset it. Poor thing probably thought it was on a rollercoaster.

"So, Tim, let's get you out of the closet. Downstairs. And you, Verna, and let's get some dinner into you two. There is more than us to think about here."

I help Tim downstairs and sit him at the table. Then I go back up and start dressing Verna.

"So, do you have names picked out for the little one?

"Edmund is a great name. Harry, yes. But Edmund is better. I was just thinking about baby names on the Tube. District Carson. I think that would be the name of my son.

"So, it is a boy then? You can use District, if you like. It is a real manly name.

"Cool, Edmund is better. I didn't want to push it for obvious reasons. But they do that, don't they? Have booms in baby names due to celebrities."

I can imagine there are a lot of Edmunds and Harry out there now. I get her dressed. Then take her downstairs. I sit her at the table with Tim.

"So, dinner. I am starving. It has been a long day. I was thinking the one-stop breakfast. Have you ever seen it?

"That's right, Jamie. We have steak, sausages and eggs.

"I was thinking about it. You do know your stuff, don't you? Do you follow me on Twitter and Facebook? You have seen all the people that I have worked with before?

"Yes. Tiffany, without word of a lie, her name was Tiffany. I couldn't believe it either. We did have a good laugh at that.

"Okay, but only if you are sure."

I sit on the floor in front of Verna and pull her top up. I hold my knife to her stomach. I am not sure where to cut. I stand up. Maybe if I flip her over and go in from behind. Or the side. Where would the baby be sitting? I sit back down again. I get back up again. I go back into the kitchen and pull a pen off the side. I stand in front of her and draw a baby bubble on her belly and then draw a baby in it.

"Would you say that was about the size of it?

"Bit bigger? Okay."

I shape the size out a little more. Think that's it. If I don't cut inside the circle, we will be fine. I take my knife and place it on her belly. I stand back up again. I then drag the knife around the belly. Barely touching her. Just to give me an impression of knowing where I am going to go. She doesn't move so she must not be ticklish. I turn around.

"Tim, I just don't think I could. Would you mind if I…?

"Thanks. Do you know, I was just too nervous? I don't want to hurt the baby. I swear, my hands were shaking for a moment then."

I place Verna back at the table and go over to Tim and lift his jumper.

"Fucking hell, Tim, are you sure you don't have two jumpers on?"

I go and fetch a bowl. One slice and I have most of everything I need out of him. There is a lot in a big guy. I would have thought all our organs were about the same size. Although his liver is a little shrunk. Smells a little pickled as well. That might be a new taste. I am always up for new tastes.

"I may have to cook this on the side as I don't think that I can fit it all in one pan. Not for the three of us anyway."

I go into the kitchen and clean it all up.

"Verna, do you mind if I borrow some... let's call it sauce? Just a little. I just think you are going to be a lot sweeter than Tim?"

I take the liver and kidneys to the table where they are sitting. I place them on the floor and slit Verna's wrist. With a little squeeze the blood starts to drop into the bowl.

"It's not to everyone's taste but I do think that women are generally sweeter. Plus, I think there may be something wrong with Tim's liver. It is an odd colour. Looks a bit dried out as well. Does he like vinegar? ... This will help. Thank you."

That should do it. I go back to the kitchen and start to make the dinner. The sausages and steak all in one pan. I don't want to overcook them. I wait until they are turning brown before putting half a dozen eggs over them to make it like an omelette. I warm the liver and kidneys through. That's all that needs doing with them. I find plates and serve up a little of everything for all of us.

I go and sit at the table with them.

"I think you will like it. And, hey you, you are eating for two, so you need to keep your strength up. It's protein, it is good for both of you."

I sit down and eat. It's amazing. The liver the kidneys, the steak. It's all good and really goes well with the eggs. The liver really isn't as bad as it looked. Has a strong flavour. Almost like that whisky in the Lake District. Eggs are a funny thing. You never think about them being baby chickens. Wonder if chickens eat eggs? That would just be weird. Eating your own kind.

"You know, I was so hungry. Tim, you not eating yours?"

I grab his plate and tuck into his as well.

"Sometimes, in this job, you forget to eat. I try reminding myself, but I just forget. I guess that's why I make the most of it when I can. I nearly stopped at the market. They have some great food down there."

I finish his plate too.

"I am going to leave yours, Verna, as you have to eat. Don't listen to all that nonsense about eggs and stuff, they are good for you. I swear, whenever I read a paper it tells me not to eat something. Or eat stuff like black pudding. It used to be bad and now a super food. Super food. I love that. Not just ordinary food, but a super food. I am not sure it can make you fly, so I am not sure how it is super. But if I was a food, I would want to be a super food.

"It's okay, you can warm it up. They are all cooked rare. So, a microwave will be fine. Just a quick couple of minutes' blast.

"This has been great. But I really have to go."

I get up from the table. It has been a long day.

"Really? Are you sure? I will put the dishes on the side and you will wash up later, okay? It is okay. I almost licked them clean. Thank you very much."

I clear the plates and put them in the kitchen. I leave Verna's in the microwave.

"How about I leave you watching a movie or something? Nice Saturday night in front of the TV?

"Oh, okay. Yes, good idea."

I take Tim and sit him on the sofa. It's one of those ones that lies back so that's good. He looks good like that, really relaxed. I then move Verna over and lie her on her back with her head on his lap. I go into the kitchen and pick up one of the books on the side. *The Intervention*. Fuck knows what that is. But sounds like something I would do. I give it to Tim and open the page.

"Wait."

I put Verna's hands on her belly.

"See, *Notting Hill*. You know when they are on the bench at the end and he is reading to her. She is pregnant. I didn't notice that the first time I watched it. Or the tenth. I was just telling someone that... I can't remember who though."

I take my phone out and take lots of selfies. I will upload them when I am back at the hotel. Looks cool. She is no Julia, but it makes me think of her. She is a good actress. Hot. Not always blonde, which is good.

"Listen, I wanted to thank you again for dinner. Thanks for helping me with the comeback, and good luck with everything. I know it's going to be fine.

"No, no, I would be honoured. Edmund is a great name. In fact..."

I grab the pen again and sign her belly. Little Edmund.

"There, so you don't forget tonight."

Not that they ever would. I take another photo. That's one for the album. She is probably going to go down to that tattoo parlour tomorrow and tattoo that signature right on there. It will be worth a fortune.

I check the window before I leave. Nothing going on. I leave them on the sofa. I head out the door. I run back in.

"It was at the school.

"Yes, that school. Think it was seventeen or the teacher. Can't remember which one. We had a long conversation about it. Anyway, sorry to interrupt the story. Hope it's a good book.

Can't say I have ever read it… These things just bug me when they sit in your head and you can't remember them."

I go back outside and look up and down the street. Nothing. Nothing going on. They all must be busy on the tube. I am knackered. Takes it out of you all this. I stand on the doorstep. I have a weird feeling. I am not sure what it is. The sight of them when I stepped outside here, lying on the sofa. Something. I don't know what. Something that tells me… I don't know.

I head back to the hotel. Nice couple. Weird tastes. Nice to be back in London. Almost feels like home. I guess it is home now. I will make Camden my home one day. I have nowhere else to be. Does that make me a cockney now? They all come from London don't they? Enough for one day. I just need my bed. But tomorrow, tomorrow is going to be something special.

Chapter 10

I stand outside the newsagents. I need to pick up all the papers
without looking at the front page. I want to read them all back
in the hotel. It will only spoil the whole thing if I see it, if I see
my name everywhere. It feels a bit like Christmas. All your
hopes and dreams wrapped up in paper. I walk in and pick up
the papers. There doesn't seem to be many? When I was a kid
doing a paper round, there were at least a dozen sorts of
newspaper. Now it seems like there are half that. Although I
can tell when I pick up *The Times* that nothing has changed. It
is still bloody heavy. That used to be a killer on Sundays to
deliver. *The Sunday Times* was fucking huge Nobody can read
all that in one day. And it was only the big houses that had that
paper. They always used to have the magazines in brown paper
too. Don't know why they were always sealed though;
everyone knew what was in them.

I pay the guy on the till and take the papers back to my
hotel room. Papers or TV first? I don't know. I am so excited.
This is going to be unbelievable... I guess the TV. I switch it
on. There is no sound. One. Two. Three... Four. Five. Six.
Fuck, this is great, nearly every channel that I switch on has a

picture of me or the Tube or the banner at the bottom saying I have returned. It will give me a big head. Wait, no, it won't. I am a professional. If I carry on watching, it may do. Fame is so addictive. I need to read what they are saying about me first. There is nothing like seeing it in the papers. I start working through them.

'The Monster Returns'. Wait, that is not very nice, is it? I am hardly a monster. That word seems to follow me for some reason. 'We knew it was you'. No, they didn't. Nobody knew it was me. Well, other than that prick in York or somewhere that guessed. Darren, yes, Darren. He didn't really know. He just wanted to be on the radio. I need to remind myself to visit him. In York.

'Evil Edmund Returns'. Evil? Where do they get off calling me evil? 'Edmund's love child drinks blood'. What the fuck is that about? Some of these papers are ridiculous. Where is the hailed return? Where are the people that are glad I have returned? Society must have missed me? What have they had to write about while I wasn't here?

Oh, yeah. They were writing about me but didn't know they were writing about me. Surely this is the news of the decade. If not the news of the world. When other people make a comeback, it's all about the bigger and better than before. Was it not bigger and better than before? Maybe that is what they are saying? They are saying that I didn't come back in a big enough way? How can they say that? I gave them loads of material. All in one day. You would think there would be a special pull-out edition just for me. Like they do with the weddings and stuff. I pick up the newspaper leading with 'The

Monster Returns'. I guess I should read it. Headlines can be very deceptive.

'Edmund Carson's assault on social media reignited yesterday as he posted over one hundred photos of his latest victims, confirming what the nation had been thinking for some time that he is in fact the serial killer that the public had dubbed Father Harry. The deranged serial killer believed he was playing the part of a character. He included scenes from all the churches that he frequented. Rectories, graveyards and even the infamous now called McDonald's burger murders. Edmund Carson's reign of terror is fast approaching two years and, yet the police seem to be unable to apprehend him.'

What? It hasn't been two years? Has it? And none of that sounds favourable to me. There should be something like, I don't know, like a phoenix from the flames. Like that wizard movie thing. Where one minute there is nothing and the next there is me. Infamous, does that mean famous or not? I did that for the advertising. Can you imagine how much they are going to sponsor me for? The world wants to see me, not hear crap about me being deranged. Surely, they have been waiting eagerly for my return? They do not want to read this nonsense. What is up with this paper? You would have at least thought that they would have said how good the pictures were.

Is it because I haven't brought a new camera yet? I am going to get one. Nothing about the scenes. They take thought and planning, don't you know? How I left people, it is hard work. No interviews with any of them. To find out how I was? What my mood was? Nothing about the five fish and the loaves of bread? People care about this stuff... Well, not all of them, some of them. Most of them. They could at least recognise the craft, if not the artist.

I pick up the next one. 'We knew it was you'.

'Edmund Carson finally admitted yesterday to playing the character Father Harry. Our sister paper *The Sun* ran this story no less than three months ago with its in-depth analysis of the cases. While dismissed by the authorities, our editor from *The Sun* would just like to point out that he has total faith in the fact that they will catch Edmund Carson. Colin Taylor said "*The Sun* newspaper is astonished by the lack of investigation from the police into our report and findings. To us it was obvious from the beginning. We are working hard to ensure that Edmund is captured. We will be running these pictures daily for the world to be able to recognise him no matter who he believes to be. This week."

Wait, what? That's more about the paper than it is about me. What the fuck is going on here? I am the star, not them. And how dare they say that they knew this three months ago? Nobody knew three months ago. That would have been when I just started. How can they say they knew? Surely that is slander or something. I should sue them. I would get millions.

Nothing about the Tube, or my friends from last night. Seems to be all about them. How clever the fucking reporters are. If they were so clever, wouldn't they realise that I am the story of their career? Maybe they should try to contact me, have interviews with me. That's what I would be doing if I was them. I would make a great reporter. It's all about the right questions. All reporters want to deal with superheroes and stars, don't they? That's why we have paparazzi? To get all up and involved in people's lives. They don't recognise talent enough nowadays. I blame reality TV. Wouldn't know talent if it slapped them round the face with a wet fish.

Wait, there wouldn't be, would there? Papers are printed the day before or at least late the night before. That's why they aren't talking about the return of the ONE and just the return of Edmund. Oh, and Father Harry. They are just talking about what has happened online. Historic stuff. They haven't seen the real return. I grab the remote and turn up the noise on the TV.

"London is back to a state of emergency with the return of the serial killer Edmund Carson. And the return of his alter ego the ONE. Yesterday Edmund taunted the authorities by uploading over one hundred and fifty photos of victims in the last three to four months. Within these victims are the people previously been thought to have been killed by Father Harry. It would now transpire that Father Harry was indeed Edmund Carson. Last night returning to London he viciously killed seven people on the London Underground just outside Camden Tube Station. Eyewitnesses said he was dressed in the now iconic black hoodie. He ran into the bar The Earl of Camden where he killed his eighth victim of the evening. Authorities are saying only travel on the London Underground if absolutely necessary and avoid travelling alone."

That's more like it. Now you are talking a bit of respect. One hundred and fifty photos? I do get a bit snap happy with that thing. It's good for the fans to see me in different poses. And it's good for the people I work with. I imagine their Twitter feeds and Facebook pages will start to erupt once they work with me. Jess will be loving this. Iconic. I like the word iconic. I think when I am immortalised in *Madame Tussauds*, next to Jack, they will have the iconic hoodie. And Father Harry in his dog collar. Maybe one in each section, looking over people. Yeah, that would be so cool. You are walking through the musicians, Elvis, Jackson, Turner, all of them and then bang! The man in the iconic black hoodie. Maybe with my knife out at Kylie. No, not Kylie. She is fit for a blonde girl. Imagine what Kylie would be like with black hair. Now that would be something. When I meet her, I am going to ask her if she would change. I am sure she wasn't always blonde. I saw a picture of her with darker hair and dungarees. Maybe it should be at that big-lipped guy. The one that screams a lot… Wait, never thought about Kylie in dungarees? Maybe she is a leso? No. Surely not? That would kill me.

I guess Edmund doesn't have an outfit. It will be all about the characters. Maybe I should start one. Something smart. Three-piece suit or something. I would look good like that. I am hot. I turn over the channel.

"Thanks, Mark. Yes, I am here by Camden Tube Station, the latest crime scene from the serial killer Edmund Carson. It's believed by experts now that Edmund is showing signs of multiple personality disorder. With yesterday's revelations in the case of Father Harry, Edmund has at least two alter egos now. This has the experts and police believing that his reign of terror will soon be at an end."

"You say end, Sally, why would this be near the end?"

"The experts, are saying, Mark, that people with this disorder often lose track of reality. This can result in mistakes, which in turn can lead to his capture. While they are not saying as much publicly, it is believed that the police are now taking advice on how to deal with Edmund and his disorder. Here is

the recorded message from Chief Superintendent Keeley McAndrew, taken earlier today."

"At approximately ten p.m. last night I can confirm the serial killer Edmund Carson brutally murdered seven people on the London Underground, dressed as the character he refers to as the ONE. After leaving the station he stabbed and killed a further victim in the Earl of Camden public house. The police were already on high alert due to his social media activity. At this time, I ask you to respect the privacy while we contact all the families. Can I further ask that you only use the London Underground if you have no alternative? Edmund Carson is a serious threat to all in London. If you must use public transport, ensure that you never travel alone."

"You can see, Mark, they are keeping things tight-lipped. I believe that they believe this is just the start of his return. They are going to need to change tactics to apprehend him."

"Sally, why do you think they can't catch this guy? It's been nearly two years?"

"I am at a loss, Mark. I, like most of the people in the country, must be looking at tall, male teenagers daily to ensure that it is not him. I am presuming that he has somewhere to work from that keeps him out of the public eye. I think he has been planning his cases well. He has unlimited resources with regards to money, as we know. Add that to the fact that we have a population of fast approaching 64 million people, I guess he can blend in. To quote a friend of mine: if we spent less time looking at our phones and more time looking up, we would have caught him by now."

"That is so true. Maybe that is the next morning news campaign slogan right there. Sally, do you believe that they are drawing closer to him? Is this disorder going to be the end of Edmund Carson? The ONE and Father Harry?"

"I wouldn't like to say, Mark. I am sure the whole world would like it to be, but I think that he has avoided them for this long. My opinion is that he knows what he is doing. I believe he is acting out some fantasy. So, the characters are just that. I personally am not a strong believer in the disorder theory. He doesn't believe they are anything but a character he is playing. There is only one Edmund Carson. Unfortunately, it could go on a while."

I like her. She is quite cute, for a blonde girl. I mean, I wouldn't do her, but I like her. At least it's all not negative. Wait, that's it, that's why some of these papers and reports are so shit. It's all about the negative press again. That's what they are doing, they are playing down everything to make it look bad. They probably have my pictures up on their walls at home. This is all trying to draw me out. Make me more accessible. Why can't they just come out and say that. Why are they doing this to me? Playing with my emotions like this? All I am trying to do is entertain them. To be the best, to be famous. They don't do this with the others. They don't treat them as badly.

And what is it with telling people I have a disorder? I don't have a disorder? I know what I am doing. I know how I am doing it. These people and their boxes. There seems to be a disorder for everything now. Even in school. They all get special treatment. Nearly everyone has something wrong with them. Makes it all the harder for us normal people, who are just normal people, to be normal people!

No, that's just the negative press thing again. They are trying to tell people not to follow me as I am ill or mental or something like that. All negative. I switch through the channels again. Still all me. They do want to talk about me. They want me on the TV. Why are they being so negative? Don't they know that will make me stop working? Imagine if I quit. Imagine what it would do to the country. Newspaper sales. TV rights. Tourism. They have no idea how pissing me off could bring this country to its knees. Who will entertain them then? I turn the TV off. I lie back on the bed.

Maybe I should quit, that will teach them a lesson. Was it not enough though? Was last night not enough of a return? I feel like it hasn't gone down well. I feel like, oh, I don't know, I feel like there was no bang. No, here is Edmund moment. When pop stars return there are always fireworks. There were no fireworks. Have I lost my touch in impressing my fans? Is it just more of the same? That's what they are thinking, isn't it? It's just more of the same? I should be doing something bigger. Bigger than the school. Something that says: Look at me. Yes, that's it. Look at me. I have returned. I am back. I am the ONE. The school wasn't the ONE, it was Edmund. Edmund did the school. Edmund didn't return last night. Well, he did but almost as an afterthought? Edmund is the real star here. So, it needs to be a big bang, Edmund style. With fireworks. Not real fireworks. Well, maybe fireworks. People like fireworks. I forget sometimes first and foremost I am a showman. I am a great showman and that is what they want.

Something people will never forget. Something that will be on people's minds forever. Maybe a university? No, that's just a big school. Needs to be staged. Needs to be scenes. People like the scenes. I can visualise all of them in the movie. That's what the fans want. Needs to be unexpected. Shocking, needs to be full-on shocking. I want people to be stunned at the sight of the return of Edmund Carson. I sit up and pick up the stupid paper. The one that has the bus on the moon. That's always shocking. If you need something different, that is where you find it. 'Edmund's love child drinks blood'. It does make you sit up and think, what the fuck? That's what I want. I want the what the fuck moment.

"Twenty-three-year-old Gail Frost is the alleged mother of Edmund Carson's first love child. After a chance meeting on a night out in Scunthorpe, Edmund allegedly took up with Gail in a night of romance and passion. Gail explained that he was gentle and sweet at first and she didn't know who he was. It wasn't until they returned to her house that she started to suspect it was in fact Edmund Carson. In her own words, she explained to us about the night:

'He was fit. Well fit. I thought he was a bit younger than me, but I like boys who are younger. I wanted to get him back to my yard as soon as I saw him. We went to Nando's and stuff first. He was polite and that. He like devoured a whole chicken. I did think that he was hard. Like, tore it to pieces and ate it in front of me in a matter of minutes. He paid as he had lots of cash. When we got back to the yard that is where it all got a bit freaky. I took him straight upstairs and we got into bed. He was really fit under his shirt. He was a good kisser. But when we got down to it he just kept asking me to lie still

240

and that. Not move. It was like he wanted to sleep with me, but for me to be, like, dead. Play dead. He didn't want to kill me as we had a real connection. He said he had never met a girl as beautiful as me. Even said he loved me. Told me that I should be a model. So, I have become one. He has those scary eyes. And a well fit body. So, I just did what he said. I lay there as he had sex with me. He was amazing. After the first time he told me I was the best he had ever had. So, we did it all night. Five times.'

Nine months later Gail gave birth to a beautiful bouncing boy Teddy Tyson Frost. Teddy weighed in at 6lb 6.6 ounces. A sign it was really Edmund's child.

'We had a pool on what the weight would be. My mate Tracy she won the hundred we had on it. He had a lot of trouble eating, like, like, I was trying to breastfeed him as soon as he came out. But he didn't like it. He kept rejecting the breast. I tried so many times that my nipples were getting sore. It was after about a day and a half they were so sore that they started to bleed. That's when Teddy started to latch on. It didn't take long before I realised what was happening. Now I have to cut myself and smear it over my breasts to get Teddy to eat.' Gail is confident that this is not going to affect her glamour model career. And she will be returning to the world of fashion in the next few months."

What the fuck!

There are some right weirdos out there. I have never even been to Scunthorpe. Where the fuck is Scunthorpe anyway? I thought there maybe something shocking in the paper, not disturbing. Although I do like Nando's. Where the fuck do they find these nut jobs? Glamour model? Please. Nobody really believes this shit, do they? Miss Walker wouldn't believe this, would she? She will know that famous people get these stalkers all the time. That's why they say five times a night. It's because famous people never want to counteract that. It makes them look good. I can do five times so it's not even flattering to me. If she had said seven or eight, that would have been better. Miss Walker will know that it is all nonsense. She won't be worried. I get up and go to the bathroom and wash my face. I need a plan. I need to get out and get some fresh air.

The beard's kicking in again. Helps to disguise me well. I guess they are all still looking for the kid in the blanket, not a real man. Maybe an airplane, not like those nutters. But release some gas or something. Not really me though. I don't want to be thought of like those people. Fucking religion. Really has a lot to answer for. Needs to be more Edmund. Something people know is me. My style. Can't be transport. That's the ONE thing. Not Edmund. Or churches. No more Father Harry. Maybe a police station? Nobody has ever done a whole police station. That would get me a seat next to Jack, for sure. Lots of guns and stuff though. One wrong move and it's all over. You can't trust a policemen not to get over excited in seeing me. There would be one smart-arse who would like to take me down. Like that JFK guy. That's what happens when you get too famous. While that doctor still thinks he is more famous than me. That can't happen. I still have work to do.

I leave the room and go and get in the lift. Thirteen floors are a lot of floors. Especially for such a quiet hotel. I get into the lift. Nobody is ever in here. This place can't stay open for much longer. The For Sale sign outside is a bit of a giveaway.

People like to be in the centre of London. I could work with an old people's home. I would be doing them all a favour. Especially that Fred. It's not like it would be difficult. I could just walk room to room. I just don't think it is spectacular enough. I am not sure anyone would really care?

What? The lift has stopped. I press the button again. Nothing. There is an emergency button. I press that. I press it again. A voice comes from nowhere.

"One moment. We are having trouble with the lifts today."

That's just great. Now I am stuck in a lift. What about an office. I wonder if you could work with a whole office. The most they would have is a stapler. Hardly going to hurt you with one of those. And they are mainly full of girls and pen-pushers. Easy to work with. Yeah, maybe an office. A whole floor and you could leave them all working at their station. Maybe not London though, too busy down here. High-rises everywhere. You would be able to see straight in as I worked. Somewhere north, like Birmingham or somewhere like that. Must be big, but not too big. I press the button again.

"Sorry, we are still struggling to get it started this time. We may have to call an engineer. How many of you are in the lift?"

"It's just me."

"Okay, sir, bear with us and we will get to you as soon as possible."

Just what I need, a day in the lift. An office is good. But I would have preferred something in London. Lots of fans in London. It's my town now. It is good to be known in a town. Maybe a small police station. Maybe one out in the villages.

That is still London, isn't it? Wimbledon isn't far from villages. Maybe close to the school. That would be popular. The people in that village are probably missing all the attention. I bet they are all famous now. And it shows I am not scared of them. Police are just humans too? I am open to work with anyone. Even them.

Police! What the FUCK am I doing?!

I am trapped in a lift. In a fucking lift! This isn't broken, it's stopped. The police are organising themselves out there. I am fucking trapped. My head is dizzy with ideas and I am not paying attention to what is happening right in fucking front of me. This is classic *Criminal Minds*. I start to look around the lift. There is nothing. Nothing. I look up. There is no trapdoor in the top of the lift. There is always a trapdoor. I start to hit the panels and there is nothing. What kind of place is this? This isn't how these things go. All lifts have trapdoors, it's in every movie. It's a safety feature. For God's sake, I am going to sue this hotel. I am going to sue the papers and this fucking hotel. Where is the trapdoor? I am pacing now. It can't happen. It can't happen here. This is not how this goes down. I need to be number one, I need to be number one. I am going to be caught in a fucking hotel, in a lift, in a fucking hotel. That's not supposed to happen. I can feel the rage getting to me. I don't even have my knife with me. What was I thinking leaving the hotel without a weapon? I can't just go quietly. They are going to say Edmund Carson, second best. Second or third. They will probably put some spin on it, the fucking papers. They want me to be forgotten. I am a legend. I need to be treated like one. Not end in an elevator. I go to press the button again. No, that's what they want, they want me panicked and scared. They are probably videoing this, there is probably a secret camera in here. I am probably on TV as we speak. Across all the stations. That is what they were waiting for, this was all a ruse. They were baiting me to come here. They knew I would need to come out of my room at some point. They want me to look scared. That would suit them. But I am not going to. I am not. I hold my hands up in the air and smile at all four corners of the lift. I then make the gesture by holding up one finger and pointing to me. I am number one. I am not going to say it out loud. They will know that I know they are out there. But when this video goes viral, they will know that I was still confident. I am number one. There is proof of that. Not like the others, actual proof. I am number one. I need to decide. Decide how I am to be caught. Do I run at them? Do I kneel when the door opens? With my hands behind my back and a smile on my face? Should I run? I am fast. I could get past some of them? Coppers are all fat, aren't they? Probably get past all of them? They are probably armed to the teeth. Probably have the army out there. Probably hundreds out there. They will have closed most of London. The press. I can hear helicopters, I am sure I can hear helicopters. They are on the roof. Because they believe that there would be a trapdoor. Everyone knows there is a trapdoor in a lift. It is the law. Dogs, there are dogs, I can hear them, I can hear the dogs. They will be those killer types. The black and brown ones. And tanks, there is a tank and guns, they are all clicking. I can hear the clicking sound. They are getting ready.

"Sorted, sir, the lift is going to start."

I bet it is. I bet it is. I bet it is going to start. Maybe I should try to get off at another floor. I press all the buttons. The lift starts. It is ignoring all the floors. It's heading straight down. They have locked the buttons. They are pulling me to the ground. Lazy bastards wouldn't even come to the door. To my door, to get me. Me, the greatest. The number one. Five. Four. Three. Two. One. Ground floor. Ground Floor. This is it. I know what I am going to do. I am going to run. They are going to have to shoot me if they can. I am fast, I am fast. I will be out of the building before they even knew what was going on. The bell rings. The door opens. Now. This is it.

Chapter 11

I am almost squeezing through the doors as they open and I run. I run. My legs are in full flow mode. I am almost gliding. I am gliding. I glide straight into the hotel manager. He grabs me by the arms. I try and shake him off to get away. He is with them. He is part of the capture squad. They are behind him, I know it. They want me to go quietly. I am not going quietly…

"Calm down, son."

His hold on me is tight. I wish I had my knife. I would deal with this. I look at my surroundings, but it is all a blur. He said calm down. I am sure he said calm down? I can't hear anyone shouting police. Or get on the ground. They must shout armed police? That's the rule, isn't it? Like reading your rights they must announce themselves. There is no click of weapons, and I can't hear the dogs anymore. I stop and look around the lobby. There is him, the hotel manager, and an engineer. I guess that's what he is, as he has a toolbox. And there is an old lady with a little dog. A little tiny dog. No police. There are no police. Or Army or helicopters. Just them. Where are they all? The lobby is empty. They couldn't even get a tank in here. Why did I think they could get a tank in here?

"Spook you a bit, did it, being trapped in the lift?"

I straighten myself up. I must have looked like a loon running out of the lift like that. He must have thought it scared me, being alone in a lift. That's what he is saying, isn't he? I can't stop looking around. There really is nobody. Nobody here.

"Yes, a little. Thank you. A little claustrophobic, I guess."

That is the right word, isn't it? Claustrophobic. Sounds like it. Stuck in a closet. I guess Tim doesn't have that? I gather my senses a little more; I must give him a reason for running. There is nobody. That was all in my head. They were never outside the lift. I knew they weren't going to be really. They would have never got to me. I am too clever for that. Nobody knows where I am staying. I used a fake name. It wasn't one anyone would have recognised. I blame the papers and the TV. They have me all wound up about this stuff. They have me thinking negative thoughts. Why don't they just report the truth and accept it? That's their job.

I knew there was a dog. I could hear the dog. I wasn't hearing things.

"It was just a fuse, I believe. Couldn't register the floor. Hence, we brought you straight back down. The lift will be up and running again in a bit."

"Thanks."

I am not sure thanks was the word I wanted to use. Twat would have been better.

"Sorry about that."

At least he said sorry. I just nod and walk out of the hotel into the fresh air. I can feel my heartbeat returning to normal. What is up with me? My heart was nearly in my mouth then. I felt like the end was coming. Those doors seemed to take an age to open. I just had this impression of a hundred guns pointing in my direction when those doors opened. I guess you just never know when they will want to take you in.

But why would they want to? I am sure they are very similar to me. They will want me to be number one. I would think it is as important to them as it is to me by now? It will be their reputation I am helping. People always remember the arresting officer. They all must be waiting to be the one to my ONE. The man that caught the most famous person in history. I am surprised they are not helping me to get there sooner.

I walk to the nearest shop, and stop to buy water. That's calmed me down. I walk a little further down the road. People are still busy on Sundays. It almost feels like it could be a weekday. Shops are all open and the pubs look like they are starting to fill up. I have no idea why they call Sunday the day of rest. Nobody seems to be resting. I pass the first pub. Looks like a carvery or something. Lots of kids. They must have one of those ball pool things. Didn't have them when I was a kid. Well, I think they did but my parents never took me. My mum never liked to put me somewhere where I might get hurt. They are only plastic. It's not like it would hurt me. In fact, I wouldn't mind a go in a ball pool. Sounds like it could be fun. I could do with a laugh. Something to take my mind off elevators. I carry on walking. I am not going in there with a bunch of kids. Maybe if it was just me and Miss Walker.

I am surprised at how many people don't look up. Especially in London. Everyone is too busy to look up in London. I always thought I would be stopped in the street more. For autographs and selfies. You see it on people's

Facebook and Twitter, always trying to take pictures with celebs. Even minor ones. Makes me wonder if they are just not confident enough to approach me. Probably all know who I am. Just don't have the courage to ask for one. Maybe I should start taking some of myself to see if anyone will try and jump in. Let them photo bomb me. That is what they call it isn't it?

I carry on walking. As I walk, I can hear the roar of motorbikes heading in my direction. I can hear lots of them. The first one passes. Then another, then another. I bet that is what I was hearing when I was in the lift. It must have been echoing down the lift shaft from a distance or something. Kind of sounds like helicopters. I wasn't going mad. It was the hotel playing tricks on me. The dogs and now the bikes. It all makes sense now. You can see why I came to that conclusion.

They all start to pull into the pub ahead of me. Must be thirty guys on bikes. I walk along to the pub. Most are standing outside with their bikes, but a few go in. I go in too. The Red Earl. Maybe it's a religious-themed pub? Earls are religious, aren't they? Or are they the ones that work for the Queen? I go inside, it's dark. Very dark considering its broad daylight outside. Most of the windows are blacked out. I go to the bar and order a drink. Hobgoblin. It was either that or cooking lager on the pumps. Not a cooking lager fan. Don't know why they call it that? Do people cook with it? I can just about tolerate Stella. It's about the only one. I take it and sit down at a table. I take one sip. It's not good. I think I prefer wine now. Of all the alcohol stuff, I think I like it best. They say you do as you get older, you become more sophisticated. But this doesn't look like the type of place you order that. I think you are supposed to be manly. I carry on drinking it as I watch the comings and goings of the bikers. They all look scary, but I am yet to hear one that doesn't say please and thank you. Who knew that they were so polite? It is odd that you expect people to react a certain way just because of how they look? Bikers have tattoos and beards and are untrustworthy because of it. It's just a drawing on your arm and a guy that doesn't shave? Some do though. Leather jackets too? Makes you look harder than you are. I don't know why they didn't kill the cow that made them. Maybe I should get a leather jacket. At least for one or two of the photo shoots.

I drink my drink and go and get another. It doesn't taste great, but it does give you that warm feeling. I don't think I could drink more than two, maybe three. I don't have the capacity for drink.

"Just passing through, mate? Or a local?"

I wasn't expecting conversation. What do I say? No, I am working? Do these guys work? Of course, he does. He is the barman. That's me thinking how they look means that they are robbers or something. I need a manly sort of job. It is a manly sort of place.

"A bit of both really. Staying in the hotel down the road."

"Oh, the Findley? I thought they were taking that place down?"

"No, it's still up and running. Well, now it is."

"Needs a bit of money spent on it and a lot of advertising, if you ask me. With these Premier Inn jobbies popping up all over the place, they are going to struggle to get any custom. Needs to reinvent itself, in my opinion. Keep it fresh."

I am not sure what to say to that. I just nod. I don't know what a Premier Inn jobbie is? But I take the advice about reinventing itself. I think he is probably talking about me. Recognised me but doesn't want to make it obvious. I need to do that. Reinvent myself.

"So, will you be with us long then? If you are staying, like?"

"Just for a couple of weeks."

Couple of weeks? What am I saying? I don't want to stay there for a couple of weeks. Is he even going to believe anyone would stay in that hotel for a couple of weeks?

"Oh, I see. What is it that you do then?"

What is this, twenty questions? What do I do? It can't be IT or something technical. I am looking to fit in. I have the beard and stuff. Well nearly. That has got to help me. Probably why he started talking to me.

"I am a lift engineer. Have some tests to do all over London."

Engineer is a tough job, I would have thought. Overalls and toolboxes. Manly enough for a bar like this.

"You would think they would put you in a better hotel than that then, mate. But there is always some good entertainment down here of a night."

What? Would they? Would they have put me in a better hotel? Do engineers earn lots of money then? I thought they just fixed stuff? I just nod and take a manly drink of my drink. Too manly, I feel sick suddenly.

"The name's Trevor."

The guy reaches over and shakes my hand, hard. He is a hard hand shaker. He looks me straight in the eye as he does. Makes me want to trust him. Makes me not want to upset him that is for sure.

"Edmund."

Fuck! Did I just tell him my real name? Why the fuck did I do that? He didn't react though, not even a flinch. I must have trusted him. He made me tell him my real name. Either that or he scared me that much I couldn't lie.

"Popular name lately. You are on every TV channel today."

He just turned and fetched a drink for someone else sitting at the bar. I don't know whether I should get up and run or not. He didn't seem to be bothered by my name. I didn't say Carson. I didn't say Carson, did I? There must be loads of Edmunds in the world. He won't put two and two together. He doesn't look the type. I pick up my drink and go and sit back down. It's a busy bar. Lots going on. People coming and going. If I get up and run, then it will spook them. They will know it is me. The barman is at the centre of everything. Packages in, packages out. Maybe he is a drug runner or something like that. This could be one of those drug dens you see on the TV. They are always at biker bars. At least on *Criminal Minds* they are. Nothing good comes out of a biker bar. I am really judging people, aren't I? Need to stop doing that. People that look like me, we get judged all the time, unfairly. Pretty boys that get everything handed to them on a plate. Models. Stars. People don't understand the pressure we are under from everyone. I take another sip of my drink. It is a sip this time, nobody is watching.

I don't really fancy finding out if this place is a drugs den. If this place is raided and I am in it, they might get my DNA tested. Then I would be screwed. Too soon to be messed up in this. When I am number one, then it won't matter. They will just want autographs or something. It will just be the next stage of fame. That's when the book deals and TV rights kick in. Movies, maybe two, maybe three. People love a good trilogy. I finish my drink and head out. The next stage of fame. That's a great name for the final film. I need to write that down.

"See you again, mate. Have a nice day."

He does say it politely. I walk out. Those two drinks have really gone to my head. My head hits the fresh air. That was certainly strong beer. I think I need a lie-down. I head back to the hotel. The manager is still at the reception desk. He smiles at me as I walk into the hotel. Doesn't take his eyes off me. He is a little weird, that bloke. Probably thinks I am a wimp now. Scared of a little time alone in a lift. There is nobody else in the hotel. Why would he place me on the thirteenth floor if there is nobody in the hotel? Wouldn't you put everyone on the same floor? Or does it make it look fuller if people are getting on and off the elevator at different floors? I stand and wait for the elevator to open. It does. I get inside. I look up. There is still no trapdoor in the roof. Maybe that is just in films. I was getting myself wound up about something as silly as a trapdoor in a lift. I don't think I have ever seen one, other than in a film. I press the button and the door closes. Makes my heart jump a little as we move up. I am just silly, got myself worked up by all of this. It stops on floor eleven. The doors take ages to open. As they do, I can feel my heart pumping, not knowing who is on the other side of the door? All I can see are the guns. They are flashing before my eyes. I almost move back as the doors open. It's the old lady with her dog.

"Hello."

"Hello."

She gets in. The dog is looking at me. It's only the size of a big rat. The lead is bigger than the dog. Looks like it wants to bite me though. Bite me or hump me, I can't really tell. Didn't even know that hotels allowed dogs? I suppose this one doesn't have a lot of choice. Will take any guest it can.

"The lift is going up, you do know that?"

I am sure she didn't notice. You don't notice stuff when you get old.

"Yes, that's fine, my dear. I am in no rush."

The doors close. Something about the doors closing from the outside makes me think of that Chocolate story. The one with the dodgy elevator that can take you anywhere. You never know what is going to be there when the doors open.

"It is so nice they have it working again."

"Yes, it is."

"I wouldn't want to be doing that many stairs, not at my age. Or Trixie. She only has little legs, you know. Don't you, my little Trixie wixie."

Trixie wixie? Who talks to their dog like that? She is looking at me now.

"No, I guess not. Lots of stairs."

I just smile at her and the dog. She doesn't like me, the dog. I can tell.

"I am eighty-four, you know."

"Really? You don't look it… Sixty, tops."

Why did I say that? I know how to flatter a woman. Any woman. But why? There was no need. It is not like I am hitting on her, is it? There is being horny and there is being horny.

"Trixie, she is nineteen."

"Nineteen, you say? That's nice."

The doors open again and I get out. Old people confuse the fuck out of me. I get into my room. Been a waste of a day so far. I was expecting great things from today. Maybe tomorrow. Wait, did she say nineteen? Dogs don't live till they are nineteen, do they? No wonder it looked grumpy. That's the equivalent of being what? One hundred and thirty-three? Was probably looking at me to work with it. Begging me, no doubt. One hundred and thirty-three? That is fucking old.

Maybe tomorrow. Once the papers have the ONE returned and my friends in Camden. Once they have said their piece, maybe that's going to make things better. I throw the papers off the bed and lie down. Staring at the ceiling, I feel like I am fifteen again. Lying in our house with my parents' downstairs making my dinner. I need a plan. I need a plan that is going to both shock and delight the world. Something that will make their hearts pump. That will make them shout the return of Edmund Carson from the rooftops. Maybe on a rooftop? Then I can use the fireworks.

There needs to be something. I need to get back on to the front pages of the paper with an amazing story. I close my eyes. Maybe it will help. Maybe it will come to me if I close my eyes and relax a little.

Three hours later I wake up. Still nothing. Should I go to work? It's what, six o'clock on a Sunday. It's too early. Even on a Sunday. I get up and wash my face. That beer was strong. I should really stick to soft drinks. Soft drinks or wine. I go out of the room and get back into the lift. Should I have taken the stairs? Too late. It stops on every other floor. Three of the floors nobody was there, but a couple and a man join me in the lift. Must have been a fault with the lift. He really needs to sort

256

that. Probably doesn't have the money if nobody is staying here. We all get out of the lift. I walk towards reception.

"Excuse me, sir, how are you feeling now?"

I turn to see the hotel manager at the desk. He is a bit creepy looking. Has one of those comb-over things. I am not sure why he doesn't just cut his hair. Lots of people are bald nowadays. I think women prefer it. Lots of movie stars have it short.

"I am fine. Thank you for asking."

I carry on walking towards the door.

"Happened to me once. Really freaked me out too."

I wasn't freaked out! I was just in a rush to get out of the hotel. I was having a moment of reflection that is all. I carry on walking.

"Yeah, it was about a year ago... I will never forget it."

I sense this guy wants to talk to me. You know when people just don't leave the conversation there, it's like they keep adding stuff until you reply. I turn and go back to reception. I didn't really have anywhere else to go. I can spare him five minutes. He is almost wetting himself at the prospect. Must be a lonely life. Especially in this hotel. Not often he gets to meet people like me.

"Really? What happened?"

"Yes. I was stuck in the lift for five hours. Overnight. I was working the night shift and cleaning rooms at the same time. There was nobody around to assist me. One of the guests tried to use it in the morning and then I got them to call my wife to rescue me."

Really? This guy has a wife? The lift thing, I can believe, but a wife?

"Doesn't the alarm in the lift go to the police or a security firm or somewhere? You know, just in case?"

"No. It used to, but you have to pay for that. One of the cutbacks in a poorly performing hotel, I am afraid."

I can see by the look in his eyes he isn't happy about the cutbacks. Probably spends most of his days moaning about the management.

"Did you complain? I would have complained. You must have a union or something?"

I am not sure what a union is, but my dad kept complaining about them a lot. Always protecting the employees.

"No, no union. I have nobody to complain to? I am the manager, the owner. I am also working night shifts and day shifts to save on wages."

Shit! I wondered why he was always here. He must never sleep.

"Things that bad, eh? Is it to do with these Premier Inn jobbies?"

I don't really care, but that's the type of thing you say to suicidal people, isn't it? To keep them stable. Plus, I want to know what a Premier Inn jobbie is.

"Yes, I am afraid so. Just too many choices for hotels around here now. It leaves me in that catch-22 scenario."

Why didn't he mention the Premier Inn jobbie?

"Catch-22?"

"Yeah. Sorry, I guess that is a little old for you. It was a book by Joseph Heller. About a guy in the army... do you know what, never mind! It means that I am screwed every way I look at it. This place costs too much to run. I can't sell it as it needs so much work on it, I will never cover the loans I have. I can't keep it open as it loses money every day. I can't close it as they will close my accounts. My mother is doing all the laundry now just to try and keep me afloat. I am trying to cover everything else myself."

I think he wants a response from me. He is looking at me as if I should be feeling sorry for him. He owns a hotel. I don't even own a house yet. There is only so much sympathy in me.

"And to top it all off, my wife left. Said it was all too much for her."

"I am sorry to hear about that."

I think that's all I can say. It is the Father Harry in me that knows what to say and when to say it. But I am not taking his confession. He is a born loser, you can tell. He must be fifty. That means his mum must be ninety and that's who he turns to for help? I can't listen to another confession with an old guy and an older woman. I can see why his wife would leave him though. Needs a bit of pride in himself. She is probably off shagging someone else.

"No chance of getting more people to come and stay at the hotel?"

"I have tried. But I just don't have the pull anymore. I can't even offer a cooked breakfast because the cook quit. I only have continental and I buy that next door in the supermarket every morning depending on how many rooms I have filled."

Fuck, this guy is depressing me. No wife, no cook and spending time with his mum… in a hotel. Wait, wasn't that a horror movie? I am sure it was. House on a hill somewhere?

He wants to say something more, I can tell. He is looking at me like I am his new best friend.

"I thought things were picking up a year or so ago. Place was buzzing. Nearly every room sold out. Worked out they were all the world's media commuting to that school. You know the school? The Edmund Carson one."

He is looking directly at me. Why is he looking directly at me? Surely, he doesn't recognise me? If he did, he would be asking for a photo to spruce this place up a bit, give it a bit of class. Wait, did he say I packed it out before?

"Lasted a couple of weeks and then after that, there was nothing again. Just about cleared a debt for a couple of months. But you don't get them type of events every day. More's the pity. We could do with a few more. Seems to have the pulling power, that kid."

He is still looking directly at me. Do I have something in my teeth? I run my tongue over them. Nothing. I can't feel anything. I do have pulling power. He is right about that. With the girls and the press, with the world, I guess.

"You know, I hear that wherever he goes, they are opening tours and everything. When they discovered a few bodies washed up in Brighton, they named a whole walk after him. They tell his story and everything. Companies must be making millions off that. Millions."

Brighton? Brighton? When did I work in Brighton? Oh yeah, Carl and family. They must be back from France. How cool is that. That will be making the top ten things to do in Brighton now. After the walking and the vineyard of course. I should have done that at somewhere more popular. Like Blackpool or something. Not that I have been to Blackpool.

He is back to the looking at me. Does he fancy me or something?

"So how long have you been here now, Mr Johnson?"

"Just a couple of days."

"I thought so. Been a quiet few days."

What is he saying? Is he saying that he knows who I am? Or is he working out who I am? That's what it is; he thinks he knows who I am. That's why he said Mr Johnson like that. Like I know your real name. Stop pretending.

"Can I interest you in a drink?"

I just nod. This guy is an odd fish. He walks to the other end of reception that doubles as the bar. Handy really as I guess he can't afford a barman as well.

"Guinness, right?"

Why would he be asking me that? I haven't drunk Guinness since, well, since BRIGHTON! He does know who I am. They must have known I was drinking that on the pier? There weren't any cameras, were there? I am sure there weren't. How else would they know? It's probably on the tour. Guinness sales have probably rocketed. I am probably their poster boy now. Jesus, I didn't even know. Wait, is everyone making money out of me now? Apart from me? I need an agent. A good agent to look after my copyright.

"Always takes a while to settle. That is how you tell it is a good pint."

I take some money out of my wallet. He shakes his head.

"It's on me. I am pleased of the company, to be honest. Not often I get it."

He hands over the Guinness and pours himself a lager. I need to change the subject to see where this is going. He is

261

starting to spook me. I can't take my eyes off the half a dozen hairs covering his head. I can see more hairs than that coming out of his nose. Maybe he should comb those over too.

"So not many people in the hotel today then?"

"No, not many. We are lucky to get thirty or forty people a night now. I mean, I am lucky. I am not sure why I still say we. Old habits and all that. Can't remember the last time that we, I, used above ten per cent of the rooms. Would have been when I just said. It was that long ago."

Why is he almost shouting the words thirty or forty? There is only me here? He can't be bragging to people. Mr Johnson and now the thirty to forty thing? Maybe he has a disorder. He looks like he could have a disorder. I don't look like that, do I?

"I was wondering that earlier. Is there a reason that they are all on different floors? Wouldn't it be easier for cleaning and stuff if they were all on the same floor?"

"It would. I started putting them on different floors to make the place look busy. Then I thought that I could leave the cleaning longer if they were on different floors. Try and use all the rooms and get a cleaner in to blitz them all. Works out it's the same either way as I am doing all the cleaning. Can't afford anyone else to do it. Picking a room to put people in seems to be my only enjoyment now. I am playing hotel bingo in my head."

This guy is a real depressive. I think if I was him I would just end it and get it over and done with. If he asked, I would happily work with him.

"Have you been following the news today?"

He knows I have. He saw me walk into the hotel with an armful of papers.

"Yes, some of it."

I say some of it just in case he wanted to talk politics or something. I don't follow that stuff.

"It seems that Edmund Carson's character, or the ONE as he likes to call himself, is back in London and back at work."

He is obsessed with me, isn't he? I guess when you are lonely and have nothing else in your life, you look to celebrities for inspiration, and this guy could really do with some.

"Yeah, I did see that."

There is a silence. He knows, and he knows that I know that he knows.

"There has been nothing else on the TV all day. They have just found a couple as well. She was pregnant by all accounts."

Why would he say it like that? It doesn't make the work any worse?

"They aren't happy about that. The press, I mean, they are going to have a field day with him tomorrow. It will be a blood bath."

Why would they be having a field day with me? And what is a field day? Is that like a school sports day? A festival? They are going to be having a party with me?

"They are saying he has gone too far with that. The world's press is saying he has gone too far. Taunting the world with what he has done. Even drew a picture of the baby on her belly to show people. Signed it to show the world that nothing was off limits for him. Funny, the things that upset society, isn't it? Been more noise about that in the last four hours than there has been about the Tube, and there were seven people on there? They are out for his blood now though. I wouldn't want to read the papers tomorrow, you know, if I was him."

What is he going on about? Why are they mad at me? I signed it for her. Verna was fine with it. I drew that not to harm the baby. She knows that. Why can't they see that? In the end, I didn't touch either of them. That picture was to preserve the baby. Tim helped instead. They should be thankful I was high on life. I didn't mind a bit of hairy meat. There is no thanks for that at all, is there?

"What do they mean, drew a picture?"

"Yes, gloating is what they are saying. He was just pointing out that he could take anyone. That he knew what he had done and didn't care? They keep talking about his disorder and how all of this is affecting him."

I wasn't doing that at all. They are making that crap up.

"Maybe he didn't know she was pregnant, when he worked with her!"

There is another silence. Shouldn't have said that. I reach around to my back and touch my knife. Just to remind myself that I brought it out with me this time. I was defending myself a little loud then.

"Yeah, maybe. She was only eight months. Maybe he didn't notice?"

I think I am going to have to work with him. Did he mean to say it like that?

"You know, I don't think he is all that bad. They have him a little misrepresented. He is doing so much good work for London. Tourism is booming because of him. Yes, he is doing a lot of good work in sales."

What! I wasn't expecting that. He is saying that to me on purpose I can tell. Trying to get on my good side.

"What I mean to say is he is bringing a lot of trade to London. In fact, trade is following him wherever he goes. I was in Oxford Street the other day and I swear people are wearing his T-shirts everywhere. Especially the ONE. There are loads of T-shirts with that on. Great marketing. I bet he wishes he was making the money out of those. Be a m ltimillionaire by now."

He is right. I should be making money out of those T-shirts. There should be advertising payments surely. He is silent again now, and looking at me. He knows who I am, but he keeps staring as if he is trying to telepathically tell me something.

"It's not only T-shirts; they reckon the sales of black hoodies has gone up a thousand per cent. Kids wanting to wear them everywhere. The police are all on overtime. So, I am sure they are not too upset about it either. The papers are selling more than ever before. I mean, this whole return of Edmund Carson with all the uploaded photos? Must have people running around like headless chickens trying to keep up with him."

This guy is talking a lot of sense now. Maybe I have underestimated him. I just wish he would stop looking directly at me. And so close. I swear, any closer and I am going to take my knife and cut his hair. Well, all six of them.

"The press has not been very favourable to him. Especially in this morning's papers. I mean, some of them are downright negative towards him. I sense that is the negative press angle. Either that or there is an underlying truth from the press they don't want to admit. I have a theory about that."

He is almost smiling now. It's a creepy smile. I can see him with that smile standing next to me and Jack in the Dungeons.

"No, they have not. I did read them too. It is the negative press thing. I don't understand why they would do that to someone. As you say, someone who is doing so much good for the country… I would be interested in hearing your theory though?"

Silence again, as he looks at me. He wants the conversation to lead somewhere. I am not sure where yet. But he wants something out of this.

"Well, I think they were expecting more. I think the press were secretly expecting another big event from Edmund and they got the return of the ONE, and a little return from Edmund. Wrong way round, if you ask me. I would have liked to have seen it the other way around. I would have liked to see Edmund Carson do something big. Maybe Preton School big."

I knew it! I knew that's what they wanted. I have been saying that all day. He is the common man. He knows it. He is what the public really want from me. I knew I liked him.

"But what about all the photos? That was big? One hundred and fifty photos of people he had worked with?"

"The uploading he did? That was all good, and the reveal of Father Harry. But what you must remember is that it was all old news to the press. A lot of the photos had been seen before. Some of them were already speculating about Father Harry and then the ONE returns on the Tube. For me, I thought he was planning another big one. Maybe bigger than the school.

Maybe something above twenty-five. Maybe thirty to forty people"

I knew I should have done that. He is telling me that I haven't done enough. Has a thing about thirty to forty though, keeps saying it loud? If this guy can see it, the whole world can. It explains it all, all the negativity? I should have done something bigger and better. I knew I should have.

"I suppose it is hard to find something to top the school though."

It is hard. This guy understands. That took thought and planning. Whatever I do next can't be a failure. It needs to be amazing. These things just don't fall in your lap.

"Anyway, I am keeping you from wherever you were going. All this talk about Edmund and how he could have done better. I am sure I have a few empty rooms to clean. In fact, I have a lot of empty rooms to clean, this place is so quiet. Just hope I don't get stuck in the lift, eh? You never know what's on the other side of those doors, do you?"

That was quick. He has stopped in mid flow. Although I suppose if he is the only staff here, he must keep working. Seems hardly worth it. He is right though, it needs to be above twenty-five. That's what I should have done. I was trying to do better with the ONE. Not Edmund, and Edmund is the real star here. He is the one that will go down in history. The ONE will just be a part he played. People won't remember the name of the character in *Pretty Woman,* but Julia Roberts will be remembered forever. It's the real person that people want. Don't know why *Pretty Woman* is in my head? That's a bit odd. Wait, that's it. He looks a bit like that lawyer bloke, the creepy one who tried to do her in the end. That's why it was in my head. I would have tried to do her too. I would have done her. She would have let me and not charged me three grand for the privilege. I wouldn't have charged her either.

"I mean, you shot out of there this morning like a bullet. I am not sure what you were expecting on the other side of the doors?"

Wait, I think he is still talking. I thought he had finished? Why is he going on about the floors and the lift? Vivian, Princess Vivian. That was the name of Julia Roberts in *Pretty Woman*.

"Sorry?"

"I was just saying, I must be keeping you from something. Something important, no doubt. All this talk of Edmund Carson's career, lifts and surprises on the other side. I ramble on. I guess it is because I am the only person working here. All night alone, with no visitors. Thirty to forty guests and I have thirteen floors to look after. They do say it is an unlucky number."

I finish my drink. I think he is trying to get rid of me. I am not sure why? There is nobody else here? He is only going to be cleaning.

"I was just going out for a walk. Maybe to the Red Earl. I quite like it there."

"Sounds nice. It is a beautiful evening out there. Be careful if you get the Tube though. Don't want to bump into the ONE, do you?"

He is looking directly at me again. I can't tell if he is trying to be funny or not. Sometimes he sounds serious. Odd little man.

I get up off the stool and head out into the fresh air. It's a quiet night. For a weird-looking man, he spoke some sense. Made me realise. I knew I should have done something. I knew it. I was just so keen to get back to work. I think that was Miss Walker's fault. She got me all excited about our life after this that I forgot what I was supposed to be doing. I am here to entertain the fans. To make myself a legend in history. As my nan would say, this is what you get to dine out on, Edmund. Dine out on the fame.

Nine. I thought nine was going to keep them entertained. Nine people to work with in one night. That is some work ethic.

I need more than that. I need more than twenty-five. He is right. It needs to be shocking and surprising. Wait, no, it was ten. I forgot about the guy in the pub. The guy. It was Dan. I forgot about Dan. Ten in one night, that is almost half the school. In the space of a couple of hours. In broad daylight. Well, nightlight.

Must be something that makes you jump. Something that makes your heart race. Like mine did this morning. More than twenty-five. He is right. Thirty to forty. Makes a lot more sense. So, there is no doubt it is bigger than the school. It can't be less than the school. The papers will pick up on it. Where am I going to find thirty to forty people in that way? Shocking, surprising? Needs to be planned. Somewhere I can plan something where nobody notices. Needs to be quiet. Needs to be staged. Not just staged, needs to be something spectacular. Something people will never forget. Better than the school. Lots better than the school. I take three steps forward and stop.

FUCK!

I turn and head back into the hotel. He is still standing at the bar and looking directly at me with a drink in his hand. He nods his head. I nod back. I acknowledge that I got it. I got what he was trying to say to me all that time. He is an odd little man. I know what he was talking about now though.

"I am going to my room."

"Okay, good evening, Mr Johnson."

"I am taking the lift."

He nods again. I walk to the lift and the doors close.

Fuck! He is right. You never know what's on the other side of them...

Chapter 12

Today is the day. Today I launch the real return. Tomorrow I will leave Al with probably the most famous hotel in the world. I don't understand why I didn't come up with this sooner. This is amazing stuff. I take all the drawings I have made and place them over the bed. Thirteen pictures for thirteen scenes, one for each floor. That alone will make the front page. The world hates that number already. This is only going to make it worse. I go and pull my new go-bag from under the bed. I have some all new cool stuff. I had to have one of these. I lift the nail gun up and take it to the desk. I put a nail in it and another and another. They go straight down to the head. It's amazing. I love this thing. It is so cool.

I take out a pen and sign the desk. It will be good for the hotel. I intend on leaving the iconic black hoodie hanging in the wardrobe and a dog collar. A sign that this was all Edmund. People will want to stay in this room. Probably conduct marriages and things here. They do that nowadays. Al will be able to charge a premium for this room for sure. Five hundred a night. To sleep where I slept. To sleep where I planned this. To have sex where I have. Wait, no, I haven't had sex in this room. I haven't had sex for a while again. I need to try and find time for that.

I put the bag on the bed and pull all the pictures back into the folder. Nobody is coming in here. Al is on the desk all day. Today I will be in the thirties. This is going to be the biggest. The biggest. I head out with the folder into the lift. I get down to reception. Al is on the desk. Al is always on the desk.

"Good morning, sir."

"Yes, it is, it certainly is."

I look around. There is nobody else here.

"Is everything okay, sir?"

"Yes, Al. Thanks for asking."

"Will you be working today, Mr Johnson?"

"Why, yes, I will, Mr Brooker."

He smiles at me. He turns the book around that is in front of him. There are sixteen bookings for the night. I read through them. Fourteen couples and two singles. I turn the book around. I smile at him.

"I wonder what they are all here for."

Wasn't so much a question, as a statement? It would be good to know.

"I wonder too. I am sure we will find out."

I don't say anything else. I don't need to. It's been what, ten, eleven days and he has never once said who I am. He knows. I know he knows, but I don't think he has even said my real name. He has never once said anything outright, but I know what he wants. I know he wants me to do this. Hell, he is helping me do this. This is his break. This is, will be, the making of his hotel. This will show his wife and his banker who is boss. I go and sit at the bar.

"Pint of Guinness and a cheese and onion roll?"

"Yes, please, Al. Sound's perfect."

He disappears and brings back the roll. It's made next door in the shop, I know, but I don't care. He pours the drink. He doesn't ask for money and doesn't say anything but goes back to the desk. I sit with my folder open. I have my lunch and today's paper. I am not on the front page. I haven't really worked in eleven days. There was the guy that recognised me in the Red Earl. But that's not really working. That was just, just crowd control. I have been working through my plan. Training up and down the stairs. Must keep fit. For the job, the press and for her. Probably should have been to see her as I am so close. I figured she would want to see me after this. After I am so much closer to our goal. Probably at our goal.

I want to be here when they check in. I want to ensure that this is planned from the beginning. No mistakes. The first couple comes through the doors. My heart is in my mouth. They don't know, do they? They don't know that they will be working with me later. It's almost like that secret camera show. I can hear Al. He is talking loud on purpose. They are just here for a one-night stay. Flying out for a long weekend tomorrow and didn't want to travel down in the morning. Just a quiet dinner and then out early in the morning. They are paying in advance due to the early departure. Al is looking at me. I am going through the thirteen sketches in my head. What's best for them? Given their build, what they look like. The fact that they aren't doing anything special. I put one finger up. He puts them on the first floor. I don't need to tell him, but they will all be near the lift.

Wait, should I start on the first or thirteenth? People don't get off on the wrong floor, do they? Can I really start beforehand? The last few nights I have sat up with Al and there is little movement after twelve thirty. But some people do get up early. Al is good at pointing out there is no breakfast till seven. Gives me a good six hours at least. If they want a three-a.m. alarm call, they will be in for an early night. Maybe I can start early with them. I don't have to make the scene. Just get them ready?

I sit and carry on reading the paper. Another couple arrives. Here just for one night. Dinner with clients and then meetings tomorrow. That's not good. Dinners can go on late. Al is a legend. He tells them about the problem with cabs and has booked them one, returning at eleven thirty. He is really working to make his hotel famous. I do hope it all works out for him. Cashing in on my name should help him no end. He is right, I am doing a service for the whole of London. They should like give me one of those keys. When famous people get a key to the city, opens every door, I guess? I don't know how. Must be like a universal remote. Floor two. He is looking, I know he has sorted it.

I sit and read the paper repeatedly. Seems to be forever. Should I have picked a bigger hotel? One with more guests. But then I wouldn't have the time to work. No, this is the perfect hotel. I am doing well here. Now that's what I am talking about. She is hot! This day is just getting better and better. Here alone for the night. There is a god. Meetings tomorrow. Early night with a bottle of wine. I agree with that. I will have time, right? Like thirty minutes, tops. Maybe forty-five. I don't want to mess it up for Al, he needs to be playing his part first thing in the morning. He is looking over at me. I hold up two fingers, floor two. Something to do while the other people are at dinner. She turns to see who he is looking at. I hold my hand up as a hi. She smiles. It's a gorgeous smile. We have a connection.

Shit, he has put her on floor seven. Why has he done that? Does he want her for himself? That's just wrong, she will never go for him. What is he playing at? I stare directly at him. He knows I am not happy. He holds up one hand and two fingers and shrugs his shoulders. I shake my head. Shit, now I see what I did… saying hi… he thought I meant seven. Twat.

We need a better signal system. Should have worked on that.

Two hours later everyone is booked in and I am back in my room. Although one couple have cancelled the room. That means there is only twenty-eight. Thirteen couples and two singles. Twenty-eight is more. It's not thirty but it's bigger than the school and that is the point. I have the plans. There will be just less people at the cross, I guess. This time I have the tools the plans and the time. It is all about the staging. Comeback of a lifetime. I am ready.

Al has a signal. He is going to let me know when they are back in the room. I will let him know when it is done by the number of rings on the phone. This key card is amazing as well. Opens all the rooms. How is that even possible? I mean, surely there is a code or something, or people would be in and out of every room all the time. I stand up and look in the mirror. There are cameras on every floor. They are all recording. The whole thing will be taped. Which is going to be amazing. They will be showing this across every network. So,

I need to look good. I have half a dozen changes of clothes. All the same. Nice shirt and trousers. Smart. Not a costume. Just me, the return of me.

Hair is good. Clean-shaven. That's good too. People will want to see my face. Remember to play for the cameras. A little wink here and a little wave there. That is what will make it special for people. I go into the bathroom and put some aftershave on. Victoria will appreciate that. She was hot. Although floor seven wasn't my plan. All rooms are opposite the lift, other than hers; hers is down the end of the corridor. He will hang up and give me an extra ring for her. That's the call I am waiting for, same as a Mrs Hutchinson. She is the other single staying on floor eleven. Didn't see her come in but Al said she was an older lady.

The phone rings. Once. I knew they would be the first. Early flight and all that. It's game-time. I check the mirror one last time and then pick up my go-bag. I take the first drawing off the bed. This is genius. I walk out of the room and head towards the lift. The camera is by the lift. I look up and give Al a wave. I am sure he will be watching. The fans will think it is for them. I head into the lift and press for floor one.

It's a slow lift. I am sure I could take the stairs quicker. Maybe I should be taking the stairs in between. The last thing I need is to press the lift and someone is already in there. Especially if it is messy. I get out of the lift and give him another smile. It's not really for Al, it's more for the millions that will be watching this when it is on YouTube tomorrow. I get to the door. I place the go-bag on the floor and take out my knife. The key works and opens the door. I push it open slowly.

"Excuse me, can I help you?"

Fuck!

The guy was waiting on the other side of the door. He can hear the lock open. It's so loud, and it takes too long. I am just standing looking at him. He is bigger than I remember. I just run at him. As I do, I can hear the screaming. Must be his wife. I am on top of him as soon as I can, but he has hold of my wrist. All I can hear is the screaming. This can't be good. I am going to have to rethink this. I head butt him. He lets go of my wrist and I stab him in the neck. I slice at it as I do to make sure. The blood spurts out everywhere. I need to shut her up. She is so loud. I turn and she is in the corner still shouting. I am not sure who she is shouting for? Probably thinks the hotel is fuller than it is. Why she is still in the corner surprises me as well. Why wouldn't she run towards the door? Probably all an act. She knows who I am and wants to work with me. I can tell these things. I walk over to her. She is trying to fight back but just by waving her arms around. I grab her by the hair and stand her up. I stab her in the stomach. It quietens her down but doesn't shut her up. I grab her again and slit her throat. I stop and breathe. I really wasn't expecting that much excitement. I guess I should have given them a little more time to get to bed. That was harder than I expected.

I go back to the door and go out of the room and use the card again. It makes a clinking noise. It's far too loud. Everyone is going to hear me coming into their rooms. I close the door and try it again, by softly holding the card against it. It makes the same sound. This is shit. I am going to have to wedge something in the doors. I knew there was a reason I needed rods. I go into the go-bag and pull out a wooden rod. I thought they would help me put people in position. I cut a piece off with my knife and place it in the lock. Feel like I am back at Melanie's flat. She was a hot girl, Shame about the rest of it, but she was hot. I close the door and push it open again. It works. I test the card. It still makes the same sound. They won't notice as long as it makes the sound. People don't try the doors in hotels, do they? They just wait for the bleep.

I take the rod and run up the stairs to my room. I get to the phone and phone reception. He takes ages to pick up. Think he was waiting for it to be a signal of some kind.

"Hi."

"Hi, Mr Johnson."

"I was just wondering if anyone else was in the hotel now."

"Yes, sir. Mrs Hutchinson is in and so is Miss Rowlands. Everyone else is out."

I put the phone down. I need to work fast. I will just have to leave those two rooms. I walk out of the room and head to the door opposite the lift. I use the rod and test the door. It works. I work all the way down to floor one using the stairs. If someone was bugging the phones they wouldn't know anything from that call. I don't want Al to get into trouble. This is not a good start. Why didn't I pick up on this earlier? I use this key every fucking day. I should have known that it makes far too much noise.

I go back to the room on floor one. They must be tired as they are exactly where I left them.

"Sorry for the delay. I wasn't expecting to be doing that.

"It is good, I found out now. It's what, nine. Imagine that this happened at twelve. I would never get all of this done tonight.

"Yes, I am. I love it when people instantly recognise me. Especially recently. Given everything else that has been going on.

"I know I have been quiet. I have been working on this. This is the start of my real comeback. After all the negative press, I thought I needed something bigger and better than before. I think I may use that as one of my straplines. Bigger and better than before.

"Look, I don't mean to be rude, but we don't have that much time. We really need to get on with things. You are going to be my first stars of the night.

"Yes, you are going to be famous, very famous. Preton school famous. Even bigger. We just need to crack on."

These people just want to talk. I understand the fame thing but not tonight. This is the first one. It needs to be perfect. Shocking and perfect. When they take the lift, this will be the first one they see.

I get them both off the floor and lay them on the bed.

"Yes. I think so. A little more shocking, don't you think?"

I get him undressed. I then start to get her undressed. There is something about a naked woman that just gets my motor running. I can't resist having a little lick of her neck as I try to undo her top. It's sweet. It's still warm and sweet. My heart beats a bit faster because of it. I whisper in her ear.

"You taste great."

I can see her smiling. That will make up for the no time to talk. She has a lovely smile. That smile when you don't want your husband to catch you. Just out of the corner of her mouth. They are both naked. Now I am not sure. Do I risk setting the scene? Or do I wait until there are more people ready to work with? People don't press the wrong number on the lift, do they? I mean, unless they were morons. They didn't look like morons?

Fuck it... I will take the risk. I can't sit around waiting. I have less than ten hours to get all of this done.

"Okay, this is my plan."

I show them my drawing.

"Yes, I did draw them myself. Thanks. I think it is right in your face. And a little bit of fun as well? I think it will make people smile, don't you?

"Yes, I agree. I don't think it will get trapped in the door though."

I whisper in her ear.

"He is not that big, is he?"

I didn't think so. It is surprising how big they can get, but I don't see that getting much bigger.

"I am glad you ask. I went to dinner at a friend's house and he had one of these. I just fell in love with it."

I walk over to the bag and pull out the nail gun. I pick up the guy and drag him to the lift. I lean him up against the lift face on. I hold him there with my body and then hold his right arm and hand to the wall. With the nail gun, I put a nail through it and step back. It held. Fuck, I was worried for a minute. I grab his other hand. Shit, it doesn't reach across the lift. Shit, shit, shit. Why didn't I check that first? I thought it would reach. I can't nail it to the door, can I? It will rip his hand off. That will ruin the effect of the whole thing.

Fuck!

I stand back. I need him dead centre of the lift, that's the point. When those doors open, the first thing I want them to see is his... well, his stuff.

FUCK!

This is going to be a disaster of a night at this rate. I stand looking at the lift. Rope. Rope is the only thing I can think of. I go to my bag. I pull out the hammer and take the nail out of his hand. He slumps to the floor. I don't think he is even trying to help me. I grab the rope and tie a piece around each of his hands and feet. I lean him up against the lift again and nail the first piece of rope to the wall. It holds. At last something is going right. I nail the other hand to the wall via the rope. Then both the feet. That's what I am talking about. I need to know what it looks like. I press the lift button.

What the fuck am I doing!

What if someone is in the lift? Twat. What the fuck am I going to do if someone is in the lift? I get on my hands and knees underneath him. When the doors open, I am going to have to crawl in and deal with anyone in there. I am a moron. I am the moron. I don't need to worry about them being one. I am waiting with my heart in my mouth. The lift bleeps and the doors start to open. They are so fucking slow. They open, and I pounce. There is nobody in there. I jump up and press the door open button. I was just trying to see what it looks like. It is in your face. But his face isn't. His head is dropping down. I need to do something about that. I get back out of the lift and let it disappear. I go back into the room to collect the chair from the desk in the corner.

"I know it is taking a little longer than expected.

"No, he isn't coming back in here. He is nearly in position.

"Ha, do you know what? There is nothing I need more now than a little tension release. Maybe if I get time later?"

I won't have time later. Although I really do need it. That Rowlands woman is so much hotter. If I am going to make time, I will be making time for her. Although at this rate. I am not getting any tonight.

I pick up the chair and take it to the lift. I grab the rope and make a loop. Not hanging him but just lifting his head up. I tie it around his head and then nail the other end to the ceiling. I step back off the chair. That will do. That will do.

I go back into the room.

"Hi. It is done."

This woman is so chatty.

"Sorry, you know, I didn't ask your name. That is a little rude, I know. I am just trying to ensure that today goes on time.

"Hi, Karen. It is a pleasure to meet you officially."

I pick her up and take her to the lift. I place her on her knees with her head and arms tucked in just behind him.

"I think he can hear you, you need to be a little quieter."

I know she is in the position. It is tempting. But her husband is right in front of us. Facing away from us admittedly. The blonde, curly hair makes it a no though. If she was dark, I don't think I would have been able to resist.

"See, star jump and leapfrogging. I think it looks real cool. When the lift opens, they are going to jump back so much.

"I would hope so. I think the papers will print them floor by floor, so you will be the first. I hope so. Anyway, it's what, ten thirty now. I am running out of time to do this."

It's done. Floor one. I need to get cracking. I smile at the camera for the fans and hold up my finger indicating the first.

I head back upstairs, using the stairs. I go back to the room and give one ring to reception. It falls silent. Then the phone rings three times. Third floor. Then the phone rings again. Nine times. The ninth floor too. Then it rings eleven times. Shit, they are all coming home. I best get the third floor done. There is nobody on the fourth or second yet, so noise won't be a problem. I head back down the stairs to the third floor and listen at their door. Nothing. I don't know how long they have been back. I should have thought about that too. I should have had some signal. Al should have thought of that. I pull the drawings out of the go-bag. I may as well keep them all with me. I planned this to be four people on this floor, but they didn't turn up. The ones that did though are perfect for the picture. I push at the door and it just glides open. It's quiet inside. I creep into the room. The bed is in the centre of the room and they are back to back. Can't love each other very much. I thought all people slept snuggled up. That's what Miss Walker likes to do. I walk over to where the guy is. I hold his head and slit his throat. It's smooth and he hardly moves. She doesn't wake up. I walk around to the other side of the bed and do the same to her. What a difference a floor makes. Reminds me of the school. There is nothing easier when people are deep sleepers. This is what I needed to catch some time up. Although it's a similar scene to floor one. I would have preferred it if there were more people. I drag him out of bed. No time to wait for them to come around. I need to get on with it. I place him against the wall opposite the lift. I quite like the fact he is wearing pyjama bottoms. It's a bit more tasteful considering the scene. I hold him up using my body and put the first nail through his hand and into the wall. It holds. This thing is amazing. I hold his other arm out and nail that too. I take some rope out and tie his legs together. He looks like he is slumping a little. I don't like it. I prop him up a little and put a nail through each shoulder and into the wall. That's better. The head is slumped again. I reach into my bag and pull out the crown I made, out of twigs. I place it on his head and then nail that to the wall too. But at an angle. I like the fact his head is to one side. Looks like the real thing. I go back into the room.

"Hi.

"No, you were sleeping. I didn't want to wake you.

"He is fine. He is in the hallway already in position."

I pull the covers back. She is in full PJs. They really weren't up for a lot tonight, were they? Back to back and dressed. Probably did them both a favour.

"If I had the time that is exactly what we would be doing"

These women are just unbelievable. How many times am I going to get hit on tonight? I take her into the hallway. I look at him and then at her. He looks all right but the cats all over her PJs don't really scream this scene to me. I go back into the room and take the sheet from the bed. I go back and wrap it around her head. Like the Indians do. Then it drops and covers the rest of her. I put her on her knees but lift her body up. I nail her hands to his thighs. She is still slumped, so I nail the sheet to her and her to the wall. I step back. Perfect. I take my phone out. I forgot to take pictures on floor one. Especially from the lift. I need to do that before I go. I take some selfies with the scene. I head back upstairs. I feel rude not entering conversations with them. That's not me. But I am not going to get time, not tonight. Maybe if there is time, I will go back and have a minute with each of them. Thank them for the support. I head to floor nine. Before I get to the door I can hear them. They do know they are in a hotel, don't they? They are full-on going for it. If I didn't know the sounds of sex, I would swear he was hurting her. I stand at the door. The bed is going like the clappers. I push the door open. I stand in the hall area and peep around the corner. Both naked and he is going at her from behind. He reaches forward and grabs her hair, she arches her back towards him. Then he lets go and keeps going at her. It's good to watch. It's been far too long. Again, far too long again. I need to get better at this thing. I miss her at times like this. I watch a little longer. Should I let him finish? Should I finish for him? She would enjoy that. A bit of changing it up a little. I watch a little more. They have no idea I am here. I bet it would be a clear turn-on if they did. Someone like me, watching them have sex. I know that sound. To be fair, her screaming I am ready, I am ready gives it away a little as well. He is going faster. Harder and faster. Harder and faster. She makes the sound. He makes the sound. I am behind him. I slit his throat as he comes. He is shaking, convulsing. She doesn't even notice at first. She must be having multiples. Her head turns and I just smile at her.

I think that's the look of shock. Shock or amazement that it is me standing behind her. I think it's the look to see if I am going to join in. She goes to scream, probably with excitement. Before she does, I have her pinned to the bed. I hold her down with one hand and slowly put the blade in her neck with the other. The blood oozes out everywhere. I lick the side of her face. The sweat and the blood mixed together is amazing. She has that I have just been fucked smell as well. The one where you know you have done a good job. She is kind of hot as well. I mean, she didn't look this hot when she checked in. I would have noticed. Maybe it's because she is naked and sweaty, and, well, I am on top of her. I lie there for a minute. It feels so great. Back in the heat of real action. I can't understand people that don't love what they do for a living. This is the best part. The part when you taste the work. Taste the success. Maybe that's why success is sweet. That's what they say, isn't it?

He is on the floor and she is on the bed. Both naked. I am not sure I want too many of the people I work with naked. It's not about that. It's more about the art of it all. I lick the woman again. Last one. Last one and then I need a break. I need to have a little fun for myself.

I leave the room and go next door. I take the mattress and covers off the bed. I need clean ones. I pull them into the hallway and in front of the lift. This is Al's money shot. This will be the one he uses in all his brochures and stuff. I lay the bed down and remove the duvet. I go back into the room. I grab the tape from my bag and tape his neck back up, so it stops bleeding. I go and wet a towel and clean him up a bit. I then pull him through to the hallway and place his back to the wall but sitting up in bed. I go back in and do the same to her with the tape. So, there is no more blood loss. I wash her too. A little slower. She is fit for an older lady. I like the stroking action. So, does she, I can tell. It is a tough job, but someone must do it. Besides, people won't stay in hotels with blood-stained sheets. I take her out and lay her next to him with her arms over his belly and then cover them up. I take a few nails and ensure he sits up straight against the wall. There, that's better. I am so tempted to move her a bit further down, so he gets the best out of the experience. He would like that. I step back and take a picture. I don't like it. Something is missing. I go back into the room. I try the drawers and bring out the Bible. You know, this thing is everywhere. When I write my book, it will be the same. In every hotel around the world. People always like to read when they are on holiday. I take it back out and nail the guy's hand to it. Now that looks better. She is having a peaceful night and he is reading. That sells hotels. I look up at the camera and give a thumbs up. I then go back to the stairs and up to my room. Signal that floors three and nine are done. He rings back. With every floor, complete. Everyone is here. We are ready to go. Even floor two. I check my watch. Fuck, it's eleven forty-five.

I really need to get on. But that woman on floor nine, she has given me a hard-on. I really need to get rid of this. I touch it through my jeans. It's huge. I could just knock one out here? It will save time. But then I might not be as good later. Fuck it, just get it done, Edmund. Everyone deserves a break at work. There are even rules about that, I am sure. I am sure my dad said fifteen minutes every four hours. I am not sure I can do it in fifteen minutes, but I will have a go. I quickly change and wash and add a bit more aftershave. She will appreciate that.

I head down to floor seven. Everything is quiet. I head to her room. It's far away from the lift and the stairs so whatever happens she is not going to cause me any issues. I go to her door. I listen. I can hear the TV on. That's good as she won't hear the clicking of the door. It doesn't make any difference, but I still softly put the key card on the door. I creep in with my back to the wall. I peer around the corner. She is fast asleep. Bottle of wine on the side and it looks like sushi. She can't have got that from here? He doesn't have a cook. Doesn't even look like she has been out all night. I stand over her as she sleeps. She is just right. Long, dark hair. From what I remember she has green eyes. I hold my hand over her mouth and cut her throat. Her eyes open wide as I do. Green. I knew they were green. I give her the smile. Her eyes close again. Probably thought it was a dream. She wouldn't be the only woman dreaming of me tonight, I am sure of that. This is going to be ten minutes, isn't it? I mean, I don't want to do anything until she wakes up again. That's just sick.

I leave the room and head down the corridor to the couple opposite the lift. I listen at the door. All I can hear is snoring. I push the door open. They are an older couple. He has one of those strips across his nose and she has one of those face masks on, to try and make her look prettier, I guess? I don't want to be rude, but it isn't going to work. Neither of them knew I was there. I was in and out in a matter of minutes. She will be thankful he isn't snoring any more. So many people sleep heavily. I wish I did sometimes. I seem to wake at the smallest thing. I would be crap to work with. I would be up as soon as the door opens. I go back to the room.

"Hey, you are awake.

"I just had to take care of something down the hall.

"Yes. Yes, it is me. You did? Why didn't you say something? I would have been happy to sign something or take a selfie. I am just surprised more people don't ask.

"I suppose you are right. If you are staying in the same hotel as me, there is a good chance we will end up working together. Especially, if I may add, when you look as good as you do."

That's made her smile. It's always good to point out what they already know. Good-looking women know they are good-looking. But it is good to tell them you know it. I pull back the covers. A black, silk nightie.

"You were hoping, weren't you? That look. I think beautiful just might not be a strong enough word."

I budge her over and lie next to her. I reach over and pour a glass of wine from the bottle in the cooler.

"I deserve to take a little me time. I think I am on track for this evening. It was a shaky start, but getting better all the time. I am getting quite fond of wine. More than beer, I would say. The white more than the red. I like it cold. Apparently, you are not supposed to have red cold? Did you know that?"

I give her a sip too. She likes it.

"I was hoping, yes. Sort of a reward, I guess, for the continued success of the night. But I never presume. Consenting adults and all that. I would never want to be accused of, well, you know."

I take a big swig and finish it. I grab the bottle again and put some more wine in the glass.

"I see you started without me. Is that one of those rabbit things next to the ice bucket?"

I look directly at her. She has gone all shy. Probably meant to put it away before I got here. I grab it and turn it on.

"Fucking hell, the head swivels and everything. That would scare the shit out of me. Is that even nice? I mean, it must make you dizzy?

"I suppose. I suppose anything will do while you are waiting for the real thing. But you can't be short of offers for the real thing? Are you?"

I place the glass down stand up and get undressed. She can't take her eyes off me. It is only natural.

"Oh, I get it. I am the real thing you were referencing. Yes, I am ready for the real thing too."

I lift her black nightie and take it off her. I lay her back down on the bed. I was not wrong. There is a well fit body under there. Sometimes I feel like I have X-ray vision and can see straight through a woman's clothes.

"I have been working out. Up and down the stairs. I am glad you noticed. Thank you. Probably lost a couple of pounds in the last week.

"More of a preparation thing for tonight. For my comeback."

I am inside her. She wasn't kidding. She has been working up to me. I glide straight in. The heat is amazing. She must have only been asleep a minute before I walked through the door. People are always sleepy after they have come. Other than me. I am always up for more. Always more. I need to be careful. I am going to probably put her in a coma now if she was sleepy after the rabbit thing.

"You are so hot, hottest I can remember."

She is really into that. Wait, she probably thought hot like sexy? I meant hot like not cold. When I went in. Oh, fuck it, she can take it how she wants. I start slow and hard. Like always. Like she taught me. I can't get the picture out of my head now of those two upstairs at it like rabbits. It makes me speed up. Harder and faster.

"You don't think they will go back to it, do you? And mess my scene up?

"Sorry, I was distracted by something happening upstairs. Never mind.

"You are right, I am sorry. Back to business."

I never thought about that. Leaving them alone. They may want to go again. That thought makes me go even faster. Faster and harder. I need to remember what tonight is about. I look down. She is stunning. She can tell I am back into it. I am giving her my full attention. Stunning. Like Miss Walker but not quite her. I can tell from her face she has been waiting for this. She is so into it. I keep going harder and faster. Maybe I should have just knocked one out. This is taking longer than I expected and I am not taking my time here. I think I am just too good a lover. It's something that is a curse and a blessing. All these people that just want a quickie. I am not a quickie kind of guy. I speed up as fast as I can. She is going to be sore in the morning, but she is loving it now. I lean in.

"Ready?"

She is. I can see she has been biting her lip for about five minutes. One final push. Push... Push... I am spent. Her eyes are rolling in the back of her head, I can tell. There is a shiver going down my spine. I only get that when it has been far too long. When all of this is done, and the world knows I am number one, I am going to ensure that Miss Walker and I are at it every day. I collapse onto the bed next to her.

"Thanks. You were pretty amazing yourself."

I lean over and lick her neck. I give her a little kiss too. The blood is a sweet taste. So sweet. It's like, I don't know what it's like. I lean on my side and face her. I can see her naked body covered in sweat and blood. So fucking hot. Candyfloss. It tastes like candyfloss. That is what I was thinking about.

"Yes, tonight.

"Of course, you are part of it. In fact, you are going to play a great part of it. I have you planned for the thirteenth floor. I think that is going to be my real masterpiece. Been planning that one for a week. The number kind of deserves it, don't you think? I am thinking they may give it to me. The number. I mean, a lot of people have laid claim to it over the years, but this hotel, the number of floors, I think it was made for me. Yes one day I will own the number thirteen.

"It is okay, he is with me. Don't tell anyone though. It was kind of his idea. You see, he has an ex-wife who is screwing him. Bills all over the place and they look like they might close this place.

"I know, with my help, this place will go down a thing of legend. He will be famous and quids in. It will solve all his issues. He deserves it. He doesn't have a lot of luck.

"I am a great guy. I don't hear that enough. That is very true.

"I am not sure, but I expect she will come running back to him. Some women are like that, aren't they? All about the money and fame."

I look over at the digital clock. Its twelve thirty.

"This has been amazing, but I really have to get on. I have what, ten floors to make scenes on. In what, five hours. That's not a lot of time. Even for me."

I get up and get dressed.

"No, you rest. You look like you need it. I bet you are sleepy now?"

I know she is, probably still going. Multiple, multiple.

"I know. Sorry, it's normally a little tenderer than that. I got overexcited. You did that to me. So, you must take some of the responsibility. You were that good."

That will make her happy. Tell a woman she is good at something and you can't go wrong. Turns their head, for sure.

"I will be back to fetch you once it is done. You will be the crowning glory. I promise."

She is smiling now. I know how to keep a woman happy. I head out of the room and back to the door opposite the lift. There is a spring in my step now. I am ready to do this. I am ready to show the world what Edmund Carson is capable of. Floor seven. Oh yeah. The ONE.

Chapter 13

"Hey, you, how was the sleep? You look like you needed it.

"I know, it took a little longer than I expected. You know what though? I think you are going to be impressed. I have really worked hard on this. It is my best work. My best work. Worthy of the name Edmund Carson that is for sure.

"Are you ready to take centre stage?

"Good. Let me help you put your nightie back on.

"Believe me, it's hard for me to dress you too. But I don't think you want to be naked in front of millions, do you?

"Yeah, you are right. You do have the body for it. But nonetheless, you will see why the black will go great in your scene. Trust me, I would never do anything to upset you. This is your moment as much as mine. This time tomorrow you will be a worldwide star."

I get her dressed and then stand her up. She is little like Miss Walker, easy to help around. I expect she is still a little weak at the knees though. Once on her own, and then multiple, multiple with me. That will do that to a woman.

"No, I want you to be the first. I have checked through it all and taken photos for the press and social media. Al has seen from the cameras, I am sure, but I want you to be the first to have the full effect floor by floor."

That will make her feel special. I place the face mask from the lady down the hall over her eyes.

"I don't want you peeking at your floor. I want you to go through them the same as the visitors will. I think they may even keep it like this. Build another lift for guests and keep this as a tourist attraction. It makes sense. I will tell Al before I leave so he can suggest it."

I carry her down to the lift. I place her sat down in the lift facing the doors for full effect.

"Okay, here we go. Let's go down to the lobby and then floor by floor up.

"Yeah, we have time. It's like five forty-five or something. Al doesn't need to sound the alarm till sometime after seven."

We go down to the lobby and the doors open. Al is at reception. He looks over in my direction. He doesn't smile to see me. I hold my hand up and wave. Nothing. That's surprising. Isn't he happy we have done all this? What could he be upset at? I think we are about to make his hotel the most famous in the world.

I press all the buttons and then turn and smile at her.

"Hold on. Here we go."

Floor One. The doors open.

"Jesus, it is a bit scary, isn't it? You open the door and his junk is right there. But jumping jacks though. Very good. I wanted something in your face. Like the dreams, the dreams I had about the guns."

"I know it's hardly a gun, I agree. More of a pea-shooter. A small pea-shooter.

"You are right, not everyone has what I have."

No point telling her the true story – that I got a little scared in the lift. A dream sounds better. The door closes. I can tell she is in shock. That was the whole point. It is working.

Floor Two. The doors open.

"I will admit to being a little lazy with this. I mean, it's just sex. Naked people having sex. I was going to use it further up, but they were in a twin room. A man and a woman in a twin room? Both fully dressed in PJs. I mean, that's not normal, is it? I don't think I could sleep in a room with a woman and not want to, well, you know. I just figured that it would be what they really wanted. They didn't talk a lot either. Something strange going on there."

The door closes. She is very quiet too. I think she is just taking it in. I supposed I need to expect that. Some people are dumfounded by art. It is making me think though have I started too softly? I feel it is teasing them in. They are the kind of things they expect from Edmund.

Floor Three. The doors open.

"Religious, yes. Crucifix, yes. It's a classic, I know. I wanted more followers, you know hanging around at the bottom of the crucifix but they cancelled the room. They will be mad when they find out they could have stayed here tonight. Imagine that. Imagine knowing that you were one night away from being in one of my masterpieces. Maybe I should find out where they came from and pay them a visit. I wouldn't want them having to live with the disappointment their whole lives. That type of thing is life-changing."

Floor Four. The doors open.

"See, now you know why I was heading towards religion. It's not the real Father Harry... because, well, I am here. But I thought it would be good to portray him in a scene. Shows those people that question me, I know there is a difference. They think I have a disorder. It's not a disorder, they are just scenes. I got the cup from a real church and there is real blood in it too, which I think gives it a more genuine feel. I struggled to get those little bread things though. Even went to a church but I couldn't find them. They are just poppadoms that I have cut into little circles. But I think they will do though. I did enjoy doing the whole body of Christ, blood of Christ thing. Made me feel like I had a real connection with people. The same tastes and all that."

Floor Five. The doors open. I am not sure she is getting the magnitude of all this. I suppose she never believed she would be this lucky. To get my full attention for so long.

"You are very quiet.

"Thanks. They are kind of amazing. I will say it again, this is the best work I have done. This again is a classic. The Scrabble board comes from one of the first families I worked with. I got to thinking about comebacks. Like pop star comebacks, they always have new material. But there needs to be a mix of the familiar. I can't tell you how long it took me to get that desk out on my own. I thought if Al was watching he would have come and helped? Do you think he is mad at me? I can't see what for? I even put his name on the Scrabble board. To tell you a secret, I did yours too. Victoria is a good name. Especially for points. It is the little things people remember. Someone told me that." That has a big smile on her face. I can tell she is taking it all in now. Not for the first time.

Floor Six. The doors open.

"This is something new. Do you like the T-shirts? I brought them in Camden. I am the ONE. That is so cool. And the Edmund Carson ones too. I like the way he is proposing to her. I wanted to show the world that I have a caring side too. You know, and I know it will help Al with the hotel. He will like the fact that we are advertising that lovers stay here. It might get him more custom. What am I saying I know it will get his more custom! He will be able to make a big deal about a whole romantic weekend packages. Make a killing. I am doing this for him too. He has become a good friend. Even if he was a little weird back then.

"Yes I can be romantic when I want to be. I think this shows it, doesn't it"

Floor Seven. The doors open.

"And that leads us into the ONE. Not the real one of course... as I am here. But I think it's good again. The girl in the chair is supposed to be on the Tube. That's why she has a model train in her hand. The windows behind her are showing that the train is moving. I wanted to give it a real feeling. Short of bringing a carriage up here, I didn't really know how else to show it. But he is iconic now. That is all they will care about. I never knew when I started what a following that guy would have. It's been great. So far, he has been the most outstanding character, wouldn't you say? But this is the real me. I am hoping this propels Edmund in front of the ONE."

Floor Eight. The doors open.

"Now, this might put you off a little. It is not my best and it didn't work out how I had planned. You see, I was in Camden and I was thinking about a new character, something that would fit in there, like tattoos, piercings, that sort of thing. So, I got the clothes and the wigs for the scene. I thought it would be good then, as they look like they are play-fighting, to give them a few piercings. I didn't really have jewellery, but I thought the nail gun would kind of give the same effect... I know... I got carried away. Before I knew it, his face was caving in under the weight of all the nails that I had used on him. Then I had to try and remove the nails with a hammer. That is not easy. And then put some more in to keep the jaw in place. It's not the best. I think the effect is okay, but I think I am going to have to give up the gun. I just can't trust myself with it... I really get carried away once I start."

I think she still likes it. That is good.

Floor nine. The doors open.

"These two, I tell you, they weren't as quiet as that when I met them. Looks good though, doesn't it? I think it's another money shot for Al. I am starting to get a little worried about Al. You don't reckon he is upset because I haven't included him tonight, do you? I mean, this way he can say he didn't know it was going on. Do you think he wanted to help me or something? He does have the look of someone destined for this career. I thought that when we first met that he had the look. And he practically had the idea. I might have upset him about that. He will see that he is in my thoughts in the work though won't he? Is that enough?"

Floor ten. The doors open.

"Yes, trying something new again. I am thinking spy, James Bond sort of thing. The man in the suit is the spy and the woman being chloroformed is being kidnapped. I can see this character coming to life. I love the idea of me in a suit. The girls will love that too. Although I will need to get real chloroform. I thought I had some. But I think the barman in the Red Earl was having me on the other night. We were talking about spies and stuff and he said that you can have home-made chloroform. Even sold me a jar of it. I tried to use it on myself, but it didn't work. Didn't even make me dizzy. Smells of coconut. I didn't think it would smell like that. But I thought it would be good to have a smell as people would try it, wouldn't they? Al reckoned it was Malibu. He drank it and it didn't knock him out. I had a sip. It wasn't bad. But I am always trying to reinvent myself. This is what this is about. Planning for the future. Letting my fans know I am planning for the future. New characters are coming."

Floor eleven. The door opens.

"Again, something new. And something old. That's the same sort of clothes that Jack used to wear, back in old London town. I like it. I think it has style. I am thinking about doing a flashback week or something. Along with new characters. You know, like they do when TV programmes run on too long. With the strapline twenty years ago. I could be Jack for a month or something? I am seriously thinking about that. It would be good for me and for my image. That's Sukey Tawdry on the floor. That's how they found her. She was one of his most famous victims. Even got in the song."

Probably shouldn't have mentioned the song. Victoria will want to be in my song now and what rhymes with Rowlands?

Floor Twelve. The doors open.

"Nearly there. That's me and a wheelbarrow and a carpet. That is where it all started. They don't know that. So, it will be somewhat confusing and intriguing at the same time. I wanted to give them a little something to make them think. I do wonder if they will then start to look for people in carpets. They will need scuba gear if they do. Could you tell that from all the floors I am trying to give a little piece of me to each of the pieces? And at the same time enhance the reputation of this place. I really need to work on that fact. The fact that I am a brand and I need to treat myself as one? I think it will make the legend of me continue long after I retire and have kids.

"Really? That means the world to me. I am glad. It is just what I wanted to hear. Feedback is critical to all artists. It makes the whole thing worthwhile."

This is going down so well. I knew it would. It is better, it is bigger. That's what they wanted, wasn't it?

"Yes, now for your masterpiece. Not really a piece of me. But more a reflection of what people must be thinking. I wanted an iconic piece as iconic as the ONE and Edmund and Harry. I think I have done an amazing job."

Floor thirteen. The doors open.

"It is quite breath-taking. I tell you, I have had this gear ready for a week. I put all the hooks in beforehand, so all I had to do was thread the rope. He does look effective though floating above the ground like that and the sheets look amazing. I think keeping is halo straight was the hardest job.

"Yes that is true of all of us." So quick I love that.

"I know, red spray paint. It was the only thing that would work on the devil. But that's why you in the middle are going to look so good. You can hardly tell it is a woman under the devil costume. And who is to say that the devil isn't a woman? It would make a lot of sense if she were. Temptation and all that.

"No, I agree. Who is to say that god isn't a woman too?

"That was the aim, torn between the devil and god. That's why he is flying and the other one is on the ground, as if she is coming up from hell. You could be pulled either way.

"Good answer. Depends what type of mood you are in, I suppose."

She is on fire now. I guess I must have inspired her in the lift. I pick her up and place her against the wall.

"Do you know, I would, I really would? That black looks amazing on you. But I think I need to talk to Al. I feel after all this, after helping me achieve my goal of twenty-eight and working towards his hotel dream, I have left him out. So, I need to talk to him before I get moving. People will be waking up soon."

I nail her hands, so they are touching the devil and god's hands. One each as if he is pulling her down and he is lifting her up. I stand back at take a photo. And then a photo of me with them. That's all of them. I have photographed the lot. All the other twelve floors and these three. I am so proud of this.

"Wait, are you sure?"

I go through it all in my head.

"You are right. That's not twenty-eight that is twenty-seven. Someone is missing."

Fuck! Who is missing?

"Mrs Hutchinson. Fuck, I forgot all about her. I haven't even been to visit her. She must be a heavy sleeper as I haven't been quiet putting all this together."

I head down in the lift and towards her room. A few minutes later I am at the door. I can hear snoring. It's amazing she has slept through all of this. How did I miss it wasn't twenty-eight? The Findley twenty-eight. The Late twenty-eight? I have been thinking of titles all night. Just didn't count the people. I go into the room. She doesn't hear the click of the door. There is still snoring. I peep around the corner.

Fuck!

It's the old girl with the dog. Al didn't tell me that. Why wouldn't he tell me it was the old girl? I walk up to the bed. She is sound asleep. Shit, she looks so peaceful. He said she was older. Not ancient. She doesn't have that long left anyway. I stand looking at her.

They will destroy me. Wow where did that come from? They will destroy me? It is the fucking papers isn't it. The papers, they will destroy me if I do this. After all the press about the baby and Verna. They said I went too far. They called me some horrible names that day. They have been calling me horrible names ever since. But they weren't there. They don't know how that all happened. They don't know I was doing her a favour. Her husband was in the closet, for fuck's sake. Fuck! What do I do? She hardly fits in any of the scenes anyway, does she? By the look of her she was probably there at the real crucifixion. I could just cover her with the pillow and let her go quietly. They might think she went in her sleep. That will be for the best.

No, that will ruin it. They would find out it was me. I need this to be a flawless launch. I don't want one paper to be negative. Even that Sarah bitch.

The dog comes over and licks me. Not a bark or anything. It rolls on its back and puts its legs up in the air. I rub its belly. It nips at my hand. Little bastard. I pull my hand out and it puts its legs in the air again. It's giving me that look again.

Fucking hell. I think it's asking me to work with it. It's a hundred and thirty-three. The poor thing is on its back with its legs in the air saying for fuck's sake, end it for me. I pull my knife from behind my back… it's smiling. The dog is smiling at me now. It is nodding its bloody head. I move the knife towards it. It doesn't move. It wants the end…

FUCK!

I can't work with a dog. They say that. Don't work with kids or animals. They always say that. What is up with me? I put the knife back behind me. The little fucker starts barking and I run out of there, ensuring the door is closed behind me. I don't want that thing ruining any of my scenes.

I head back to the lift and then down to my room. I pack my stuff, leaving just the iconic hoodie and dog collar in the wardrobe.

They will see that as the end of those characters. I am still not sure. It may be the end of them. I am not saying that I will not bring them back if the fans demand it. Maybe this is the beginning of a few more tonight. James Bond. The flash back Jack. That is a cool name. I head back to the lift and down to the ground floor. Al is at reception. Well, to the right of reception at the bar area.

"I bet you could do with a drink, Mr Johnson."

"Yes, please, Mr Brooker. I really could."

He pours me a Guinness. He doesn't say anything. I sense he is not happy. I knew I should have included him more in tonight's activities. He did come up with the plan to save both our careers. Well, to save his. Mine was on track. This just puts me more firmly on track. And his marriage, I would guess this is going to save his marriage. She will probably come back to him now, once the money starts rolling back in. He is back to looking straight at me. I need to thank him. I need to ensure he knows I couldn't have done this without him. He is a good guy. He tops up the drink and leans over and places it in front of me. I jump forward and grab the back of his neck with one hand. With the other the knife goes straight in. I pull hard and almost pull some of his neck out.

The blood gushes everywhere across the bar and into my drink.

"Thanks, Al, and I think you can call me Edmund. We are not kidding anyone anymore."

He drops to the floor. It was the least I could do. To make him a legend in his own hotel.

I take a sip of my drink. The blood makes everything taste better. There is sort of a red tinge to the Guinness now. I would recommend that they do this. Add a bit of colour to the drink. I should contact them. See if we can jointly advertise.

I take out my phone and start to attach the pictures to emails. I am going to send them to all the newspapers. This is the real return of Edmund Carson. I prepare them all ready to post to all the news contacts I have and all the social media sites. I want the world to see this all at the same time. This will be the big bang they have been waiting for. I drink some more of my drink.

"Hey, you are back with us. That was quick. Didn't want to miss anything, I bet. I don't blame you. We have done a great job."

I go around to the other side of the bar and pick up Al. I place him on the reception stool and take my drink along to him.

"Yes, thank you, an amazing night. I couldn't have done it without you.

"I know, I am so sorry. I just didn't think. I could tell something was up when we came down in the lift. It just hit me. I never once talked about you being part of it. Luckily, I didn't work with Mrs Hutchinson so there was a space. Twenty-eight, as we said earlier. I had worked out all the slogans, so it works perfectly. And you will be the number one they see. Perfect for both of us.

"Yes, not just better but over ten per cent better. People will forget about that school now.

"And bigger, yes, bigger. The scenes are amazing. I am sure you have seen then on the screens? Of course, you have. Best night's TV you have ever had I am sure of that.

"Al, I hope you know you are about to have the most famous hotel in the world? How do you feel? Excited? The banks will be sorted. And I tell you, your wife, what was her name Alex? She will be here by lunchtime, I can almost guarantee it. Begging you to take her back. Tell her you helped me. I don't mind. It will get her old juices going.

"I know, right. The difference one night can make. I wish you all the success, mate, I really do."

I finish my drink. I was thirsty.

"No, I will get it. It's thirsty work. Let me get you one too. We can both toast to new beginnings."

I go back to the bar area and pour us both a Guinness. He will enjoy this more than cooking lager. He had never heard of that saying till last week. Now he calls it the same thing. It s good to have friends. Keep them close as well. Another saying from my nan. She should have written a book on them.

"I know. I have watched you. The key is to let it settle, and then pour a little more. Settle and then a little bit more. Takes time but it is worth it."

I take us both back a drink.

"Here is to new beginnings. New characters and new chapters in both of our lives."

I nearly down the pint in one go. I was still thirsty. I need to hydrate more when I am working. I just get carried away with it all. Maybe have a packed lunch. That will keep my energy up.

"Al, don't really know what to say now. I know you have breakfast and stuff to start so I will get out of your hair. I am so glad I have made a true friend here in London.

"I will be back and often. This will become my favourite hotel. Maybe we can plan it, secretly, like personal appearances on the dark web. I am not sure what the dark web is, but it seems the sort of place we would advertise.

"No, I will do all that. Most of it is loaded and ready to go. They will work it out quickly where we are. Before ten o'clock, if I was a betting man.

"Mate, no, thank you. I just needed a little guidance and that has come from you. You will be a success, Al. Trust me. Headline news by lunchtime.

"I don't know. I was thinking the coast. Maybe down to Brighton. I would like to pay my respects to my nan. I think that is the best place to do it. I hear they even have a walk named after me. I think it was you that told me that. Could be good for a visit. I can rest up there for a week or so and wait for the news to really break tomorrow. I need a kip, I know that."

I go and shake his hand. That guy is an absolute legend. I walk out of the hotel and head to the Tube station. Think I will train it down for a change. I don't use public transport enough. Maybe due to the freaks you get on it?

Chapter 14

I open my eyes and look at the ceiling. I did it. I managed a whole day without looking at social media. The news or any reports on TV. I wanted the papers to be the first. I wanted to see it in black and white the real return. With all this negative press, they have not been favourable to me lately. Now is their time to make it up to me. The amount of work I have done, is going to make them realise that I deserve the headlines. I get dressed and head out of the B&B. There is something about waking in the sea air. No wonder my nan loved it. I can't believe I haven't spent more time in Brighton. I love it here. The air just seems so much fresher. Makes you glad to be alive.

I walk along the front and past the pier. The café is called Edmund's. That can't be a coincidence, can it? It wasn't called that last time I was down here? Was it? They must have changed the name because I sat there. Because it's near the pier. I wonder how many other places are cashing in on my name. They are really milking my fame here, aren't they? The flyer in the hotel for the ghost walk with Edmund Carson, and now this. I should be getting some money out of this. One day. I don't need it now, but one day I want my cut.

I walk into the newsagents. There is a spring in my step. I pick up the papers. I am trying hard not to look at them. But I see the front page of *The Sun*. Hotel Hell is the headline. I smile to myself. That's what I am talking about. A bit of positive press. I put the rest underneath, so I can't see them. I pay at the counter and walk back to the B&B. This is what the real return is about. It's about the wow factor. I place them on the bed. My hands are shaking, I am so excited about this. I may as well go through them in this order.

I look through the first paper. It's amazing. They have done everything I asked. It is literally the first twenty pages of the paper. Every scene. All thirteen. Plus, reception. I should have done more for reception. Just for Al. Victoria looks amazing in these photos. She is going to be so happy. I am so glad that I convinced her to put clothes on. So gorgeous. There is even a piece on Al and his wife. The fact that the place was struggling. Not anymore. You can't buy advertisement like this.

They mention whether these new characters are going to come to life. They got everything that I was trying to say. This paper is amazing. This hails the return of Edmund Carson. How it was supposed to happen. I feel so good about it now. It was worth the wait. It was so worth the effort. They are finally learning to appreciate me. Like they did in the beginning.

Okay, the next one... *The Times*. What the fuck is this? Russian planes fly too close to our airspace? That's not a headline? I scour the front page. Not even a reference or a line about me. How have I not made the front page? I flick through the paper. There is nothing. Nothing on me whatsoever. I check again. Is there a section missing? Should there be a pull-out special or something? This paper does that. A paper within a paper. But nothing. Nothing about me. I have a good mind to go back to that paper shop to see if he has forgotten to put it in. There is no reference to a pull-out. There is always a reference. That's that bitch, isn't it? That Sarah woman. She works there. The one who started this negative press thing. I pick up my phone just to check. Yes, three email addresses. I had three email addresses to *The Times*. There was no way they didn't receive the pictures. Bitch!

I pick up the next paper. The Russian plane is on the front page as well. That is all that is on the front page. Nothing, nothing about me. I check through the whole paper. Nothing. I spread all the papers across the bed. One paper, only one paper has printed anything about me. Even the fucking weirdo paper doesn't have anything about me. It's leading with some slapper that slept with some footballer? What the fuck is going on? That is not news. That is an everyday event. I sent it to all. I know I sent it to all. I sent the fucking pictures to all of them. All they needed to do was print them. I grab my phone and check the emails again. Yes, all of them. All of them have received. I even get a note to say they have been delivered. I did the fucking work for them. They can't say I didn't help them. This is a fucking joke. They can't say they didn't have time. They had a fucking day, for Christ's sake. I grab all the papers and rip them to shreds. Bastards! Bastards all of them!

Do I have to do everything myself? The paper world is dead. Fucking dead. It's a good job we all have our own social media now. I grab my phone again and click into Facebook.

Fuck!

Deactivated account! What do they mean, deactivated account? I try and log on to my other accounts. None of them. None of the Facebook accounts are working. Some aren't even in my name. How do they know they are mine? I try Twitter. It's the fucking same. I can't get on. None of them. None of the accounts. It's like they are banning everything to do with my name. They have a right to keep these open. Freedom of speech, it is one of my rights. It is a human fucking right. Even the ones that aren't in my name. How do they know? Not even the fan pages are there. What the fuck is going on? I switch on the TV in the room. I flick through the channels. There is nothing? Nothing! No special news bulletin, nothing. What the fuck is going on? I throw the remains of the papers off the bed. I sit down on the edge. What the fuck is going on? This is the greatest return in the history of comebacks. They must have found them. They must know, it's in *The Sun* newspaper. I just fucking read it. I pick up the paper off the floor. I start to read it. They have been there. It clearly says so here. It says police were called by Mrs Hutchinson, the only surviving guest. So, they all know. It even says the world's press turned up so what the fuck is going on? I guess that is Al's ex-wife. So, she is there. Why isn't it on the news? In the papers? This is my fucking comeback! I grab the papers again. I try and piece them together and start to look through them. There is nothing. No mention of me. Or the hotel. I flick through the TV again. The news, the news is starting. I turn the TV up.

"The Sun newspaper this morning has made a public apology for its early edition. They were set to print this before the UK government ruling that we are simply to refer to as The Blackout. Some locations around the country will have

received this first edition. This edition reports on situations before The Blackout. The Sun newspaper has asked that they all be returned. These editions have been predominantly distributed in the south of the country. The Sun's editor Matthew Welch released this statement. 'The Sun is fully behind the government's decision of a full media blackout, known only as The Blackout. We were, as with most newspapers, already preparing today's edition. Our south London printing house had distributed the early edition before the government ruling of the law which passed late last night in the Houses of Parliament. This law is the first of its kind in the UK. In fact, the first of its kind in the world. The world's press has agreed to adhere to the terms and conditions of The Blackout. This is until such time that this threat to our society has been captured. Social media sites have also agreed that any account mentioning, uploading or displaying of anything to do with situations referencing The Blackout will be taken down immediately.' In other news, Russia has apologised for flying to..."

I switch the TV off. I am in shock. The Blackout. They are calling me The Blackout. They have, they have what? Banned me from my fans? What? That can't be right? Who do they think they are? What do they think they are doing? I don't do this for me? I do this for them.

They can't black me out! The fans? The people? This is the reason I do what I do. What the fuck are they playing at? I sit on the bed. I don't think I have ever been this stunned. What does it even mean? No more social media? No more papers? No more TV? How are people going to know? How are they going to keep updated on my events? I go to my bag and grab my laptop. They can't stop everything, can they? They won't know it is me? I will just post as someone else. I open the laptop and set up a new email address. Alan, Alan Brooker. Easy. Now set up Twitter. Done. Now upload a photo. I will use the one of me and Victoria. That should get people's attention. I will get a thousand followers like that. People want to see what I have done. It's not so much punishment to me, it's the fans they are hurting the most. I post it. See, it works. Try another. I start to upload it.

It's not uploading.

Your account has been deactivated. What the fuck? How do they know it's me? Do they have people just sitting there waiting for me? That's it, isn't it? They have people online waiting for me. Just to fucking block me. I slam the lid down on the laptop. I then throw it on the floor. I then stamp on the fucking laptop. Probably want to track me. I stamp and stamp and stamp. Fucking governments. They are here to support people, support enterprise. After all I have fucking done for them.

I should go out to do something. I should do something that they can't ignore. Something that people are going to see. In a crowd. A fucking stadium. I have lots of fans here. I am going to go back to the pier. Work with all the people on there. They want to stop publishing me? Blackout me? Really blackout me? Then I will get others to do it. The world is snap happy with cameras and stuff. They will put it up for me. They can't control all the accounts in the world. They can't be everywhere at once. That's what I will do. I go into the bathroom and wash my face. I look at the mirror in front of me. Bastards.

That's it. That's what they want, isn't it? They want me out there doing something stupid. That's how they see this is going to end, don't they? They want me off my game. Don't they know they are just giving me more time? Do they know the number of hours I work on keeping my presence online? I am totally dedicated to my fans, even if they are not. They will give in. The fans will be demanding it. I bet the Houses of Parliament are covered with protestors now. All demanding to know what I am up to.

What am I up to? I mean number wise. I must be close to two hundred, if not over it. I am! I am over it! Hell, I worked with twenty-eight yesterday. That doctor fella, he is well in the number two position. Well in. It begs the question then, doesn't it? What do I do now? What do I do? I go back into the room and lie on the bed. I thought this would be more of a celebration weekend. I thought it would have been something special. They are trying to ruin my holiday down here. I expected today to be a real launch. I don't think I will ever forgive them. Even when I am retired, and they want to talk about it, talk about my fame at its height, I will never forgive the press. Should I just stop now? I should.

Is that a knocking on my door? I get up and open it.

"Well handsome, are you going to let me in?"

I almost lose my breath. I don't know why I knew she would come. She will have seen *The Sun* newspaper. She always knows the right time to come. Dressed to kill as well. Always dressed in what she knows I like, what I need. She knows that is my thing. I fling my arms around her and bring her into the room. I close the door behind her.

"I am so glad to see you. Your timing couldn't be better. I am sorry about the mess though. I was just catching up on my reading."

I wasn't lying to her. I wouldn't lie to her now. I was reading but I didn't like what I was reading.

"Or lack of things to read?"

"Yes, lack of it. Have you already seen the papers today?"

She just nods at me. I can see by the look in her eyes she knows everything. She always knows everything. I sit back on the bed and she comes and sits next to me. She grabs my hand and gives it a squeeze. She always knows what I need.

"Edmund don't worry so much. You are going to be okay?"

"Yes, I am. It just came as a bit of a shock really. It's everywhere. They are calling me The Blackout. Did you know that? I am The Blackout. I have worked so hard over the last couple of weeks to achieve this. So hard. I thought it was a masterpiece. It is a masterpiece. I am just upset that the whole world isn't going to come on that journey with me. It is them I feel sorry for."

"I know, that is the kind of caring person you are, Edmund. It all happened last night. The whole of the government has been involved. They say for the first time ever, it has come to this."

She is half smiling at that. At saying the first time ever.

"No media whatsoever? I just, I just, how will they know? All the fans. And Al? What about Al? He helped me, and this was going to launch his hotel. He has debts and everything. Don't they know how much he needs this? The Blackout is going to affect trade. People depend on me. I am good for the country."

"I am sure people will still hear about it. Word of mouth, that sort of thing. You are very famous, Edmund. People will be keen to talk about you. They can't stop the world talking about you." She is right. She is always right.

"Yeah, I just don't think it will be the same for him. It won't happen quick enough to get the debtors off his back. He is my friend. I wanted to do the best by him."

I feel like I am coming across as childish. I don't want to seem that way. Not to her. It's not that I need the press. I think they need me more. I have increased sales. Everywhere. This is going to hurt them. What about the T-shirts and stuff? The lady on the market? The Edmund Carson walk? Are they all going to be shut down too? That is hardly fair on those good people. I am in The Blackout T-shirts. Feels like another great opportunity. Maybe every blank black T-shirt is now a brand, is the ONE, The Blackout? He is all black. The marketing opportunities alone are huge for me. For the country.

I can see them on Camden market. Shhh, it's a Blackout. I can't tell you, there is a Blackout. The markets would, will, make a fortune. I don't think the government has really thought any of this through. Do they realise the amount of people they are hurting with this? She squeezes my hands again. I swear she is inside my head. She can read my thoughts. She knows exactly what I am thinking.

"Edmund, you need to think about who you are doing this for? Don't worry about others. It's not just for the fans, is it? Or your friends. You really need to think about yourself. For once, Edmund, think about yourself. Is this it? Have you accomplished everything you need to? Or is this just another bump on the road to worldwide stardom."

"No, it is not just for them. I just wanted to be the best at something. I wanted to show the world I was the best at something. I have never really said this before, but I feared at times people didn't notice me. Not how they should. I wanted to impress, well, you for one? When you noticed me, in the class? When we did the play. That made me realise that I could capture anyone's imagination. If you noticed me, then I could make anyone notice me. I wanted that. I wanted to make you proud of me. Make my nan proud of me. I am sure she was. I am sure you are. My nan told me, she told me, every day."

"Edmund, you do impress me. Every day. I don't have to read about you for you to impress me. And your nan. She loved you. And was loved by you. Which is so much more important. You know that."

She is kneeling in front of me now, holding my hands.

"You had a goal, and you wanted to reach it. You have been striving for this for years now… Have you reached it, Edmund?"

"I was just thinking that. I was just thinking I must be close. I used to keep count, but I lost some numbers somewhere. I think I must be close. I have probably reached it. I am more than probably over it.

They have never done this to anyone else, have they? So, I must be number one? That's how they would have sold it to the government, isn't it? To stop the best, they must do something different. They can't do what they have always done?"

"No, they haven't. You are a world first. I am sure that is why they did it."

Those words are ringing through my ears.

"Because you are the world's number one. The press, they will return. They won't blank you forever. Everything you dreamed of is coming. The books, the TV programmes, the movie deals, they are all in your future, Edmund. You are doing this for you. You always need to remember that."

"For us."

"Okay, yes, for us. Once it is done, we can move on together and start our lives."

She is right. I started this for that reason. To be the best. I am the best, and the whole world knows who I am. I do enjoy my work, and I think I have been focusing too much on what everyone else wants. It's not about them. It's about me. The press are just pausing. Pausing to take it all in.

I look straight at her. She is the most beautiful woman in the world, and she is mine. I think that is one of my major accomplishments. I need to always remember that. I know she feels it too. It is why she does what she does. She knows I love the black dress. Every time I see her, she is in that black dress. Not for long. But she always wears it. It's a real sign of love. I only mentioned it once. Once that I liked it. The first night, I think. I am sure I told her when we were in the car.

"You are right, as always. This is about me. And it's about getting this chapter done so that we can start our next one. Together. Plan our lives together. Our lives were always meant to be together."

She is nodding at me now.

"Exactly like we discussed in the Lake District. What our future held for us, Edmund. Everything we ever dreamed of. Seems like a long while ago now though, Edmund."

I knew she wouldn't forget that conversation. Women like to talk about marriage and babies. It is probably all she has been thinking about over the last, what is it, a couple of weeks? A month since we have been together? It may have been longer. She seems to think it was longer. I don't know where the time goes.

"Yes, exactly like we discussed up north. Little District Carson."

I smile at her. We both know what that means. It is time.

"I have really missed you."

"That's good to know, Edmund. Now I have been here for what, ten minutes and I am yet to get a kiss, let alone anything else? That must be a record? Either that or you have gone off me? Is that the case?"

I smile at her and she smiles back. It's the playful smile that makes her whole face light up. She pushes me back on the bed and then climbs on top of me.

"Edmund. First you are going to take me. Because it's been far too long, and I am as horny as you are. It has been far, far too long. We are then going to stay in this room until we decide on our future. Come up with a plan together. Once we have a plan, we are going to start living it. Time is running out for us, Edmund. I want you back in my life full-time, so we can start the next chapter of our lives. It is going to be amazing, Edmund. Really amazing."

She has that I am in charge look in her eyes now. She means it. I love that look. That almost drunk with happiness look.

"Yes, Miss."

She likes it when I do that. Remind her she is the teacher. I smile at her. I will let her be in charge today. Just because she made the trip.

"Now. Get me done. That's your next job."

She lifts the black dress over her head. I will never get bored of that sight. I do as I am told. Never contradict the teacher, is what my nan used to say.

Chapter 15

I open my eyes. I am staring at the ceiling again. I am having that déjà-vu thing. The ceiling is not always the same, but the feeling is. I turn over. She has gone. That is déjà-vu as well. She loves the disappearing trick. I can hear a pin drop when it comes to night-time. Unless it is a night with her. She really tires me out. There is a note on the pillow. Gone to school. See you soon with a question mark and a kiss.

I love spending the weekend with her. We have hardly left the room, but it has been good. I needed that to get my head back in gear after what they have tried to do. I get up and shower. I don't think we concluded though? The choice is mine. That is what she said. I know what she wants though. If I continue, it needs to be for the right reasons, and what are the right reasons? To be number one? When I already am? The main reason would be to prove to the world they can't blackout me. I am too popular, and the country needs me.

I would need to get a car. Just head north and stop off to work wherever I feel. Make the fans know that I am still around. A UK-wide tour would be the only option, if it is going to be word of mouth only. I need to be seen and heard everywhere. I can do what she said. Tag walls and stuff. They have given me a new name. Maybe even a new character? So,

I should I use it? The Blackout sprayed everywhere. They will appreciate that I have made the effort to come to their town.

If the government doesn't want me to be in the press, that is fine. I could make so much noise they won't have a choice. I get dressed.

Then again, who am I proving myself to? She is right. I am done. I am the best. The movies are coming. The books will be released. The trilogy, quadriology even, will write itself. I am not sure that is a word. Four times movie just doesn't sound right. Is it time for us to just be together? Holiday, I really need a holiday. Together. I could certainly spend all my mornings waking up next to her. Saying that, I am not sure it is very often we wake up together? This is the beginning of the rest of our lives. Sex every day, living in Camden. It would be good to walk through the market every day and see my name. Probably make a personal appearance once a year on an anniversary or something just for my fans. It is time. District Carson. Miss Walker, sorry, Mrs Carson. I grab my bag and head downstairs to reception.

"Checking out, sir?"

"Yes, thank you."

"Did you have a good weekend? I am sorry about the weather. It is that time of year."

"Yes. It was an amazing weekend. Just what I needed. No need to apologise, the weather can't be helped. The joys of our country, I guess."

The joys of our country. I do love our country. I wouldn't want to live anywhere else in the world. I pick up the leaflet off the counter. It's a picture of me. Well, it is a hooded figure. It is not actually a picture of me. The ghost walk including the

Edmund Carson story. I guess they will still be doing this. He hasn't taken it off the desk. The Blackout hasn't reached the B&Bs of this world. People will still want to do these things. The fans will never give up on me. The government can't take it all away from them. They can't Blackout the feeling that I gave to them, the history that I gave them. For generations to come they won't forget.

"Off somewhere nice, sir?"

"Yes, to spend some quality time with my girlfriend."

He smiles at me. I open the leaflet. There is a whole map and everything. The Pier, the bar. They must have been tracking me.

"And did you do the walk while you were with us, sir?"

"No, no, I didn't. Never got around to it."

"I hear it's very good. Takes you through the whole Edmund Carson story too. Up until the time he visited us here in Brighton. He worked, I love the way he always says worked, with one of his old school friends and his family over by the pier. Good story. Well, I say good story. You know what I mean. As horror stories go. We only found out about the case recently. I do wonder what else we don't know about him. I think we will be discovering his stories for years to come."

I wouldn't say we were friends at school. I think we are now though. Yeah, I would class us as friends now. I bet Carl is loving the press, and his sister. It is probably him doing the tour. I think that would be a fitting job for him now he has left school. He has left school, I presume? Never struck me as the university type. I wouldn't be surprised if the whole family haven't moved down here to cash in on the fame. Fame that I have given them. Now that they are back from their holiday in

France. They didn't stick around to help me in the beginning but now, now they want to use my fame to make money. I have made this country so much money. Really put some of these places on the map. I am a national treasure. That is what they call them, isn't it? People that embody the country and its values. Bring joy to millions.

And they have the gumption to treat me like... No, not going down that rabbit hole again. I have made my decision. She was always the right decision for me. She was always going to be the right decision for me. She was my future.

"I do hope that you come again, sir."

He hands me a receipt, and smiles at me.

"Maybe do the walk next time. I am sure that would be fun, and you never know how long it will last given this blackout thing."

I lunge at him and grab the back of his neck. My knife is in his neck and I tear out his throat. I drag him across the counter and lay him on the floor. I climb on top of him and stab, again and again and again, everywhere from his head to his stomach. The blood is everywhere. I can't stop. I keep going again and again. It is not even spurting any more. That makes me stop. It is no longer fun. I stand up and I take the flyer and put it on his chest. I then stab my knife straight through it. I leave it there.

I am not happy about the fact that people are making money out of me. It's starting to grate on me. The government need to know that they can't have it both ways. That's Brighton done. Brighton. I have been here enough. This town has made enough money out of me. I am not coming back.

Fucking Brighton. The word is stuck in my head now. Brighton.

Maybe. B. Maybe, that's what I really need to do. It will ensure I still have the following. I will have people looking out for me. Expecting me. That is what I need. Fuck the Blackout. That's your choice. I will make you eat those fucking words.

Somewhere with an A, start somewhere with an A. Then work my way through the whole fucking country by the alphabet. The Alphabet Killer. That's another character. No, the Alphabet Killers. There is no saying that I must use just one character. I am going to show the world they haven't seen anything, fucking anything. It is about the Alphabet. I could be a million people. I could be Jack. I could be anyone.

I walk out of the hotel and into the fresh air. They thought they could stop me? They thought The Blackout would make a difference to me. If the world thought it had seen something before, if it thought it had seen the best I had to offer, it needs to think again. I can reinvent myself at a drop of a hat.

I can become anyone. I mean, anyone. I grab my phone to send a hashtag. Arggh… fucking forgot. Fuck it. Don't they know who I am? Who I really am? I can still scream. You can't censor that, you pricks.

"I am Edmund Carson! Do you fucking hear me? Edmund Carson. The ONE, the Only. You haven't seen fucking anything yet!"